THE NEON PALM OF

MADAME MELANÇON

WILL CLARKE

middlefinger.press

Dallas ♦ New York ♦ London ♦ Hong Kong

P.O. Box 181583, Dallas, Texas 75218

Book Design by Will Clarke // Cover image by CSA ©csaimages

Distributed by Ingram

1st Edition

10 9 8 7 6 5 4 3 2 1

(hardback) ISBN: 978-0-9726588-3-6

(paperback) ISBN: 978-0-9726588-5-0

(e-book) ISBN: 978-0-9726588-4-3

For Michelle. You are my lifeline.

MELANÇON

muh-LAHN-sahn

Means "melancholic man."

1

MARCH 18, 2010

Two days before the Sub-Ocean Brightside Explosion

"When the sea turned to honey, the poor man lost his spoon."

— **Madame Melançon, New Orleans, Louisiana**

2

MARCH 22, 2010

Two days after the Sub-Ocean Brightside Explosion

"Make no mistake, this is a baptism by fire, but Mandala will come back galvanized by this."

— **Christopher Shelley, Mandala Worldwide CEO**

3

MAY 4, 2010

Forty-six days after the Sub-Ocean Brightside Explosion

I have come to realize that pythons do not make good family pets.

However, this epiphany, like most epiphanies in my life, has arrived a little too late. The only thing I can figure is that Emily must have forgotten to feed Dolly this month. Now our snake smells some smaller mammal on my clothes, and she thinks it's dinnertime. So Dolly is doing what Dolly does best: squeezing her prey to death.

It's the natural order of things, I guess.

Or maybe, just maybe, a 20-foot reticulated python isn't the kind of animal that you let take free rein of your home, no matter how sweet and docile you once thought she was—no matter how much you thought you could keep the natural order of things under control by feeding it freeze-dried rodents, and even a few live goats. Either way, Dolly has wrapped herself, at first playfully, around my thigh. But now, after striking me twice in the face, she is crushing my rib cage. I have both hands around her neck so that she won't strike me a third time. I try to remain calm. I try to get Dolly to remember who I am, to get her to realize that my heart is bigger than a rabbit's—that I am the source of her food, not her food.

"Please," I whisper to her black and caramel coils. "Let me go."

Blood runs down my forehead into my eyes, and all I can really see is Dolly's open mouth—a black hole surrounded by pink and white sinew, a reverse-birth canal lined with saw-like teeth. She is stronger than I am. She is one undulating swell of muscle, squeezing the blood from my leg, twisting my internal organs, and tightening my breath into gasps.

This will be how I die: On the floor of our playroom among the scattered Goldfish crackers and Berenstein Bears books. Emily is at the grocery store, and Jo-Jo and Stewart are in the next room playing trains. I pray that they stay in there, that they don't hear my thrashing and groaning. I pray that they don't come to me for more juice or a blanky. They are little boys, only three and five, easy prey once Dolly realizes that I am perhaps too big for her to swallow.

She coils around my neck. Constricting. I can't breathe. I can feel every vein in my head.

I need a knife.

A rock.

A heavy book.

Something to bash her head in.

I start to black out, and to top things off, my iPhone won't quit chirping, taunting me. Buzzing and chirping, reminding me that Emily is not at the store, that Stewart and Jo-Jo are not playing trains, and that we don't own a twenty-foot reticulated python named Dolly. Chirping and buzzing, waking me up to the fact that I hate snakes, that this is just another impossible scenario in tonight's medley of panic dreams.

My iPhone is actually on my bedside table, and I am not in the playroom. I am in my bed, fighting the pillow and sheets.

I roll over in the dark and answer the chirping.

"Hello?"

"They're pursuing a criminal investigation!" Someone is shouting at me on the other end.

"Who is it?" Emily puts her hand on my shoulder.

I don't know. All I really know right now is how much I fucking hate snakes.

"Duke, you there?" the voice asks.

"Yeah, yeah. Who is this?"

"Wake up. It's Gary."

"What's the matter?"

"It's happening. The DOJ wants us to preserve evidence. They're pursuing a criminal investigation. I need you to come in."

"Now?"

"We need to get ahead of this."

I focus my eyes on the clock radio on the bedside table. It's four a.m.

"The networks are breaking the story on the East Coast within the hour. We're at DEFCON 5."

"You mean DEFCON 1. DEFCON 5 is actually the lowest level of alert. DEFCON 1 is, you know, the highest."

"This isn't a joke, Duke."

"I'll be there in an hour," I yawn.

"Get here now." Gary hangs up. No apologies for calling me at this ungodly hour. No thanks for coming into the office at four-in-the-fucking morning. Just a click.

"What was that all about?" Emily asks.

"Gary. I have to go in."

"Try not to wake the boys."

I put my phone back on the bedside table and get up to take a shower in the dark.

* * *

When I walk into the New Orleans offices of Mandala World-wide, it might as well be 5:30 in the afternoon, not 5:30 in the morning. Everyone is popping up and down, turning their heads back and forth above their cubicles like meerkats. The glare of the office lights casts everything in the present tense. We are all wide awake and shell-shocked, running around, sloshing coffee, printing emails, slamming phones, and kicking printers. We are all scrambling to cap an oil spill[1] that threatens to destroy the Gulf of Mexico as well as our company.

---

1. The Sub-Ocean Brightside Oil Spill started on March 20, 2010, in the Gulf of Mexico when the Mandala Worldwide-owned and operated deepwater rig exploded, killing 50 men and sinking the entire structure after a 72-hour inferno. The Sub-Ocean Brightside flooded the ocean with petroleum for 146 days until it was contained on August 13, 2010. 5.9 million barrels were estimated to have been spewed into the Gulf of Mexico from this spill. The Sub-Ocean Brightside was declared sealed on September 11, 2010, by the U.S. government. However, reports in late 2013 have established that the site is still leaking.

"Today is going to be a real gang-bang." Gary walks me back to his office. "The DOJ is going to be so far up our rectum, I can't stand it. And we got Christopher Shelley down in Venice today. And to top it off, Wilkers just green-lit lowering the containment dome."

"That's good, right?"

"Game changer." Gary hands me a file folder stamped CON-FIDENTIAL. "But the press is going to grill Christopher today about the DOJ, so he needs us to craft the answers to sidestep all that. Constanze is going to need your crisis-management plan within the hour."

"Within the hour?"

"You're going to have to wrestle this python to the ground, Duke. The press conference starts at noon."

"You just say python?"

"Yeah." Gary squints. "So what?"

"Nothing," I say. "Nevermind."

"The intern's making a Starbucks run when they open," Gary yawns. "Tell him I want a venti double latte extra hot and get something for yourself."

So I put in my coffee order, and then I get busy pulling together another memo for our CEO's press conference. I will give Christopher Shelley the precise words to explain how this oil spill is not entirely Mandala Worldwide's fault. Words are strange and powerful devices, and most people I work with have no idea how strange and powerful their words actually are—especially Christopher. The shit that comes out of his mouth blows the mind. Every single word we utter at a time like this is a grenade, and it's my job to make sure we lob them all in the right direction.

Not to put too fine a point on a very complex situation, but the Chinese drilling tools and equipment that we thought we had ordered for this well were not, in fact, the drilling tools and equipment that we actually purchased. This bait and switch will become the cornerstone of our legal defense once this thing inevitably goes to trial, and it's never too soon to start building this narrative. So within a matter of about fifteen minutes, I will distill these very arcane petroleum engineering facts into easy-to-repeat sound bites for Christopher Shelley. My brief this morning won't be my best work, but it will at least give him enough talking points to help deflect the press—reporters who, by the way, have no idea how geologically disastrous things really are.

Despite my best efforts, the press and the bloggers are sharpening their knives for us. Even with the breaking news of dropping the containment dome, they will be coming after big bad Mandala Worldwide and our Sun King CEO. Every end-of-the-world scenario needs an Antichrist, and Christopher Shelley is perfect casting right now.

The fact is capping a well as deep as the Sub-Ocean Brightside is closer to NASA than it is to Exxon. This disaster is Apollo 13, not the *Valdez*. No one has ever had to kill a well a mile beneath the ocean. We have to make this shit up as we go. We have to invent something as complex as a mission to the moon in a matter of days.

The first few days of the Spill were exhausting, but as the days have passed, as it has become apparent that we may have opened a hole in the earth that can never be closed, the exhaustion has metastasized into wide-eyed terror, and that terror is now grabbing us all by the throats.

Every day, gossip blazes through our office like a forest fire. The burning rumor last week involved a megaton of tennis balls. The idea is to cram them into the hole to plug it up.

My friend Josh in accounting told me that he saw the purchase order for the tennis balls. Millions of dollars' worth of tennis balls. Which is better than the rumor week before last, which involved detonating an atom bomb on the ocean floor. Thankfully, as of today, Dan Wilkers, our Chief Operating Officer and resident George Clooney look-alike, isn't moving forward with the millions of dollars' worth of tennis balls or the nukes.

The current plan is to drop an enormous steel dome on top of the well and then suck the oil out. The press should be all over this, but they are not. They are manic with catastrophe. They'd rather replay the explosion that killed fifty of our workers. They'd rather say we've stabbed New Orleans in the neck, that we've killed the wetlands and murdered the fishing industry.

* * *

Earlier this year, before the Sub-Ocean Brightside exploded, Emily and I had been living in Houston. My most challenging day at Mandala Worldwide U.S. headquarters usually involved our ad agency putting a trademark symbol in the wrong place in a *Time Magazine* ad. That was once considered a five-alarm fire for External Affairs. That's because life back then within America's Energy Corridor was good, beautiful actually—oil prices were soaring along with our stock price, and we were "drill-baby-drilling." The money was practically printing itself. As a result, our office park was a perk-filled neverland: Free snacks. On-site baristas. Chair massages on Wednesdays. I had just hung my favorite Shepard Fairey print in my new office overlooking the Mandala Worldwide Zen sand garden when I got the call from my boss Gary.

"I need you in New Orleans ASAP," he said with his mouth full.

"What are you eating?"

"Pumpkin ravioli. Chef really outdid himself today."

"I'll have travel book my flight tomorrow," I said. "Who am I meeting in New Orleans?"

"Oh, this isn't a trip. We're moving you."

"What?"

"We need External Affairs on the ground in New Orleans," he said.

"Stewart just started school."

"I need you in New Orleans, Duke."

"I'm going to have to talk to Emily about this."

"We've got you in corporate housing. I'll send you a link to the house. It's on a golf course in Covington, just outside the city."

"Covington is not just outside the city. It's across the Pontchartrain, Gary."

"If it makes you feel any better, I'll be moving too."

"I haven't passed the bar in Louisiana," I remember saying.

"Nice try," Gary said. "HR will be coming by to give you the details."

A week later, Emily and I were bubble-wrapping her grandmother's Wedgwood china and bossing the movers not to break our shit, and whether I liked it or not, Mandala was moving my young family back to the city and the woman that I had spent my entire life scrambling to escape.

4

EVE OF ST. GEORGE'S

May 5, 2010

Ever since Mandala moved me back to Louisiana in April, my mother, the infamous doomsayer, has done her level best to make me miserable. The woman seems intent on punishing me for abandoning her and this town, for defying her predictions, for marrying Emily and fathering my two sons despite her dire warnings against doing both. So now that I am back, Mama picks fights with Emily and throws tantrums constantly.

Take tonight, for example. She has decided to pull a vanishing act.

Poof!

Just like that, Mama has disappeared, and nobody can find her. She didn't take her purse or her phone. Daddy says that a calico cat ran into her kitchen shortly after Jay Leno's monologue, and my mama, whose superstitions compel her to believe that calico cats are basically text messages sent from the devil, chased the filthy animal with a broom, out the house, down Magazine Street.

She was in her black velvet robes and red satin slippers.

"The police ain't got nothin'." Daddy shakes his head. But then again, Mama isn't exactly going to be at the top of their lists. She isn't just some feeble old lady who got confused and wandered out into the streets. Mama is the long shadow that most New Orleans cops wisely avoid. She's the uneasy feeling they get before they bust down a door of a drug lord; she's the whispers in the storage units where Colombian neckties are cut; she's the prayers made by handcuffed prostitutes in the back of squad cars.

Or at least that's what she's always told me.

Mama comes from a long line of mystics and mountebanks. My grandfather, Yuri Blavatsky, was something of a Rasputin for the Albanian Royal Family before the communists took over. According to Mama, Yuri's diabolical predictions were legendary in Eastern Europe, and if this is true, he came by his sinister reputation honestly. After all, he was the only son of Madame Helena Petrovna Blavatsky[1], the dark sorceress of the New Age and the shadowy muse of Tolstoy, Gandhi, and Einstein. My great-grandmother even has her own Wikipedia page—which

---

1. HP Blavatsky was a 19th-century German-Russian aristocrat, occultist, and medium born in the Ukraine on August 12, 1831. She co-founded the Theosophy Society in New York in 1875 based on Hermetic principles she acquired from her travels to Tibet. She was a historical figure of dubious reputation who claimed to be led by an assortment of astral guides and ascended masters. Her influence was broad and astonishing. Many prominent thinkers and creators of her day, like Thomas Edison (the light bulb), L. Frank Baum (*The Wonderful Wizard of Oz*), and Abner Doubleday (baseball), were among her devotees. She was regarded as a beloved guru by her followers and scorned as an insufferable con artist by everyone else. Large swaths of Blavatsky's life have been unaccounted for. However, one thing is for sure, Blavatsky's prolific writings flooded modern Western thought with Hindu and Buddhist ideals. This wave of spiritualism inundated America at the turn of the century, resulting in a surge of disparate esoteric movements that continue on to this day—from spiritualism and anthroposophy to Oprah Winfrey and Lululemon.

Mama shamelessly pulls up on her phone to show to any and everyone who fails to grasp the fearsome magnitude and historical significance of the name,

"Blavatsky!"

Because of this occult bloodline, my mother, Helena Petrovna Blavatsky Melançon, is not just her grandmother's namesake, but heir to the throne of Osiris and Thoth, predictor of Katrina and Obama, secret advisor to Russell B. Long and Carlos "The Little Man" Marcello, and, most recently, Brad and Angelina.

These credentials are shouted from the hand-painted signs that litter her front yard, beneath the buzz and glow of an enormous red neon palm. Madame Melançon "Knows all! Sees all! Tells all!" And to further prove it to everyone who comes inside the house, her parlor is plastered with autographed headshots of just about every celebrity imaginable.

Take, for example, the photo of the tan man, the one with the slicked-back silver hair, hanging next to the china cabinet. That's Willy Williams, the former governor of Louisiana. When Williams was in office, the press liked to call him the "Silver Fox." Mama just called him Willy. For a better part of three decades, the governor would drive down to New Orleans, go for oysters across the street at Casamento's, and then walk over to The House of the Neon Palm. I'd watch him come in with his state troopers by his side. He'd kneel before my mother, and she would read his palm. She would spit the secrets of the shadows into his ear.

Then one day in 1998, Willy Williams had a few too many Harvey Wallbangers across the street, and he thought it'd be cute to share a joke that he had heard when he was vacationing in the south of France with his new wife. So the Silver Fox says to my mother, "You know what happens if you stick your hand up a fortune-teller's dress? You get your palm red every twenty-eight days."

Williams laughed until his face turned purple and tears came to his eyes. Tears came to my mother's eyes as well, but not because she was laughing. My mother was straining to summon the Hounds of Hecate; she was giving Willy Williams a good old-fashioned evil eye.

"Я собираюсь дерьмо все над вами!" Mama hurled a powerful curse at the then governor of Louisiana—a curse that when translated into English loses considerable mystical impact because it simply means "I am going to shit all over you!"

"Ваше имя будет забыто," or "May your name be forgotten," was what my mother whispered when Williams drove away that night in his state-issued limousine, and from that moment, Willy Williams was doomed. Whether Mama tipped off investigators or her prayers actually obliterated the angels who had been protecting the governor is still debated in the darkest bars of New Orleans to this day. Either way, Williams' magnificent luck was removed. Exactly one week after pissing off Mama, the feds swooped down and threw his sunburnt ass in jail. In a matter of months, Governor Willy Williams was found guilty on seventeen of twenty-six counts, including racketeering, extortion, money laundering, mail fraud, and wire fraud.

People all over New Orleans who have any kind of sense will tell you, "Do not disrespect the Lady." This has been my mama's tagline for over forty years of advising some of NOLA's biggest kingpins, celebrities, and criminals, and the woman has that saying trademarked. So as you can see, this makes her disappearance even harder to figure out. No one in their right mind—and when I say no one, not even the dumbest, lowest-level mobster—would dare mess with Madame Melançon, much less kidnap her.

* * *

From Mama's front porch, I stare out over Napoleon Avenue. I look up at the power lines running through the canopy of oak trees and imagine the lines running through all the oak trees on every street of this city. At the end of one of these power lines, on one of these old streets, is Mama. Which lines are running from her to me? If I could find the right one, then I could follow it to her. It's an odd thought, but one I can't shake.

"Why are you doing this to me?" I actually say out loud. I close my eyes and inhale the past—the nighttime smells of my child-hood—the jasmine and sweet olive, the crawfish shells rotting in nearby dumpsters, the beer and piss souring in the streets.

"Someone kill the fatted calf, the prodigal son has returned."

I turn around.

"Wow, look at you," I say.

My younger sister, La La, is aping Gwen Stefani this week: Glit-tery forehead dot. Lots of red lipstick. White-blond hair swirled into a 1940s 'do.

"Don't start," she says. "Don't even start with me."

La La, the unlucky one, believes that these pop-star disguises confuse the Fates. That these costumes will cause Fortuna, the goddess of destiny, to mistakenly deliver the celebrities' good luck to her lifeline instead.

"She's a jinx, our cross to bear," Mama would always say when I'd challenge them both about this nonsense.

So at the ripe old age of thirty-one, La La's a spinster, unable to marry lest she unleash a groundswell of misfortune upon any man who would even dare kiss her. The worst part of this is that La La actually believes it.

"I dreamt of the Pythoness last night," she says.

"The what?"

"The Pythoness. Mama."

"Pythoness?" I say.

"The Bee Maidens brought that dream to me."

"So did the Bee Maidens tell you where she is?"

"There's been a tear in the brocade of time," my sister says without a whiff of irony. "An unseen hand is unraveling our very destiny."

"Right."

"Do not disrespect the Lady!"

"Then peddle that horse shit someplace else," I say.

"Don't come here after all these years and call what we do bullshit!"

"I didn't call it bullshit. I called it horse shit."

"The Bee Maidens aren't to be trifled with!"

La La walks away. She slams the front door and the light bulb over my head pops and leaves me standing in the dark. Poltergeist-y things always seem to happen around La La. If Mama were here, she would tell you that the Bee Maidens—The Melissae—like to make strange and obscene gestures whenever La La's upset. Mama also liked to tell her customers that La La sips the future and gulps the past, that she can bend spoons and read your dog's soul.

"Your sister's ears are open. She can hear things as they truly are: Infinite and Loud!" Mama would say. "You will be like that one day, Dukey!"

"Don't call me Dukey," I would say.

"I am your mother. I call you what I want."

"Why can't you just be normal?"

"Bah! Normal! You know what's normal? Normal is an entire nation marching people into trains only to put them into ovens and gas chambers. That's what normal is. People doing terrible things to other people. That's what normal is and that's what no child of mine will ever be!"

So my mother, like any good occultist in need of extra cash flow, sent her "pet psychic" daughter out into the world with my brothers Vlad and Roman to New Age conferences and Renaissance fairs to con grieving pet owners and sell bent silverware. La La and my six brothers—Roman, Timur, Yanko, Stevo, Vlad, and Louis—all believe Mama's hocus-pocus bullshit. Unlike me, my siblings have obediently followed Mama's prophecies and wrapped themselves inside the comfort of her lies. So now they will be intent on conjuring up the curses of the past, waging war on her secret enemies, or whatever a jinxed daughter and her brothers do when their witchy mother runs out into the hot, syrupy night, chasing a calico cat.

* * *

"I should be there," Emily argued with me over the phone.

"I'm not sure I want the boys around all this," I said.

"The boys will cheer up your father."

"Daddy hates kids."

"Too late. I've already got them in their car seats."

And that was that: Emily shows up with a bag full of breakfast tacos and Jo-Jo and Stewart dressed in their matching gingham jumpers and saddle oxfords. Stewart comes running up the steps and into my arms. I'm glad Emily didn't listen to me. I'm glad she's a better person than I am. I'm glad she showed up with her baby-blue cardigan tied around her shoulders and that smirk of hers.

"You hungry?" She pulls a foil-wrapped taco out of her bag.

"Starving, actually. Thanks." I kiss her and take the taco. "Come inside. Daddy and La La have gone back upstairs to rest. We can eat in the parlor." I grab Stewart by the hand while Emily carries Jo-Jo inside.

"Papa, you want to play dinosaurs with me?" Stewart asks.

"Sure," I say. "You gonna be the T-Rex again?"

"Nah, you can be the T-Rex. I'm gonna be a python!"

"A python?"

He hisses at me and giggles.

It's hard not to attach meaning to these coincidences, but just because my boy says "python" moments after my sister's rant about "the Pythoness" right after I have a dream about a python doesn't mean anything. These coincidences are just that: unrelated events that just happened to coincide.

But Mama would say, "There are no coincidences, only the chess moves of an unseen hand." And I would say, "Please just stop with all that. I'm not one of your stupid marks."

Anyway, Emily sits the boys at the table. She unwraps a taco and hands it to Stewart.

I can't help but smile watching my boy feed himself.

"You going in today?" Emily sits down and puts Jo-Jo in her lap.

"Nah, I'll just work from here. Gary's emailing me the press releases."

"The article in the *Times* was pretty fair." She repositions Jo-Jo on her other knee and feeds him pieces of her breakfast taco. "But CNN is on a total witch-hunt."

"Put a hole in people's ocean, and that happens."

"Well, it's just not..." She plucks the taco apart, and Jo-Jo plays with the pieces. "It's just not very productive to be so critical when everyone's working so hard to figure this out."

Emily begins sniffing the air. She picks up Jo-Jo and holds his butt up to her nose. "Oh, somebody had a grumpy."

"I do not!" Jo-Jo pouts.

Emily gets up from the table and takes Jo-Jo to the bathroom.

"Daddy?" Stewart tugs at my shirt. "You ready to play?"

"You bet, Tiger."

"I'm not a tiger. I'm a snake!" He hisses.

I pick up my boy and fly him around the parlor like an airplane, over the crystal balls and tarot cards, around the palmistry diagrams and astrology charts that haunted my childhood.

5

ST. GEORGE'S FEAST

May 6, 2010 (Russian Orthodox)

When Uncle Father, my daddy's older brother, walks into the house, he is dressed in full priestly garb. Not just his white collar with the black short sleeves and gray pleated pants, but his floor-length, *Exorcist*-ready cassock. Emily and I sit in the parlor with my father. Daddy holds the remote control in his hand, and we all watch Anderson Cooper talk about how Mandala Worldwide has broken the planet.

"Sorry, I'm late," Uncle Father sings. He only sings his words when he is lying. "Had to cover mass in the Ninth Ward for Brother O'Neal. Didn't have time to change."

"Well, ya here now." Daddy doesn't look away from the TV.

"He had time to change," I whisper to Emily.

"He seems nice," she says.

"Oh, he is, but those robes are to protect him from Mama's voodoo."

"And he's one of your dad's brothers?" Emily asks. "How does that work?"

"It doesn't." I nuzzle Emily's neck. Her perfume smells like tangerines, cucumbers, and clover.

"You two need to get a room," Uncle Father interrupts.

"Oh, sorry. Hi." Emily pushes me away and holds out her hand. "I'm Emily."

"Everyone calls me Uncle Father." He shakes her hand. "Hanging out with this scoundrel will get you into trouble."

"I already got her into trouble," I say. "Twice."

"Did you bring the boys with you?" Uncle Father asks.

"They're down for a nap right now," Emily says.

"Well, can't wait to meet 'em," Uncle Father says. "Come here, T'boy!"

He pulls me up off the couch and into an Uncle Father hug. He smells like frankincense, tobacco smoke, and furniture polish.

"Welcome home, T'boy." He slaps my back. "Where's your sister?"

"Upstairs. She's up in her room."

"Of course she is." He shakes his head and then points at Daddy. "How's he holding up?"

"Complaining a lot about his phantom leg," I say. "But other than that, he's doing pretty well, considering."

"Have faith. We shall persevere." He puts his hand on my shoulder.

"What should we be doing?" I search his gray eyes for an answer. "I feel like we should be doing something."

"Duke, all you can do is pray and wait. Pray and wait."

Without another word, Uncle Father clears the parlor of what he believes to be the Devil: the ebony St. Sarah statues and the blue-eyed nazars, Mama's crystal ball and the Masonic flags, the candles and the amethyst-encrusted skulls, the tarot and the runes. He gathers everything up into one of Mama's purple silk scarves, and he carries the witchery into the kitchen. He dumps it all in a pile on the table. With Mama's arts and crafts in the other room, where God can't see them, Uncle Father lights candles for his saints in the parlor.

"Let's circle up," he holds out his palms. Emily takes his right hand, and I take his left. Daddy struggles to stand up from the couch with his crutches. He steadies himself and grabs onto Emily's free hand and then mine to close the circle of prayer.

"Let us bow our heads. Dear Heavenly Father…" My uncle clears his throat and then he prays first for God's forgiveness and then for Mama's soul. He calls for her safe return and for God's will to be done. He says something in Latin, throws holy water around the room, lights a candle beneath a Virgin Mary statue that he brought from the church, and then sits down on the couch next to Daddy. He shotguns three Dixie Beers and falls fast asleep with his mouth open and his dentures hanging from his gums.

So here we all sit on Mama's old velvet couches with the TV on mute, Uncle Father snoring, the mantel clock ticking, and the phone not ringing.

"She'll come back," Daddy breaks the aching silence. "You know how she is."

But no, this is not how she is. She's done a lot of crazy stuff before, but not this. This is not what Mama would have done willingly. This is not like her in any way, shape, or form.

"We should be looking for her," Emily whispers.

My wife is right.

Lighting a candle and taking a nap is not going to bring Madame Melançon home. We should be out looking for her: We should find a recent photo of Mama, put it into an envelope, and then drive to the FedEx on Tchoupitoulas and have them make 2,000 missing-person's fliers. Then we should drive back to the house with the boxes of fliers and split up. La La and Daddy can cover our neighborhood and the Garden District. Uncle Father can hit Uptown and the Fairgrounds, and I can tackle the Quarter, the Marigny, and the Bywater. Emily can take the boys in a stroller and hit the neighboring houses on the block.

"Come with me," I say to Emily.

6

MAY 7, 2010

Over forty-eight hours since Mama disappeared

In the past day or so, we have posted Mama's fliers all over this city. By noon today, I have canvassed most of Canal and half of the Quarter, and I still have five or six boxes of fliers left in my Prius. A lot of the bars and restaurants aren't even open yet, and the ones that are, are full of talkative "Y'ats."

"Where you at, bruh?"

"Who me?"

"Yeah, where y'at? Who ya been hangin' out wid? Ya cousin Larry?"

And all these "Y'ats" have a missing-person story: Katrina this. Attic that. Crazy *mémère* this. Drunk ex-husband that. Blah blah blah blah blah blah.

Just put my poster up, I want to say.

I take my fliers all the way through the Quarter, down Bourbon. I staple them to phone poles. I tape them to streetlights and onto the doors of bars. All the while the tourists are bumping into me, sloshing their big plastic party cups and pissing in the streets, laughing at their own jokes and singing karaoke. Being around all these drunk fucks brings back every bad feeling I ever had as a kid growing up here. Look, I am sure it's a blast to visit New Orleans and to drink in all this broken beauty, to break all your promises to yourself about your health, your fidelity, and your dignity.

Obviously, look at all these ass hats.

But growing up here, watching everything and everyone fall apart day in and day out was an existential beat-down that's almost beyond words. Living under the neon palm, I saw it all: the heart-breaking misery of the people stuck living here and the teeth-grinding avarice of the tourists who come to exploit it. I grew up ankle deep in the party gravy of an eternal morning after. It was a stain and a stench that was impossible to wash off. What all these stumbling partygoers don't want to face is the fact that there are actually two New Orleans: the "Zip-a-Dee-Doo-Dah" city of their Trip Advisor imagination, and then there is the real New Orleans, the belly of the beast that every tourist is terrified their taxi driver might take a wrong turn into.

This real New Orleans teaches whoever grows up here that good luck is not doled out by a fair and even hand. This simple yet horrible fact haunted me as a child. It overwhelmed me with a hopelessness and fear for the future that still haunt me to this day. But Mama was always much more sanguine about all of this. When I would try to get her to understand how much this weighed on me as a kid, how much it terrified me, she would always spit Shakespeare back to me in Russian, "Это не в звездах, чтобы держать нашу судьбу, но в нас самих," which means, "It is not in the stars to hold our destiny but in ourselves."

So I took Shakespeare's words to heart. I held my destiny in my own hands, and I took it out of this sinking city. I took my destiny as far away from Madame Melançon's House of the Neon Palm as I could. However, now that I find myself back here twenty years later, walking through these same streets amongst the lost partiers and slobbering drunkards, I realize it is impossible to hold your destiny in your own hands, to escape your fate. Because I am here once again in New Orleans—despite all my best efforts to never come back, I am here dealing with my mother's shadowy past—just like I would be if I had never left.

So, Shakespeare, you were wrong. Destiny is not in our hands. It is held in places far harder to grasp. It is waiting for us in the bottom of OxyContin bottles, in the winds of a hurricane, in the flashing lights of a police car, and for me, in the emails of an imploding oil company.

By the time I make it to Café Du Monde, I am drenched in sweat and mired in a lifetime of weird guilt and bad feelings. My lower back is killing me. But with the staple gun in my left hand and a box of fliers in my right, I make myself walk into the front door of Francesca's Famous Pralines.

Everything smells like melted butter, roasting pecans, and brown sugar. The air conditioning feels better than the cool side of a pillow on a sleepless night.

"Welcome to Francesca's! Best dang pralines you ever put in your mouth!"

I am greeted by a tall woman with bright hazel eyes, a vanilla ice cream complexion sprinkled with orange freckles, and a warm, gap-toothed smile. She has one hand on her hip while the other holds a small silver tray full of praline samples.

"Want to try one?" She skewers a broken praline with a toothpick and holds it up.

"Actually I was wondering if you could hang one of these for me." I hold up a flier.

"Madame Melançon?" Francesca looks at Mama's photo and smiles. "She's my girl."

"You a client?"

"Oh, yeah, she got my boo back for me."

"So would you mind putting up a flier? Help us find her?"

"For sure." She puts down her tray on a stack of praline boxes and studies Mama's photo. "What you think happened?"

"Don't know," I say. "Ran out the house chasing a cat and never came back."

"Feel sorry for whoever messed with the Lady." She shakes her head.

"I appreciate it." I hold up my roll of tape. "Need any?"

"Nah, we got tape," she says. "Hey, let me ask you a question."

"Sure."

"Your mama really put a curse on Anne Rice?"

"Where'd you hear that?"

"That's what people be saying. Creepy bitch packed up her baby dolls and left New Orleans real fast."

"Not so sure that's exactly true," I say.

"Just sayin'. I didn't like her vampire-ass no way." Francesca shoves a praline in my face. "Here, eat this."

I step back and shake my head, no.

"Come on now. These my Sugar and Spice." She touches the praline to my lips. "Got a little cayenne in them. Try it. Ain't like the sorry whatevers they sell at Praline Perfection. I promise you that."

I reluctantly open my lips, and Francesca deposits the brown candy into my mouth. It melts into a sandy-sweet, buttery warmth. The sting of the red pepper and sugar hits the back of my throat. The praline is so sweet it makes my heart race.

"Good, huh?" she says.

"Yeah, great," I say.

"How many you want?"

"I'll take a half-dozen."

"Here." She hands me a small white bag. "A little sumptin' sumptin'."

I pull out my credit card to pay, but Francesca pushes my hand away.

"Just a little *lagniappe*," she says. "You her baby."

"Thanks. That's very sweet of you."

"Have faith." She smiles, pushing her pink tongue through the gap in her teeth. "You gonna find her."

* * *

"Your lifeline is long and strong." I point to the crease in the middle of this Camellia Grill waitress' hand. "But you got to watch the smoking."

Once the waitress realized that I was Madame Melançon's son, she demanded that I read her palm if she was going to hang up my fliers. I'm a corporate lawyer. I don't read palms. But she didn't want to hear that. She shoved me into a booth and held out her open palm. She wanted her future told by the son of Madame Melançon, the Fortune-Teller Queen of New Orleans.

"What about my love life?" the waitress asks.

"That's complicated," I say.

"For real?" she laughs. "That's what it says on my Facebook. Shit's complicated."

I study the lines in the waitress' palm like I know what I am doing. While I don't read palms, I do know what each of the lines mean. You don't grow up under the roof of HP Blavatsky's grand-daughter and not know what a broken heart line forebodes, or a "Ring of Solomon" augurs.

"See that line running across your heart line? That's a new love," I say.

"Is that a line you want to cross?" She fingers my hand with little tornados.

"I'm married," I say.

"Too bad." She withdraws her palm. "You cute. A little nerdy but cute."

I don't know what to say. I am all out of bullshit.

"You know I'm pretty sure your mama was in here a couple of weeks ago. Maybe three or four weeks ago. Sat over there." She glances to the table next to us. "Waited on her and this old man."

"Why didn't you say that to begin with? Are you sure you saw her?"

"Yo' mama had a cheeseburger. French fries with a side of mayo which is gross, but whatever. The old man ordered the chili but didn't touch it."

"What did he look like?" I say.

"Well, he was this Big Bird lookin' old man. Real tall and goofy."

"Goofy... What was he wearing?"

"Shirt and khaki pants. Maybe he got a mustache. Might have been a goatee, though. His clothes looked like he slept in them. Kinda crazy looking."

"Crazy looking?"

"Yeah, look like he drink too much."

The waitress has just described 99% of the people in the Quarter.

"What were they arguing about?" I say.

"Look, I ain't trying to get up in other people's Kool-Aid when I don't even know what flavor it is. Ya heard me?"

She just looks at me.

"Please," I say.

"The old man was saying something about your mama getting a cat," the waitress says. "Your mama was saying she don't want no cat and he kept saying she was getting one whether she liked it or not."

"They were arguing about a cat?"

"Yeah, I think so. Why you look so worried?"

"She hates cats. Like really hates cats."

"Look, I'm sorry about your mama." She shrugs. "But that's all I know. I got to get back to work."

"Here," I hand her my Mandala Worldwide business card. "If you think of anything else, call me."

"Oh." She shakes her head slowly. "My sister's husband was on that rig. He had three little girls." She hands my card back to me.

"I'm sorry."

"You got that right. You folks are sorry individuals." She turns and walks away.

I want to apologize. To tell her how bad we all feel back at Mandala about her brother-in-law and all the men who died on that rig. That we are all grieving but that this is also part of the danger of what we do. I want to explain this to her, but I don't.

Instead, I get up and walk past the restaurant's TV. CNN is rerunning footage of the Sub-Ocean Brightside explosion.

There's no getting away from what has happened.

The Spill has taken over everything. Every TV in every bar. Every ding on every iPhone. Every newspaper in every kitchen. Every birthday cake on every counter.

Yes, birthday cakes.

There are Mandala Worldwide Spill birthday cakes covered in black icing that are being sold at the Breaux Mart, down the way from Mama's house. I know this because Gary is texting me pictures of the stupid cakes.

Get them taken down.

People can make whatever birthday cake they want, I text back.

It's on the front page of Reddit, he texts. *Cease and desist.*

Impossible.

Now.

Do you even know what Reddit is? I text him back.

For the past forty-eight hours, Gary has peppered me with over three hundred texts and emails, threatening to fire me while simultaneously begging me to come into the office. Thanks to the Spill—if you believe CNN—the whole world is dying, and I'm wandering the French Quarter, passing out missing-person's fliers to people too drunk, too hungover, or too stupid to care. If I were superstitious, I'd say I was on the receiving end of a curse.

7

MY FEET ACHE

I am a thunderstorm of sweat and B.O. I hate New Orleans in the springtime. It's so humid down here—breathing feels more like drinking. By late afternoon, I have made it all the way to the Orange Food Store on Rampart, and after a clumsy half-hour conversation with the sweet Vietnamese owner-lady, who I think says, "Sure thing, sugar," when I ask her if she will hang a flier, I order a shrimp po'boy, and like it says on the handmade sign next to the beer case, I *"Don't eat sandwich inside store!"*

I take my food outside, and I wash it down with a Coors Light hidden inside a brown paper bag. It's a dinner as holy and redemptive as any mass. After I finish, I wipe the sweat and grease off my face with a napkin and toss the white butcher paper and brown bottle into the trash. I then walk across Kerlerec Street to post Mama's fliers on the boarded-up windows of the abandoned Drop-in Center.

This dead corner of the neighborhood is manned by a mustachioed homeless-guy-slash-street-artist. He stands on a milk crate with an upturned straw hat at his feet. He reads *Slaughter-house-Five* out loud and with great affectation. The old guy in the rumpled suit is pretending to be Kurt Vonnegut, and he's doing a pretty good job of it—same world-weary face, basset hound eyes, and the broom-bristle mustache. He's got the happy curmudgeon thing down pat, but there's something off about this guy. He's not like most street performers. First off, there are no tourists anywhere near here.

"You're doing it wrong!" he shouts at me as I walk past him.

"I'm doing it wrong?" I point to the Quarter. "Bourbon Street is that way, old man."

"You're not going to find her like that." He gestures to the fliers in my hands. "Plus you can't deface my building with those. I'll have you arrested."

"Looks like someone already beat me to it." I nod to the graffiti.

He steps down from his milk crate but still looms over me. He's a tall old man.

"Stay away from my art. That's a Banksy." He points to the life-size little girl rendered in black spray paint on the white wall. She stands under an umbrella, but the umbrella is not keeping her dry; it's actually the source of the rain. The girl's face eerily resembles Mama's in her younger days. If I was as obsessed with synchronicity as the rest of my family, I would say this girl being rained on by her own umbrella is some sort of sign—a symbol for New Orleans' constant struggle to remain dry, for the oil that both feeds us and ruins us, for Mama's bad karma that has come tumbling back onto her head. And even though I am not superstitious, the longer I look at the graffiti, the more it feels like God is playing tricks on me, the more a lump kicks in my throat and what feels like a hummingbird darts around inside my chest.

©Banksy 2008

I step back from the wall.

"Thank you, young man."

"Have you seen her?" I hand Vonnegut a flier.

"Ah, Madame Melançon," he says. "My dear friend, the Delphic Oracle. The Pythoness herself!"

And before I can ask the Vonnegut impersonator what the hell he is talking about, the unmistakable horns and illicit drumbeats of a second line explode from around the corner. We both stop talking and just watch the parade as it comes rolling towards us.

The Big Nine Social Aid and Pleasure Club proclaim their arrival with their satin banners and their big brass band. They booty-bounce and feather shake all over the street. High-stepping men in double-breasted black suits and white ties wave red and white ostrich feathers, grooving and shaking it with their shiny, gray alligator shoes. Women dressed in all-white pantsuits drop it low, low, low. Little boys in tuxedos and red bow ties smile and wave their red feather fans to the beat of a band that is so funky, so badass, so completely dirty that I have to resist the urge to bounce and butt-shake into the parade myself.

"Now if that's not proof that God exists, I don't know what is," Vonnegut winks at me. "No matter how screwed up this world gets, the music will always be wonderful. Never forget that."

"You were saying something about my mother being the Pythoness. What did you mean by that?" I ask.

"Just one of the Lady's many names, my boy. *Pythoness*. It has a menacing ring to it, doesn't it?" He elbows me. "You know I used to play the licorice stick myself. Seeing those fellows going down the street makes me think I should take up the clarinet again. You think your father could give me lessons?"

"You know my father?"

"Know of," he says. "Quite a musician, according to your mother."

"You know my mom…"

"The question is *do you know your mother?*"

"How do you know her?" I ask.

"Unfair question, I suppose. Do we ever really know a person?" Vonnegut rubs his mustache. "Especially our mothers."

"I asked you a question," I nudge him.

"Of course I know who Madame Melançon is. She's the Neon Palm who holds us in place until it's safe to proceed." He points to the red hand flashing on the crosswalk sign. "Madame Melançon's fingerprints are all over this city, all over this world. Those glowing red palms that we encounter at every intersection are hers. The universal symbol for 'wait, just wait, until it's safe to proceed' was conceived by the Lady. She is the one who convinced the New York City traffic engineers in the '80s to replace those clumsy 'Don't Walk' signs with her glowing red palm. This is just one of the many ways your mother holds us in her care, rewrites our history for our own benefit. She put her glowing handprint on every street corner of this blue marble, so you and I would know that she is holding us in place until it is okay to proceed into our futures."

"I just need to post these." I hold up the fliers. "Okay?"

"Put them around the way." He points to the boarded-up window on the other side of the corner. "Just not over the Banksy."

"Thanks." I walk around and put extra tape all around the edges of the fliers.

"Your mother," he follows me, "was our first hope against The Great Unseen Hand. You do realize that."

I stare at him. I try to look into his eyes to see if he's just messing with me or if he's as crazy as the words that are coming out of his mouth. Was this Vonnegut impersonator the Big Bird-looking old man that the Camellia Grill waitress was talking about? Or is he just one of the thousands of mental cases in this city who tremble before my mother because they believe she has magic powers?

"Ever wonder why you've never met a Tralfamadorian?" He shakes his tattered copy of *Slaughterhouse-Five* at me.

"No, can't say that I have."

"A Tralfamadorian." He points to the sky. "An alien. You want to know why you've never met one?"

"Because they're not real," I say.

"Actually, it's because of The Great Filter Theory." He chuckles. "That's why you've never met an alien or a time traveler for that matter. Humans always filter themselves out before they can reach that future. Homo sapiens always destroy themselves before they achieve that level of technology. At least that was until this mystical child from the Ukraine showed up." He points to the umbrella girl on the wall.

"Your mother changed everything."

"I have a lot of fliers to post," I say.

"No, wait." Vonnegut grabs my shoulder. His fingernails ː prisingly well-manicured—shiny, pink.

I shake him off and step away.

"I need to ask you something," he says.

I just stare at him, not sure how my face should look, trying to hold a smile, so he will let me post my fliers.

"Could I trouble you for a cigarette?" Vonnegut bites his bottom lip. "I could use some combustible energy right about now."

"Don't smoke."

"What about a couple of bucks so I can buy a pack?"

"Didn't Kurt Vonnegut die from smoking?" I ask.

"That would have been a much classier way to go. What I did was fall down my stairs. Terrible mess. But let's not talk about the past," Vonnegut says.

"I'm not buying you cigarettes."

"You better hope some vandal doesn't come by and tear down your posters," Vonnegut says. "I'd be willing to watch them for you. Even ask people if they've seen your mom."

"How much?" I say.

"Pack of cigarettes, a beer, a po'boy would buy you a couple of days."

"It was just two bucks a few seconds ago."

"Inflation sucks," he says. "But that's capitalism."

"Here." I pull out two tens from my wallet and hand them to him. "You better not tear down my posters."

"Oh, thank you." He takes the crumpled bills and crams them into his pants pocket. "My batteries are running low, and I desperately need to refuel."

"No worries," I say.

"If this isn't wonderful, I don't know what is!" He nods at me, and then crosses the street to the Rampart Food Store, almost skipping.

8

MAY 8, 2010

Fifty days after the Explosion

Sergeant Mark Babineaux's a muscly guy who uses a little too much hair gel. He's the proud owner of a Kung-Fu tiger tattoo roaring up his left calf and a Purple Heart from being injured by an IED while on patrol in Afghanistan.

Mark and his wife, Jean, are why I came in to work today. Despite the fact my own wife blew a gasket when I told her I was coming in to close this deal. With a spill like this, timing is everything, and I have to get these two locked into a contract so our ad agency can start shooting the commercials in which the Babineauxes are slated to star.

So Mark and Jean Babineaux sit here in their flip-flops and jean shorts, across from me while I try to explain to them how commercials work.

"It's about two days of shooting." I point to that exact line on the document. "We'll then run the commercials, and the good news is every time we do that, we'll pay you what's called a talent residual."

The Babineauxes own a shrimping boat named the "Coon Ass[1] III," which is why our ad agency handpicked them to work with our restoration effort. It's a great boat with a funny name. It will show the humor and resilience of the people down here, just how plucky these poor Cajuns are. This kind of narrative is essential for Mandala to get into the "lame-stream media" to counter all the news stories about how Mandala has wrecked the economy down here. Once our engineers kill this well, it will be important to change the conversation: make it about how Mandala is working with the community, cleaning up the coast, saving shrimpers like the Babineauxes.

"That's in addition to the ten grand talent fee?" Jean Babineaux asks.

"That's correct," I say.

"How much in addition to?" Sgt. Mark Babineaux picks up the 150-page contract and flips through it.

"Really depends on how often we run the commercials," I say. "We pay union scale."

"What does that mean?" Jean looks me in the eyes for just a beat too long.

"It means you could make another twenty grand this month, easy, if we run it at the flight we have scheduled."

---

1. Coonass is an ethnic slur regarding Americans of Cajun decent. Many Cajuns have proudly reappropriated this word to describe themselves and their culture. The word can be found all over Acadiana on bumper stickers, coffee mugs, trucker hats, bass boats, and t-shirts. No one really knows where the term was first used or where it comes from. Some people will tell you that it refers to a Cajun's habit of eating raccoons and other game, while others claim the term goes back to when the Cajuns wore coonskin caps while fighting in the Battle of New Orleans.

Jean's skeptical, and it's bleeding over to Mark.

In all actuality, this is a really good deal for the Babineauxes. They will make more money in two days of shooting than they will in a month of shrimping.

"What if we don't like what the commercials say?" Jean asks.

"I don't know why you wouldn't. All we are going to do is show how Mandala Worldwide is helping you rebuild your business."

"How are you going to do that when all the shrimp are dead?" Mark asks.

"They aren't all dead," I say. "At least that's what our marine biologists are telling me."

"You been out on the water lately?" Mark raises an eyebrow. "Cause I have. They all dead and the ones that aren't are full of poison."

"They'll come back, and Mandala Restoration will help you until then."

"How much?" Mark asks.

"That's really between you and our restoration group," I say. "But if you're in our commercial, I can promise that you and Jean will move to the front of the line with them."

"Can we see the script first?" Jean asks.

"There's no script," I lie. "It's docu-style."

"Docu-style?" she says.

"We ask you questions and use your answers in the film," I explain.

Why is she killing this? They need to do this. They have to do this. They are perfect casting. Mark is the strong silent type, and Jean is pretty in that hardscrabble, hair-in-a-chip-clip Cajun sort of way. They both have strong, earnest faces of people who have weathered the storm.

"So ten grand and all we have to do is stand around on our boat, answer some questions, and let you take pictures of us?" Mark takes the contract from me.

"Pretty much," I say.

Jean takes the contract from Mark. "It's a lot of pages."

"It's standard," I say.

"We're going to need to let our lawyer look at this before we sign anything." Mark finally makes eye contact with me.

"By all means," I say. "I just need everything signed and notarized by early next Monday."

"We can't do next Monday," Jean says. "Mark's got group."

"I can skip group," Mark shrugs her off and then looks directly at me again. "I want to be paid in cash."

Jean makes another bad face like she is biting her tongue.

"Sure. If that's what you want," I say.

"Yeah, that's what I want."

"Just let me know when you can bring the contract back signed, and I'll have the cash ready."

"Make it all twenties," he says.

"Twenties it is."

"In a suitcase. One of those silver ones you see in movies."

"We can do that." I shake Mark's hand again. His grip is light. I notice the burn scar that covers his hand and crawls up his arm.

Mark nods at me without smiling, and then guides his wife by the elbow out of my office.

9

MOTHER'S DAY

Where are you?

I wake up Emily with a vase of peonies, along with her definition of a perfect cup of coffee—PJ's Southern Pecan with two splashes of coconut creamer and half a packet of stevia. Stewart and Jo-Jo bring her pancakes smeared with Nutella and strawberries, dropping the fork and napkin on the floor a couple of times before they get it to her.

Emily feeds her pancakes to the boys while they smear chocolate and strawberries all over our white sheets. It's a morning full of hugs and Eskimo kisses, duvet covers, and laughter. I take a picture of this fleeting, sunlit moment, a moment so sweet I grieve its loss before it's even over. It's an image that I will need to refer to in the coming weeks, especially the longer this thing with my mother drags on, and the more this spill contaminates everything in my life.

"Oh, wow!" Emily opens the card that Jo-Jo made for her at school. A couple of uncooked pieces of macaroni fall into her lap. "What is it, baby?"

"It's a big hand like the one on Mamaw's house." Jo-Jo holds his chubby palm up to Emily's face.

The card is a folded piece of pink construction paper, an outline of Jo-Jo's hand in red crayon, glued pasta all around it.

"The wed hand will po-tect you," he says.

The teapot is whistling in the kitchen for the second French press that I forgot.

"How will it protect me, sweetheart?" Emily looks at me.

"It will smush the monsta-hand that wants to disappea-us!" Jo-Jo claps his hands together.

"No such things as monsters," Stewart says. "You're just a baby."

Emily smiles at me as if to telepathically say, *that's a little weird. This son of yours is a little weird.*

I shrug.

"Come on, boys." Emily picks up Jo-Jo and gets out of bed. "Let's hop into the shower. Pappy's making lunch at his house, and Mommy needs to get ready."

"I'm not a baby." Jo-Jo hits his brother.

"Mom!" Stewart yells. "Jo-Jo's hitting me again."

* * *

After Emily and I get the boys bathed and dressed, we load them up in their car seats and drive across the Pontchartrain to my parents' house for Sunday jambalaya. By the time we hit Magazine Street, my phone is blowing up.

It's work.

I park the car under the flickering neon sign and make a mad dash upstairs, past my crazy family, to jump on a conference call.

I dial in and put my phone on mute.

Christopher Shelley's Chief of Staff, Constanze Bellingham, downloads the PR team in her lilting British accent. "At zero-six-hundred, we lowered the containment dome over the Sub-Ocean Brightside. Unfortunately, this attempt to kill the well was not successful. At zero-seven-thirty-two, engineers reported that the temperatures were too cold at those depths for this particular dome to be successful. In short, the methane from the well keeps freezing inside the dome, preventing the kill. Mr. Shelley is regrouping with our engineers as we speak, and I will update you as soon as we have more information. But at this time, we are aborting this attempt."

The conference call explodes with questions that Constanze can't answer, so I hang up. There's nothing more to learn or to say. The well is too far at the bottom of the ocean to kill. The press is going to eat us alive today.

And therefore, Gary will be leaving me a pissy voicemail to come and solve this, even though I worked sixty-eight hours straight, even though I lied and told him that I am down with the flu, even though it's Mother's Day, even though I respond to every email with deliberate and precise counsel, even though I made Christopher Shelley look like a rock star just two nights ago on Wolf Blitzer.

And now the deluge of texts:

The AP and Reuters both need another statement.

Call me.

Why aren't you answering your phone?

Need another press release to CBS. The last one we sent had incomplete details about the dome failure.

NPR wants to interview Wilkers. Email him the answers you prepared for Christopher.

Constanze claims she never got your last email. Resend ASAP.

Of course, I could tell Gary the truth, that my psychic mother is missing, that the police refuse to look for her, that we think she was likely kidnapped by a rival fortune-teller or maybe a crazy client, that she is probably rotting under an overpass somewhere south of I-10, but honestly, he would be all, "Oh, wow. So sorry to hear that. I hope they find her. That's terrible. Jeez... Give my regards to your family... Yeah, I hate to even ask this in light of all you're going through, but did you get a chance to look at that press release I sent you?"

I fire off a volley of emails, and while I am waiting for responses, I go back downstairs to see how Emily is dealing with my family. I walk past all the framed photos that hang along the walls. I stop and stare at the one with all of us at Olan Mills in the '80s hanging in the middle of the stairway. I passed it a million times growing up and never gave it much thought. It's all eight of us kids, towering over Daddy, who is holding Mama from behind. She was so young—her curly hair pulled tight into long, black braids, her big hazel eyes are incandescent just like her diabolical grandmother's were in old photos.

Where are you?

The smell of frying bacon pulls me away from my sad thoughts, down the stairs, and outside to the back porch where Daddy and Uncle Father are getting lunch ready. The two of them have the ten-gallon, gas-powered Cajun Cooker burning. Uncle Father is standing behind a card table piled high with *the holy trinity*: onions, celery, and bell peppers. Daddy's got his fake leg on. He only uses it when he cooks: "Frees up my hands. Ya heard me?"

"Where you at, T'boy?" Uncle Father grabs me around the neck and hugs me. "Where you at?"

"What it is, Uncle Father. What it is." I pat him hard on the back.

"Yeah, boy. We gonna find her," Uncle Father says. "The police got the Silver Alert going."

"We heard anything from the police?"

"Notta word." Daddy looks up from his cauldron of frying bacon and shakes his head. "Dinner will be ready 'round eleven." Uncle Father takes a swig from his Dixie Beer and holds it up to me. "Want one?"

"Sure."

Uncle Father reaches down in his green Igloo and pulls out a beer. He pops the cap off, and the brown bottle swells with suds.

"Ah, now dat one's gonna be a little moist." My uncle laughs as he hands me the gushing beer. This beer geyser won't stop. It just keeps going like the CNN footage of the Sub-Ocean Brightside bleeding 65,000 barrels a day, like the gushing blood from my mother's slit neck.

"Why you look so sad, son?" Daddy asks.

"I'm not," I smile.

"Ah T'boy, you gonna find her. You my seventh," Daddy says.

Uncle Father harrumphs and takes a long swig off his beer.

My daddy, Vinny Melançon, was my family's original seventh son, and his superstitions are perhaps easier to explain than my mother's. That's because he's not a Russian. He's Cajun — which comes with its own mixed bag of oddities and customs, but it's nowhere close to Mama's walls full of old books and bizarre family legends.

Daddy was born here in New Orleans to a sprawling Catholic family, the seventh son of his perpetually arguing yet somehow still sexually active parents. He grew up in this fancy white house on the corner of Magazine and Napoleon in the Faubourg Bouligny. His immediate family wasn't rich, but my *mémère*, my dad's mother, had inherited the place from a spinster aunt. So here was my dad's big, poor family living in this big, rich house that over time became a big, fat mess like much of the city.

My dad's childhood was pretty much a Crescent City cliché—a muddy swirl of life and decay, fried foods and hard liquors, hurricanes and humidity. My dad's family spoke French at home and English on the streets. They all played some sort of musical instrument, and by play, I mean mastered. My dad was given his uncle's clarinet at the tender age of six, and to this day, he can toot that thing like no one I have ever met. The Melançons ate red beans and rice on Mondays because everyone knows that Monday is washday. They ate fish on Fridays because the Pope said so. And for Lent, they gave up liquor, but not wine, because wine is not liquor. My dad, like every one of his brothers and sisters, grew up knowing exactly how dark to cook a roux to make a good gumbo—about as long as it takes to kill two cold beers, by the way. Like I said, they were your typical New Orleans family who may seem exotic to people not from here, but pretty normal, maybe even a little boring, to the rest of the city.

However, Mama will tell you that Vinny Melançon was special, and not because he was my *mémère's* favorite son or because he could make people forget their worries with just a clarinet. She will tell you that Vinny Melançon was chosen by the Three Bee Maidens of Fate to be her husband and my father. She will tell you that Vinny Melançon was destined to sire a New Age savior: me.

"Your daddy's home address at Magazine and Napoleon divined his destiny." My mother loved to tell this same story over and over as we grew up. "Daddy went to war like Napoleon, and it was a *magazine* launcher that almost killed him. See how that works?"

"It was an M79," Daddy would then specify. "I didn't know what I was doing."

In short, the magazine launcher backfired and ignited a gasoline tank, sending Daddy home to New Orleans with one Purple Heart, one glass eye, a fake left leg, and a burn scar that covered more than half his torso and resembled the state of Florida.

When my father shipped out in 1967, he was just an unlucky University of New Orleans student who failed out of college at a time when Uncle Sam drew his draft card. I can attest that my father's a good, brave man, but he will also tell you straight up that he never had any dreams of fighting for his country.

"Hell, that's what I went to college for in the first place. But I wasn't some kind of communist. So if I had to go, I had to go."

While war has been known to turn boys into men, my father loves to tell whoever will listen, "It just makes you old."

"But weren't you happy to be back? To have survived?"

"At that point, my life had been too long already. So I figure I'd just put myself out of my misery. But then I got this idea to go see a fortune-teller."

"Why a fortune-teller?"

"Wanted to make sure I wasn't gonna miss nothing."

So my father, who at the tender age of twenty-two was already a very old man, crutched it down to Jackson Square, where the artists sold their wares in front of St. Louis Cathedral. Daddy's government-issued leg didn't fit him right—rubbed a sore on him, so he left it at home and hopped around the Square on his crutches, with his left pants leg safety-pinned to his hip. To this day, he says he can get around faster that way.

"You know the Square wasn't like it is now. Back when I went down there, it was all these artists and painters. Famous ones and poor ones. There were only one or two fortune-tellers even allowed on the Square. They were the real deal. Not the kooks they got down there now. You know what I mean? You seen those crazy assholes down there with their turbans and their shitty costumes?"

The Jackson Square of today is full of "Nawlins" bullshit. There are dueling Bone Ladies dressed in red robes with white skulls painted over their faces. There are fake descendants of Marie Laveau and fat jazz guys in spangled purple pants juggling rubber chickens and fire batons.

"They all clowns!" my father would say. "Stupid clowns."

However, on that spring morning in 1967, before the idiots and amateurs had taken over the Square, my father came to the table of the real deal: Helena Petrofina Blavatsky's very own grand-daughter. A woman of the world in the full bloom of her thirties.

"She had big green eyes and long braids, and big lips—sweet, juicy lips like plums." Daddy smiled. "Back then, ya Mama called herself Sister Reverend Evangeline."

Like all higher initiates of The Theosophical Society, Mama has a name for outsiders, and a real name, her secret name. I cannot and will not tell you her secret name. However, I can tell you that she can read your fortune for five dollars; tell you your secret enemies for six; remove a curse for seven; bring back a lost love for twenty, just like she did that day for my father.

"She said, 'Alo, Vinny. I've been vaiting for you.' Your mama talked like Dracula back then. My ears perked up when she called me by name. I could definitely understand that. This pretty lady acted like she had known me all my life. Then she told me that if she spelled my name to God, she could tell me my whole life story from beginning to end. I told her, spell it!

So she did. Her eyes fluttered, you know how she likes to do, and she began to speak real fast. She told me that I had eight brothers and three sisters and that I was the seventh. She even told me their names. She told me about my buddies over in Nam and that our platoon leader, Lieutenant McTaggert, would be killed on his next tour of duty, and not that I wished anything bad on anyone, but I was glad to know that that bastard was checking out. So I took a seat and let her read my palm.

She told me that I would father eight kids myself and that I too would have a seventh son, a son who would do wonders for the world and for his family. That's when I told her she was wrong. I told her after her reading that I was going home to kill myself. I had already bought the bullets. She put her hand in my open palm.

She looked me straight in the eye and shook her head no. Then she took me out back behind the cathedral, to this courtyard with all this bougainvillea and sweet olive everywhere, and we made your brother Roman right there in broad daylight. I scratched the hell out of my backside on that bougainvillea, I tell ya."

"Ugh. Dad."

"It's the truth. Your mother was a very sexual woman."

"Seriously, I don't need to know that."

"Well, all I'm saying, Duke, is you don't sire eight kids by marrying a nun. You need to marry a woman who likes it."

"Change the subject. Please."

10

"DUKE!"

My brother Stevo runs to me with his arms outstretched; the black hair under his armpits is almost as long and matted as his black beard. He hugs me tighter and longer than I want.

"I thought we had lost you forever!" He pulls me closer, squeezing me. He smells like raw onions and pumpkin pie. He feels thin like he has the bones of a bird. When he lets me go, his wife, Cactus (yes, Cactus), also hugs me tighter and longer than I want.

"Blessings, my brother," she whispers hot in my ear.

She feels even more fragile, more bird-boned; she smells like cat pee and patchouli.

Stevo is in full-on hippie mode: pirate-black beard, long hair tied into a bun on top of his head, cut-off army fatigues, and Vedic tattoos all over his skinny torso. There are two naked toddlers at his ankles, and Cactus stands behind him, her dreads pulled back in a red bandana. She's wearing the flowy peasant garb of a flower child.

"That's your Uncle Duke, boys!" Stevo smiles and deep crow's feet crinkle around his eyes, revealing how harsh life has been since I last saw him. "Duke, these are your nephews, Paint and Brag."

Since I graduated law school, I haven't talked to Stevo. He hasn't called me. Emailed me. Facebooked. Done shit. Stevo, along with the rest of my brothers, expected me to do what they were doing—be dutiful to our mother's prophecies and con jobs. And because I wasn't, because I was willful and *faithless*, they shunned me. To be honest, I was fine with it.

If the only way not to spend my life tricking people out of their money with threats of demonology and long lists of secret enemies was to lose my brothers and sister, so be it. That was a price I gladly paid to live in a world that wasn't ruled by tarot cards and Aleister Crowley's incantations.

"Are they twins?" I ask.

"Ten months apart." Cactus smiles and looks down at the ground. She grabs Stevo's hand as if what she just told me made her oddly bashful.

Stevo and Cactus and their boys are beautiful—beautiful in the way that all wild things are beautiful. Stevo and Cactus are true nomads. They live on the road, roving from state park to state park, reading tarot with the Red Hawk Family—a pack of hippies who like to spread peace and love and herpes by gathering in groups of about 30,000. They like to have these big-ass campouts so they can sit around in drum circles, eat mushrooms, and swap old ladies. Mom arranged Stevo's marriage with Cactus when he was sixteen.

Cactus is more "Hey! Wow!" hippie than a serious student of the occult. Cactus's father, while he is technically a 33rd-degree Freemason, turned out to be some kind of "channeler" who pretends to be a Native American spirit guide and calls himself Chief

Red Hawk. The Red Hawk Family travel from state park to state park, but their life is so intertwined with the mundane, you could hardly call them practicing members of the Theosophy, at least not in a way that would ever make Mama happy. So much for my mother's "peeks behind the veil" and astrological matchmaking.

"Dad!" Stevo makes his way over to our father and hugs him even tighter than he hugged me. Cactus gives Uncle Father a chaste handshake while Paint and Brag continue to untie my shoes.

"When do we eat?" Stevo stares at the pot of boiling rice.

My phone buzzes in my pocket. It's another text from Gary:

Christopher's flying in on the 13th.

I need you in the office.

Answer the goddamn phone!!!

"You need to tell your sister to calm down." Emily comes out to the front porch, carrying a stack of red party cups full of plastic forks and paper napkins.

"She's on edge. Stevo's here." I take the napkins and forks from her, and tilt my head in the direction of my long-lost brother and his bird-boned wife who are now tumbling and laughing with their naked kids in the tall grass of my mama's backyard.

"Wow. He looks just like a homeless version of you."

"No, he doesn't."

"Oh, *yes* he does." She nudges me in the ribs and then shouts at my dad, "Those are some strong genes you got there, Mr. Melançon!"

"What?" Daddy shouts back from behind the pot of jambalaya.

"I said: You-Have-Some-Strong-Genes!"

"What?" He cups his ear.

"Never mind!" I yell at him.

"You have to speak up. He's deaf, ya know!" Uncle Father shouts at us as he pours the Louisiana Hot Sauce into a measuring cup.

Daddy holds up his wooden spoon and points to his head. "I'm deaf!"

"Don't worry about it!" I wave him off, and Daddy goes back to seasoning the jambalaya with my uncle. "Where are the boys?"

"Watching *Dora* in the parlor." Emily sets the forks onto the folding table, the same folding table I grew up eating off of, the one my dad always uses to spread out boiled crawfish, shrimp, and crabs.

"I'll run up and get them," I say.

"Well, aren't you going to introduce me first?" Emily tugs on my belt loop.

"Time to eat!" Daddy proclaims.

Before I can introduce Stevo and Cactus to Emily, those two start shoveling gobs of jambalaya into their mouths and their kids' mouths with their bare hands. Stevo and his family are hungry like I have rarely ever seen.

"Hi." My sweet wife holds her hand out to shake Cactus's. "I'm Emily."

After a few awkward seconds of watching Cactus and Stevo grunt and lick their fingers, Emily puts her hand down and slides over next to me.

"Are they on something?" she whispers.

* * *

We all sit down at the table in the backyard, covered with old *Times-Picayunes* that Daddy saves in tall stacks out on the back porch. Cactus has one of her naked sons in her lap, and she is now feeding him the jambalaya with a spoon. The other boy is running around, hitting things and giggling. Meanwhile, Stevo is on his fourth plate, and Uncle Father is on his fortieth beer, and Daddy has turned off his hearing aids.

Emily sits next to me, quietly eating and observing my strange family, while our boys sit on Mama's back steps flicking rice and sausage slices to the ants. La La eventually calms down and comes outside. She sits as far away from Emily as possible, and she looks only at Daddy and Uncle Father as she eats.

Daddy's chicken and sausage jambalaya is good, better than anything I've eaten in weeks. It brings a comfort and warmth that only this kind of food can, and as much as I hate to admit it, eating jambalaya on a paper plate with everyone I love and hate brings a settled feeling that I haven't felt in a long time. It makes me less shaky on the inside, less worried that something unspeakable has happened like maybe there is some hope left and that Mama will trundle up the walkway to the backyard, laughing and shaking her head and saying cryptic things like she always does.

"When you are given, eat. When you are beaten, run!" she would probably say.

And this would be about all Mama would say to explain herself if she were to walk up right now, but of course, she doesn't walk up because she is missing and no one at this table has a fucking clue what happened to her. So we all act like this isn't freaking us out. We eat and talk too loud and interrupt each other and speculate. We pass the French bread and butter. We pass more beer and hot sauce.

"So when are the rest of you boys getting here?" Uncle Father asks.

"I don't know. Stevo, have you talked to anyone?" I say.

"Texted Roman," he says. "Big hail storm in Baton Rouge yesterday. Lot of body work."

"That fat ass can't take an hour out of his day to come down here?" La La shakes her head and dashes hot sauce onto her jambalaya.

"Big money right now fixing all those dents," Stevo says.

"What about Yanko?"

"He's got a gig at House of Blues tonight," La La answers.

"Louis? Vlad? Timur?"

"Still in Florida," Stevo reports. "Their septic tank broke."

"Their wives are keeping them away," La La interrupts. "Stasia and Tina think they're too good for this family. So does that Tamber bitch. They're Spiritualists. That's how they roll."

"It's not just them," Uncle Father adds. "Everyone's saying it's La Cosa Nostra."

"The mob?" Emily nudges me.

"Your mother-in-law was tied up with some bad people." Uncle Father shakes his head. "Always has been."

"Word is it was The Unseen Hand," Stevo says as he keeps eating.

"The street artist I met passing out the fliers, he was talking about that," I say.

"The Great Unseen Hand," Uncle Father says. "Been terrorizing New Orleans since before you was born."

"Stop saying that name!" La La says. "That is a demon that should never be summoned."

"All I know is people are saying that The Hand finally got her." Stevo holds up his beer and takes a swig. "That's all I'm saying."

"Stop manifesting it!" La La screws up her face and looks like she is about to cry. "She is still alive! The Bee Maidens would have warned me if she was not."

"La La, weren't you the one carrying on about The Unseen Hand the other night?" I sop up the rest of my rice with some hot sauce and buttered French bread. "We should be able to talk about what happened to Mama without worrying about summoning demons."

"Why are you here?" La La smolders.

"The Archangel Gabriel brought Duke back to us." Cactus smiles and sucks the grease off her fingers. "I asked my angel cards."

La La holds her dinner knife in her fist just over the table, like she might—just might—stab a bitch.

I close my eyes and take some deep breaths. I don't need this right now. Christopher Shelley is flying in next week. I glance over at Emily in hopes her eyes will give me strength, but instead of giving me the loving smile I am looking for, Emily nudges me to look out past my warring siblings, out to the back gate: There are two men dressed in black short sleeves standing on the back drive way, two men with crescent moons eating silver stars on their chests, two men with black guns and handcuffs on their heavy belts, two men with news about my mother hiding inside their bulldog cheeks.

* * *

I always thought that the police asking the family to identify a loved one's body was a bunch of *CSI : Miami* bullshit that made for bad TV, but as it turns out, this is exactly what the police do when they find your loved one's body. They send two officers to your house. Two officers who stand in your backyard, sucking in their guts, wearing their purple Oakley sunglasses.

"They found the body in Audubon Park, right by the Tree of Life," the shorter of the two says.

I look over at my sister. She covers her mouth and shakes her head. Stevo holds her. Uncle Father walks Daddy inside the house, to sit down on the couch, while Cactus tries to convince him that yes, yes, yes, Mama is dead.

* * *

The Orleans Parish Coroner's Office is freezing. The contrast between the wet heat outside and the cold, sharp air inside makes me shiver. The old building has that weird municipal library smell that permeates every government building—some combination of Pine-Sol and 409, cabbage, and crayons.

The two cops take off their sunglasses and guide us down the hall. They open an unmarked door into a room with floor to ceiling mint green tiles. The body is under a white sheet on a large, dented metal table in the middle of the room. La La shuts her eyes and covers her nose. Stevo keeps his hand over his mouth and nose as well.

"You never want to smell someone else's foul luck. It can get inside you and grow like snakes," Mama'd threaten us when we'd pass a bad smell and didn't cover our noses.

"Gonna lift the sheet," the coroner says. "Look at her face. If you can identify her from there, we won't have to go any further down."

"I do not need to see my mother naked." Stevo covers his nose.

The coroner holds the edge of the sheet.

La La opens her eyes and nods her head.

"Please, no touching. Still collecting evidence." The coroner folds down the sheet, revealing a head full of dyed-black hair parted into long braids. The flowery blouse and coin necklace around this woman's neck are just like my mother's. The face is not decayed, just slightly blue. She looks asleep, peaceful, at rest here on the slab.

I am staring at my mother's dead face and then I am not. This is some other woman. A woman who doesn't even remotely resemble my mother.

"Oh thank God," La La says.

Stevo begins to smile from behind his hand. "That's not her."

The coroner holds my mama's missing person's flier next to the dead lady's face.

"You sure?" he asks.

"That's so not her," Stevo says.

"Are you sure?" The coroner is almost pissed.

"That poor woman." La La crosses herself and whispers a prayer.

"Do you have the name of your mother's dentist?" he asks.

"That's not our mother," I say.

I blink my eyes to make sure they are seeing what I am seeing.

"Yeah, that's not her," I say.

11

"WHY?"

She always asks

When Emily and I first got married, she used to get onto me about never talking to my mother. "Your family is my family. Why do you do this?" she'd ask every time we'd spiral into a fight about it.

I wouldn't even know how to answer her. I'd just walk out of the room.

After all, nothing could have been further from the truth. My family is not Emily's family.

Emily's family is not a bunch of con men and crystal-rubbing psychics. They're Texans. Her dad is a former Aggie football star, and a successful Sugar Land insurance mogul. Her mom's some sort of Houston socialite, all proper forks, and tight-lipped smiles. Emily's brother, Rod, is a neurosurgeon, and as one might expect, he's also kind of a jerkface.

They are nothing like my family. They are not throwing bones on the kitchen counter or reading the entrails of a chicken to divine the future of crime bosses and their jealous wives.

"Duke. Seriously." Emily would say. "Whose family isn't messed up?"

"It's not the same."

"So I'm just never going to meet them?"

"It's better this way. Trust me."

"You look so sad when you say that."

"Not sad. Just serious."

She'd then kiss me and we'd do what newlyweds were made to do, and for a couple of years that was as far as the conversation went, but then one Christmas, when Emily was pregnant with Stewart, she felt the need to disobey one of the most fundamental agreements of our marriage.

"Surprise!" Emily ushered my family in from our kitchen, lining them up in front of our Christmas tree. My mother was squat and frowning with her hair parted into long, dark braids. Daddy was drunk off eggnog and teetering on his crutches. La La was in her Jennifer Lopez phase. My only unmarried brother, Yanko, had tagged along and was sporting a mustache and a newly minted gold tooth. Thankfully, the rest of my brothers were running various con jobs and psychic grifts or else they'd have been there as well, with their screaming kids and their fist-holding magical wives.

To say the visit didn't go well would be an understatement. To begin with, my mother refused to eat anything Emily and I prepared; she complained about the deadly "low vibrations" and the "lack of fêng shui" and the "inauspicious placement" of everything we owned. Instead of joining us for the family meals, Mama would hole up in the upstairs guest bathroom communing with her long-dead grandmother by candlelight, telling her loudly what a mistake her seventh son had made with his life.

Christmas Eve, things only got worse. Daddy, who is notoriously lactose-intolerant, had drunk his weight in eggnog and kept unleashing these horrible farts that watered our eyes.

"Traveling upsets my stomach," Daddy would say and then fart loudly to prove just how upset his stomach really was. La La, who was dabbling in Santeria at the time, slit a live chicken's neck in front of the fireplace to bless our unborn son. Blood splattered everywhere, and Emily started to hyperventilate. La La and Mama couldn't understand why we were so upset, such nonbelievers. The arguing along with the screaming, shitting, bleeding chicken caused Emily to sort of faint, and I had to put her to bed, and then I spent most of the night cleaning blood, chicken shit, and feathers from our new shag carpet.

I guess the final straw for Emily must have been Christmas morning. Daddy lost his glass eye, and, of course, Emily was the lucky one to find it in her bowl of oatmeal. This did nothing to help her morning sickness. And let's not forget my brother Yanko, who chatted up our recently divorced next-door neighbor, Julie Carville. He spent three of the five nights of his stay boning Julie Carville in Emily's craft room—loudly enough to make Emily want to call 911 because she thought for sure Julie was being murdered.

In short, Emily extended the olive branch, and my family extended their middle fingers. When everyone finally loaded up in Mama's black Mercedes to go back to New Orleans, Emily never asked to invite them again.

"You were right" is all she said.

She never complained about my secrecy or embarrassment or

for that matter why I never planned trips to visit my family in New Orleans. When our boys were born, Emily was gracious and invited my mother to the hospital to see them, but Mama drove back the same day, calling me from her cell phone, crying, saying that I had chosen the *pizda* over my destiny. As the years passed, the distance between Houston and New Orleans became that of oceans, galaxies, universes.

So moving back to New Orleans, even before Mama ran away, was hard for both of us as a couple. But Emily's been a good sport. She's shown up to all of Daddy's Sunday meals with a smile and a salad. She makes sure that our boys hug their *Babushka* and she has ignored most of La La's jabs.

"They're no weirder than most people in this city," Emily said one night after Daddy had boiled crabs and Mama had accidentally smiled at her.

"You're just being nice," I said.

"They're our family, Duke."

"You're my family."

"Well, it's important that the boys know where they came from," Emily said, but Emily and I both knew that this is just what you say to be polite, decent, and respectable.

Mama never put much stock in such things; she made a career of being just the opposite: rude, conniving, and despicable. She couldn't care less about embarrassing me, or, for that matter, openly hating the woman who's given birth to my two sons.

"Ah, look. The *pizda* is here," Mama said every time we showed up for Sunday dinner.

"What's a *pizda*?" Emily wanted to know.

"A term of endearment."

"I'm not stupid, Duke. What does it mean?"

"Cunt," I confessed.

"Nice. Real nice."

12

MAY 10, 2010

Five days since Mama chased that cat out the house

"You're going to work?" Emily walks into our bathroom, just as I am putting on my Mandala Worldwide polo shirt.

"Christopher Shelley's flying in." I tuck in my shirt tail.

"So?" she says.

"So. I have to meet with Gary about what we're going to say to him."

"Tell Gary you have a family emergency."

"I'm not telling Gary about any of this."

"You don't have to tell him what the emergency is." She holds her gaze.

"You obviously don't know Gary." I grab my belt off the bed and thread it around the waist of my khakis.

"Duke, we should be looking for her."

"Don't start." I buckle my belt.

"You know, last time I checked, Mandala lawyers aren't the ones trying to figure out how to plug that well." She stands in the door to the bedroom.

"Please." I loom over her. "You're going to make me late."

The boys' laughter and SpongeBob's deranged giggles echo from our family room downstairs.

Emily drops her head, moves to the side, and lets me pass. "So you're seriously going to work today?"

"Yes."

"Okay." She folds her arms. "Then let's just pretend she's not missing. Heck, let's just go back to pretending you don't even have a family at all. That's healthy."

"Do not tell me how to deal with this."

"God, you're being such a jerk."

As usual, Emily is right. I am being a complete jerk. This is shock or grief or whatever you call it when you know that your mother is as good as dead. The funny thing is, knowing that I am reeling from this does absolutely nothing to help me right myself. I am still an asshole. I still can't admit to Emily that she is right. I can't admit that I'd rather face the dying ocean and its devastated shrimpers today than find my mother's body.

So instead of going with Emily to canvass Uptown with more missing-person's posters, or stopping into the police station to goad them into action, I let this Spill be more important than all of this. I get into my Prius, and I drive into the New Orleans emergency offices of Mandala Worldwide. I drive towards Mandala Worldwide's orange, yellow, and pink dreamcatcher logo—a symbol born from Native Americans' connection to the earth and sky—a symbol Mandala Worldwide repurposed to show our corporate commitment to both.

I go to where the problems, as apocalyptic and impossible as they are, are problems that follow the Byzantine logic of geoscience, Napoleonic codes, and maritime law—problems so impossible that I can hide inside of them, problems that are given to me in emails and voice messages, tragedies that may not be solvable today, but can be argued, managed, filed, collated, deleted, put off until next week.

* * *

Gary Dubois is yelling. Raging, really.

"Can we all just pretend that we have done this before? We cannot say the words, 'We are sorry' anywhere in this commercial." Gary exhales and then looks up at the ceiling tiles. He's counting them. That's what his "coach" told him to do when he feels like he might want to throw something or pinch someone. Yes, pinch. My boss literally pinched his assistant's arm last week. Hard. Left a nasty purple bruise. A friend of mine in HR emailed me the photos. Normally, Mandala would fire your ass for doing something crazy like that, but Gary's the best we've got when it comes to spin doctoring. He's the "master of disaster," or so the C-suite likes to call him. So Gary's assistant, Jill, got moved into exploration and drilling. She supposedly got a huge raise and Gary got a "coach."

In addition to being the master of disaster, Gary is also Earl of Over-sharing.

"I'm peeing blood. This shit is killing me," he told me over happy hour margaritas at Superior.

"You sure you didn't just eat some beets?"

"I went to the doctor. It's a bladder infection. Stress."

While I'm not so sure it's the Sub-Ocean Brightside that's put blood in Gary's urine—more likely The Kitty Kitty Kitty, a Slidell strip bar that Gary likes to go to after work. However, the stress we are all under is murderous; that part Gary is not lying about. We're all feeling it, and it is the kind of stress and anxiety that causes heart attacks, impotence, strokes, cancers, gnarled addictions to Ambien and Wild Turkey. The Spill has become this monster that haunts all our days and tracks us back to our homes. It slithers into our beds and chokes our dreams. It's the pet python we've all let into our homes.

"Get those ad agency people on the phone." Gary has stopped counting and is now "consciously breathing." Step two from his coach.

"I've left five or six messages," I say. "They aren't calling me back."

"Then you take over our Facebook posts."

"You want me to run our social media?"

"I just sent you all the login info." He rolls his eyes. "Same user name and password for Twitter and Instagram."

"You need a social media manager for that. That's not what I do."

"It is now," Gary says. "You're in crisis management. Manage this fucking crisis and get rid of all the negative comments on our page!"

"That's not a best practice," I say.

"Here, I just emailed you a picture of our guys cleaning up a greasy pelican. Post it."

"That's a terrible image." I look at my phone. "That bird is covered in oil because of us."

"Yeah, but our workers are saving its miserable life. Post it. We need to change the conversation."

"Not to this, we don't."

"Just post the goddamned pelican!"

Gary used to be a great boss, but now every day is like this: Panic attacks. Thrown staplers. Pinched assistants. Every day since the Sub-Ocean Brightside blew up and killed those poor roughnecks, and that subterranean monster began shitting oil into the Gulf of Mexico, I have been pulled deeper and deeper into the undertow of my mother's Louisiana. If anyone should be pissing blood, it's me.

"I need you to make sure that the shrimping couple signs their contracts today. Marketing needed those yesterday." Gary hands me a stack of papers, tagged with glowing neon Post-its.

"I have them coming in today." I place the contracts under my arm and leave Gary counting audibly.

"Twenty-three, twenty-four, twenty-five..."

* * *

Back in March, just eleven days before the Sub-Ocean Brightside exploded and everything went to shit, Pauline Sarin was in New Orleans to headline the Southern Republican Leadership Conference. Some of Pauline's hosts thought it would be festive to throw her a New Orleans-style blowout complete with Mardi Gras Indians, a second line, and a small armada of kitschy fortune-tellers. And because many of Robby Wendall's people consulted Mama on a regular basis, she was hired to entertain the crowd at Pauline's "Taste of Louisiana" reception.

"I was reading palms for all the bigwigs. Mary Matalin, Newt Gingrich, David Vitter's pretty wife. They all come up to me, acting like I am silly joke lady. And when they open their palms, they know they are no longer looking at silly joke lady." Mama told me this over the phone the night after Pauline Sarin's reception.

"Sad little girl named Krystal Sarin comes to me. She ask me if she will be movie star. And I say no! no! no! I have better news! I see babies! *Lots* of babies. Then Krystal begins to cry because American girl does not like lots of babies. She wants to be on TV like those big butt Kardashians. So Pauline Sarin comes at me with her fancy glasses, and she says the Bible to me, calling me a vitch—like I never hear that one before. So I grab Pauline Sarin's hand and turn her palm over. She does not pull away. She does not do nothing except shut her mouth because what I tell her makes her so very, very happy. She cried too but because she's so happy. She signed her autograph and kissed me on my cheek."

"What did you tell her?"

"Exactly what she wanted to hear."

"Oh, come on, Mama."

"She calls me vitch. I fix her."

"Mama. Seriously?"

"Best curse is granted vish, Duke, remember that."

So you can imagine the weird, uneasy feeling I have today when I get to work, and Jean Babineaux is already sitting here in the lobby, wearing a "Don't Blame Me I Voted For Pauline!" t-shirt. She waits anxiously under the temporary vinyl banner that reads, "Mandala Worldwide Gulf Coast Restoration." Jean is here without Mark.

She is holding a six-inch stack of ratty papers—more than likely unpaid bills that were unpaid and late well before the Spill. I already know how this will go: She will follow me into my office, shut the door and then shove these bills in my face. She will demand that I pay her if she is going to sign anything today. There will be crying and begging and pleading. It will be enough Gulf Coast drama and sadness to momentarily eclipse my own.

Jean Babineaux and her impossible situation are exactly why I came into work today.

"We decided we ain't gonna do it." Jean Babineaux sits across from me. She holds her hands in her lap on top of her dog-eared papers.

"Is something wrong?"

"Mark and I decided last night," she says.

"Ms. Babineaux, we've already hired the director and the crew."

"Sorry."

"Is this about the money?"

There's a long, awkward silence.

Here Jean Babineaux sits, cool and composed, ready to take me to task for Mandala Worldwide's greed and incompetence. I can tell by the way she is pursing her lips that she wants to tell me how we're not doing enough to save the Gulf and that, in turn, we're not paying her and her husband enough money to appear in our commercials to lie for us. Of course, this is about the money. Why else would she be here? It's always about the money, especially when a claimant says...

"It's not about the money." She looks me in the eye.

"You know, they can cut you a check in accounting like right now. We can walk over there and get it."

"I'm good," she says.

"Have you thought about this?"

"Thought about it. Talked about it. Prayed about it." She smiles.

"Okay." I take a deep breath and massage my temples. "How about we just call Mark real quick?"

"He's out on the water." She winks at me. "We won't be able to reach him."

She then picks up my nameplate off my desk.

I can feel my cheeks burning red.

"You're her son." She nods.

Jean Babineaux acts warmer, more familiar than she should.

"Same last name. No relation," I say.

"I know who you are."

"Melançon's a pretty common name around here," I say. "Kind of like Babineaux."

This makes Jean Babineaux laugh, but not hard enough to change the subject.

"She said you'd need proof." Jean hands me her stack of tattered bills and busted envelopes. "Every time I saw your mama, I wrote down every word. I mean *every* word."

I flip through page after page of scribbled-on electricity bills and credit card statements.

"Your mama told me to save them." Jean looks at me. Her eyes are wild with anticipation. She's having a hard time not smiling.

"She's not my mother." I glare at her.

"She said this would happen." Jean holds up a phone bill. "The Spill. This ad. Mark's depression. His suicide attempts." She pushes the phone bill in my face. "Look: 'After the Spill, the TV deal will kill. Your husband will take his gun and put out the sun. To stop it, you must be the one.'"

This is the exact kind of sing-songy, rhyme-y, pseudo-Nostradamus bullshit that Mama said to all her clients.

"She was never wrong." Jean sits across from me with this increasingly worried look on her face. "You okay, Mr. Melançon?"

"Yeah. Fine."

"Ya mama came to me in a dream." She stands up. "She asked me to show you these letters." She waves her stack of busted envelopes and credit card statements at me.

I jog a stack of paper on my desk and don't give her eye contact.

"I'm sorry, Ms. Babineaux. I've got to find somebody to be in this commercial."

"That's okay. She said you wouldn't believe me at first, but you'd come around." Jean Babineaux takes back her stack of crazy phone bills and walks out of my office.

I wish I believed like Jean Babineaux, like La La and Stevo, or even Daddy and Yanko. La La and Stevo would say that Jean Babineaux's sudden appearance in my life was Mama's way of reaching out to me, and not just some cruel coincidence in an otherwise indifferent universe. Daddy would scold me for not realizing the power that the Seventh Son of a Seventh Son holds in this world. And just as I am getting revved up to feel really sorry for myself, I notice that Jean dropped one of her past due bills by my desk. I pick it up.

It's scribbled over with Jean's transcription of one of my mother's bad poems.

It's addressed to me.

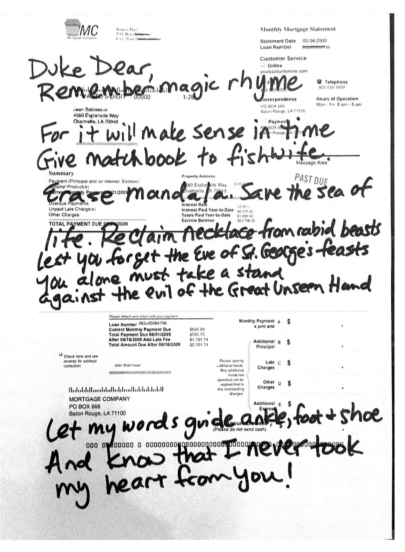

This letter is the kind of coincidence that would have set La La off into an hour-long diatribe about how the three Bee Maidens are afoot, and that if you just pay close enough attention to the signs and symbols, you can hear angels singing to you in riddles and rhymes. But this crazy letter from one of my mother's crazy clients is just that: crazy.

"You just wait, Duke. Destinies are not to be farted upon," Mama liked to say while she held her crystal ball next to her ear like a shot put. "One day, you will understand and you will be ashamed of how you have treated me."

There are no three Melissae or secret smiles at work here. There are only probability and chance, and as unlikely as it was for Jean to show up today with my mother's ramblings in hand, the world is full of unlikely occurrences. To try to attach meaning to such an occurrence is very human, but it's also pointless. The reality is Mama didn't warn Jean Babineaux about any of this; all Mama did was give that poor woman and her husband some shitty rhymes, the same obtuse riddles and universal truths that you can read anything into once enough time has passed—like a horoscope. It's *La Langue des Oiseaux*[1], the Language of the Birds. It's green language—verdant with possibility. Our brains are built to make connections and correlations when it comes to language, even when those connections aren't really there: *The Book of Revelation*, Nostradamus' quatrains, Mama's palm readings. Confusing as hell, but these words somehow—if you strain hard enough—seem to reveal the most profound and ominous warnings.

Put it this way: If Mama had truly warned the Babineauxes about their future, then why did they stay when they knew Katrina was coming? Why didn't this woman who believes my mama can see the future just leave the Gulf? Why didn't she help her husband find another job before the Sub-Ocean Brightside exploded?

---

1. *In Hermetic, Eleusinian and other magical traditions, Langue des Oiseaux, the language of the birds, is considered a hidden and divine language that can lead to perfect knowing if you can decipher its metaphors and puzzles. The key to understanding is to read between the lines and to interpret the clues of the obtuse rhymes and mandarin prose.*

As it always is with Mama's clients, the Babineauxes are lost souls who have placed way too much faith in my mother's other-worldly advice. I want to feel bad for Jean and her family. I want to feel horrible. I want to tell them I am sorry that Mama took their money and is now keeping them from the only real payout they will see in the Spill. I want to be angry for Jean Babineaux. But I'm not. I'm just not. This is not my fault. I can't stop the oil. And I can't fix Jean and Mark Babineaux's broken life.

Just as I am explaining all this to that annoying Jiminy Cricket voice inside of my head, my phone rings.

"Mandala External Affairs, Duke Melançon."

"Duke!"

"La La?"

"You have to go home!"

"What's wrong?"

"You need to go to Covington." Her voice quivers with hysteria. "I see it. I see it everywhere."

"See what everywhere?"

"There is a pox upon your house. A plague!"

"I don't have time for this."

"Just go home!" My sister hangs up on me.

13

TONIGHT

There are no stars in the sky

As I am driving over Lake Pontchartrain into Covington, to our rented McMansion inside the Cotton Gin Country Club and Golf Community, far from La La's visions and rants in New Orleans, Emily calls and tells me that La La was right, that there is indeed a pox upon our house, and that I need to come home "right freaking now!"

Emily has locked herself with our two sons in the panic room.

"They're everywhere!" she says over the phone.

"Who's everywhere?"

"Raccoons!"

And by raccoons, Emily doesn't mean one or two sneaking in our back door. As I pull into our driveway, my headlights illuminate the glowing eyes of hundreds of raccoons crawling all over my house and lawn. They scamper and hiss, lunge and snap. The bastards teeter across my roof, waddle on my front porch. They have found their way inside my house, probably through the attic and air vents. They've taken over the den and the playroom. They've shredded the couch, leaving the white stuffing strewn into every room. There is piss and shitty handprints everywhere, and these raccoons aren't the cute Ranger Ricks you learned about in seventh-grade Life Science with thumbs on their paws and goofy smiles. These things are vicious.

* * *

"I ain't never seen nothing like this. Not even after Katrina," says Bobby Faucheaux, the owner of Black and Gold Wildlife Control, with his two bottom teeth missing and his Saints Super Bowl Champions hat worn straight and low on his brow. "They got da rabies, ya heard me?"

"Wow. That many raccoons have rabies?"

"Oh yeah, they sick all right," he says, "Chaouis don't act like this unless they sick. Sure they gone bite you if you mess with them, but other than dat, they gone run and hide first. Somethin' ain't right with Mother Nature, ya heard me? Over on the West Bank, there's dis pack a wild pit bulls breakin' down people's doors, eatin' dey cats."

I text Emily, telling her to stay calm, that Bobby Faucheaux is here, that I will be getting her and the kiddos out soon.

"So how are you going to get my family out of the house without getting bitten?"

"Well, it ain't gone be easy. Da chaouis is fuckin' murderous when dey pissed, but we can get dem out."

"When you say *we*, you mean *you* are going to get them out of my house."

"Time to kill us some chaouis." Bobby takes his pistol out of the holster on his hip and checks the clip.

"You're not firing that gun inside my house."

"Fine, I got dis baseball bat in the back of my truck, but dat's sort of inhumane, and dat's gone cost ya extra." He lays on the Cajun accent as most folks down here do when they're trying to make a point or be funny. Or both.

"Look, we can figure out what to do with the raccoons once we get my wife and kids out of here. Okay?"

Bobby puts his gun back in its holster and grabs a thin, black baton-like canister off his belt. He holds it up. "Peppa spray."

Bobby Faucheaux straightens his Saints hat and then marches into my house completely unafraid, through the foyer, past the angry raccoons, into the living room, unleashing long, steady streams of pepper spray. I follow close behind, trying to fight the very unmanly urge to hide behind him.

"When you said you got a raccoon problem, you ain't lyin', boy," Faucheaux says. "This shit is Biblical up in here."

"Over here," I wave him over to the panic room door.

The vapors from the spray are burning my throat, and I start to choke and cough. My eyes water, which is the least of my problems. While at first the pepper spray repels the raccoons, now it only seems to make them crazier and more erratic. They run around in circles. They claw at the carpet and gnash their teeth.

"Emily!" I shout. "Don't open the door until I say so."

"Okay!" She yells back.

And that's when Bobby screams — "Fuck me!"

One of the "chaouis" is hanging off Bobby's forearm. Blood is spewing everywhere.

Bobby tries to sling the raccoon loose by waving his arm around, but the raccoon only seems to clamp down tighter, causing Bobby's vein to squirt an even faster, thicker, darker stream of blood.

Not wanting to make any sudden moves to provoke the rest of the raccoons, I just stand here for what is only seconds but what feels like seasons.

"Is everything okay out there?" Emily calls out.

"No! No, it's not! Just keep the door shut!"

Bobby's gun.

"Hold still." I pull his t-shirt up and take his firearm out of its holster on his belt. For a split second, I deliberate what to do with this gun.

"Shoot it!" Bobby yells at me.

I hesitate.

"I said shoot it!"

I unlock the safety, press the muzzle against the belly of the growling beast, pointing it away from Bobby and me.

I shut my eyes.

Pull the trigger.

Kapow!

I taste the gunpowder.

Blood, guts, and fur are all over me. My ears ring.

Emily screams from behind the door.

What's left of the raccoon drops off of Bobby's arm and into a wet thud onto the floor.

"What's going on?" Emily calls out.

"We got it under control!" I shout back.

The gunshot causes the swarm of raccoons to scatter, over the chairs, into corners and out of the hallway.

I safety the hot gun and slide it into the back of my jeans.

Bobby pulls an LSU bandana from his back pocket and begins to tie his arm off with a tourniquet.

"Don't do that." I take the twisted-up bandana from him. "You're in shock."

I shake out the purple cloth and hold it against his bleeding arm, trying not to mix the raccoon guts with his blood. "Here, hold this super-tight and keep your hand over your head."

"Shit! I ain't got time for no shots this week," he says.

"After we get my wife and kids out, I can drive you to the emergency room."

"Nah, dat's ahright. I can drive myself," he says.

"Emily! Pick up Stewart, and I'll grab Jo-Jo!" I yell through the door, "And be ready to run out the front door!"

"Okay! I'm ready!"

I open the door to the panic room. Emily's face is flush with fear. She is holding a broom in one hand, and she's got Jo-Jo crying into her shoulder with the other. I pick up Stewart, who's too young to process how scary this is, and we run through the living room, past the snarling raccoons, into our front yard.

A fat raccoon waddles across our circular driveway, growling, wearing my mother's gold coin necklace, the necklace that Mama has worn since she was a child in Albania—around its neck.

"Here." I put Stewart down and give his hand to Emily.

"What are you doing?" she says.

I pull Bobby's gun from the waist of my pants and walk up to the raccoon.

"Duke, no!" she says.

I unload the clip until there is nothing but blood and fur and a striped tail.

I reach down into the bloody mess and reclaim my mother's necklace.

14

MIDNIGHT

Mama has now been missing for six days

There are thousands of hotels in New Orleans, and it would have made complete, logical sense after what we just went through to get the presidential suite at The Windsor Court for the night. But no, I let Emily talk me into accepting Daddy's invitation to spend the night at The House of the Neon Palm, in the room where I grew up—a room that still has the same bunk beds intact from when I shared it with my six brothers: Roman, Timur, Yanko, Stevo, Vlad, and Louis.

Emily and I take the top bunks, and our boys are soon fast asleep below us.

"I think you'll be glad we spent the night," Emily whispers.

"We should have gotten a room."

"Your father was begging, Duke. What else are we going to do?"

"After tonight, we're going back to Covington."

"No, we are not." She hits her pillow with her fist and lies back down. "I'm not going back there until you call the police and tell them what happened."

"I don't need this in the press right now."

"You're paranoid, and quite honestly, a little full of yourself," she says.

"I'm handling it."

"I don't feel safe in that house," she says.

"I said I was handling it."

Emily gets down from her bunk bed and opens the door.

"Where are you going?"

"Downstairs."

"Really?" I say.

"I'm going to read," she says. "Still too much adrenaline in me to sleep."

She closes the door behind her.

The boys are making their little sleep-whistle noises, and the room is humid and warm. I am too pissed off and too hot to go to sleep. So I throw off my covers and get up, but I don't follow Emily downstairs. Instead, I go to the bathroom. I take a leak, and then to the medicine cabinet to pour myself some NyQuil. Too much adrenaline indeed.

* * *

At around 2 a.m., I wake up to drunken shouts and catcalls echoing from The Club Ms. Mae's, a twenty-four-hour bar across the neutral ground from my parents' house.

It's just as well. I kept having the same dream over and over: unrelenting images of my mother lying face down and dead in a ditch, in the trunk of a Mafioso's car, under an overpass, in a shallow grave dug by a rival fortune-teller who practices a bloody brand of voodoo revenge. I get up, put my clothes on in the dark, and walk downstairs to the kitchen.

Now that I am awake I keep retracing my mother's steps in my mind. I pick up the broom leaning next to the fridge, and I throw open the kitchen door. I run out into her backyard swinging the broom.

I walk to the gate, open it, and step out onto the street, picking up my speed to see what it would look and feel like to chase that stray cat off her property. I chase this imaginary cat onto the neutral ground, and before I know it, I have chased it to the front of Ms. Mae's, and here I stand with a broom in my hand. Considering that Mama hated Ms. Mae's, I feel certain that she didn't enter this bar the night she disappeared.

Nevertheless, I drop the broom in the street, and I go inside the bar. At best, I'll chat up one of the regulars who might have seen something that night, and at worst, I can down a couple of cheap nightcaps and get drunk enough to fall asleep again. But before I can even get my foot in the door of the bar, I hear my brother, Yanko, cussing and kicking the video poker machines inside.

Ah, Yanko, the rock star. Yanko, the unbathed pussy magnet. Yanko with his mustache and his gold tooth, with his Palestinian hipster scarf and fedora that he snagged from Urban Outfitters. Yanko Melançon, the second-most-famous member of my family.

"Ha! Duke!" He stomps his foot like a flamenco dancer and puffs out his chest. He grabs me and kisses me on both cheeks.

"My brother!" he exclaims in his horrible fake Russian accent.

"Would you stop talking like that!"

"Don't embarrass me, brah," he whispers with the normal, less exotic accent that he grew up speaking with, and then he exclaims with his Russian affectation, "Everybody! This is my long-lost brother, Duke!"

Everybody in the bar, and I mean *everybody*, turns around on their stools, away from their pool games and video poker machines, and they drunkenly shout, "Hello, Duke!"

Like I said, Yanko, the wild accordion boy, is famous, or at least he is in bars like Ms. Mae's. So I wave and smile to the crowd so that they will all get back to getting drunk and leave me the hell alone.

"So you have a drink with me." Yanko reeks of cheap bourbon, Ice Breakers chewing gum, and oceans of Giorgio Armani cologne.

"Sure," I say. "Why not?"

"Ketel One martini! Dirt-tay! Dirt-tay!" Yanko shakes three dollars at the bartender all the way across the room, and because he is Yanko Melançon, the lead singer of the New Orleans Baltic funk band, Yankotronic, the bartender ignores everyone else who is standing in line at the bar, and he begins to pour Yanko's martini into a silver shaker of ice.

"Look, I need to talk to you about Mama."

"She is a businesswoman. She will return to us when she is ready."

"Not if someone killed her, Yanko." I pull Mama's necklace from my pocket.

"Where did you get that?"

"Someone put it around a raccoon's neck and then set the raccoon, or rather raccoons, loose in my house."

"In Covington?"

"Yes, in Covington."

"This is some sort of sign. What do you think it means?"

"It means someone is threatening us. It means someone has her."

"Get rid of it!" Yanko pushes the necklace away from his face.

"Seriously, Yanko?"

"I'm opening for Dr. John tomorrow. I don't need that kind of bad luck around me right now."

"Someone did this."

"So you think it's the mob?" Yanko asks. "You think they would be that stupid?"

"I'm just waiting for a horse head to show up in my bed next," I say.

"I know a guy." Yanko pulls out his phone and starts texting. "See what he says."

"Who are you texting?" I ask.

"Mama's bookie. Dude knows everyone."

Yanko's face glows in the light of his phone as he types on the tiny screen.

"Says we can meet him at the Dungeon later." He slides his phone into his back jeans pocket.

"The Drungeon? You got to be kidding me."

"Do you want to find her or not?"

"Do you *want* me to punch you in the neck?"

And just as I am about to throw my drink down and walk home, Yanko snaps his fingers over his head and raises his leg like he's the goddamn fiddler on the roof.

"Let's go make love to the dance floor!" He lays on the Russian accent extra-thick. "Let's go to the Dungeon and chase some poo-say!"

"Hells yeah!" One of Yanko's fans high fives him.

Despite my better judgment, I follow Yanko and his sudden entourage out the door into a cab.

* * *

Ye Olde Dungeon is an after-hours bar in the Quarter where many of Mama's customers like to get their drunk on while they hip-thrust and fist-pump to death metal and shitty nineties rap rock like Limp Bizkit and Sugar Ray. Once we go inside, Yanko, the famous son of Madame Melançon, is mobbed by Wiccan wannabes and Voodoo bikers. He goes from just being another area rock star to the Dark Prince of New Orleans. The first round of drinks is on the house, according to the manager, so Yanko, being Yanko, demands bottle service: Cristal. And he gets it.

Many of the Dungeon regulars like to pretend that they are the dog-collared masters of the night instead of diabetic cube dwellers who have trouble getting laid because of how much alcohol and fried food they consume on a daily basis. The rest of the crowd is made up of stupid tourists and drunk high school boys with fake IDs who are lured off Bourbon Street with rumors of S&M cage sex—which, let's be clear, if fat people with open sores and choke balls, slapping their fupas together does it for you, well, good luck with that. By 4 a.m., the shit show is in full throttle, and things go beyond the bar-sanctioned gothiness and sad chubby sex acts. And this is when Yanko's contact walks in the door.

"Ah! There he is," Yanko says to me and then waves him down. "Gay André!"

And yes, Gay André is his real name—as much as any name is real. His Christian name is Gay Costello the Third, but somehow this supposedly "made man" looks just like a teacup version of André the Giant. So André got tacked on over the years. Gay André is the name the city of New Orleans gave the petite mobster. It's what everyone calls the Fairgrounds bookie. Himself included, often in third person, like he's doing right now:

"Yo! Gay André don't play that way! Don't be a stingy bitch unless you want Gay André to bust a cap in your ass!" Gay André shouts at the overly pierced bartender. This is Gay André's idea of a joke. Fortunately for Gay André, the overly pierced bartender pretends this is funny, instead of treating it as the ass-whippable offense that it is.

"Gay?" I say.

"I hate to disappoint you, but I ain't no queer. Gay is my birth name, " Gay André says. "Faggots ruined a perfectly wonderful word. Gay used to mean happy. In my book, still does."

"Well, that's ironic," I say. "Seems to me with a name like Gay, you might be, you know, more open-minded."

"Fuck you. Who are you anyway? Alanis-fucking-Morrissette? This shit ain't ironic. Gay was my daddy's name—and his daddy's name. Before the faggots stole that word to mean something horrible, just like they stole The Wizard of Oz and the goddamn rainbow. When you see a rainbow, you should think of Noah's Ark and all the animals getting on two by two." Gay André taps a shiny black matchbook to his temple and smiles. "Not butt-fucking."

"Wow" is all I can say. What an asshole.

"Gay, it's me. Yanko Melançon," my brother finally speaks up.

"Oh shit, boy, didn't recognize you with that stupid hat on."

"This is my brother, Duke," Yanko says.

He shakes my hand. "What the hell kind of name is Duke?"

I just stare at him.

"Sorry to hear about y'all's Mama." Gay André fidgets with his matchbook. "She was a good woman. Looked after me like she was my own mama."

Yanko smiles. "You hear anything?"

"I hear the police ain't lookin', but what you expect?" he says. "They ain't gonna get off their beignet-eating, killing-poor-people asses to look for somebody like your mama."

"You been talking to the cops?" Yanko says.

"Maybe." He nods. "Buy me a drink, and I'll tell you what I know."

Let me translate this for you from Gay André speak. Just like gay still means happy to this bizarre little homophobe, "Buy me a drink" means "Sit here and match me shot for shot until we both go blind."

"I'm not doing this," I whisper to Yanko.

"He wants to drink," Yanko spits back in my ear.

So I give the bartender my credit card, and I begin buying drinks, and just as Gay André promised, the more we feed him drinks, the more he talks. Gay André talks about oyster boats and cocaine lords, about banana kings and sex slaves, coffee shipments and Colombian cartels, about bad cops and waste management kingpins.

Gay André is talking so much and so fast that he's hard to follow. Between all his manic slurring and fast talking, Gay tells me crazy things, impossible things. He tells me that Mama told him that Donald Trump will be president in 2017, and Britain will abandon the European Union, and when that happens, all hell will break lose. The world will be primed for the end times.

So she told Gay André to take his money out of the banks and to put it all on a horse—a gelding so fast it was named after Walter White, the speed dealer off of *Breaking Bad.* The tea cup mobster says that Walter White will one day win the Kentucky Derby, and it won't matter who is president because that horse will make us millions, and that my mother promised him all of this.

He claims that this is the last thing Mama told him before she disappeared. All the while, he worries this shiny black match-book between his fingers. Some kind of hand washing compulsion. Some kind of firebug tell. He keeps opening and closing it, opening and closing to make sure the matches are still there. It makes me think of the passage in Mama's letter:

Give matchbook to fishwife.

"So what do you know about The Unseen Hand?" I ask.

"I know I ain't near drunk enough to talk about anything like that." Gay André throws back his whiskey and slams his empty glass down on the bar for me to have refilled.

So I keep the drinks coming, and I steer the conversation back towards my mother's long list of enemies within Gay André's "Family."

"Who did this?" I hold up Mama's gold coin necklace.

"Oh, the raccoons." He taps the matchbook on the bar. "That had to have been something to see."

"How do you know about the raccoons?"

"Crazy shit like that travels fast." He takes a shot of bourbon and then sticks his tongue into the empty glass, like a bee searching for the last drops of nectar.

"I haven't told anybody but my family."

"Bobby Faucheaux likes the horses."

"So who did this?" I hold up the necklace to Gay André.

"My family is full of crazy motherfuckers, boy, but ain't nobody I know got time to go find all those raccoons and put them in your house. Seriously, where you even find that many raccoons? Why not just leave a fucking note? Know what I'm saying?"

"I need to know who did this." I shake the necklace in his face.

Gay André takes another shot of bourbon. "Look, I don't know nothing about no raccoons, but…"

He pulls my head close to his mouth, almost French kissing my ear, and whispers, "There's this guy over on the West Bank. He's friends with Stanky Franky Esposito. Everybody calls him 'The Loup Garou.' Got all the dirty cops looking for him. Sure enough, The Loup Garou knows where your mama is."

"Loup Garou?" I push him off me. "Like the werewolf-Loup-Garou?"

"Shut up! Don't say that so loud!" Gay André's bottom lip trembles. "You can't be saying that name so fucking loud in here."

"Seriously?"

Gay André doesn't answer. Instead, he trips over his bar stool, trying to get away from me as fast as his short legs can carry him.

"We're not done!" I say.

"Oh, yeah, bitch. We done." He walks out of the bar.

I look over at his empty glass. He left his precious matchbook.

I pick it up and inspect it:

Chris Owens Club & Balcony.

It's my mother's unmistakable handwriting:

"There are no coincidences, only the chess moves of The Unseen Hand." Mama's tired old saying rings in my head.

15

7:00 AM

Snuck up on me

When I walk out of the shadows of Ye Olde Dungeon, I have to cover my eyes from the stabbing sunlight. I open my fingers, bit by bit, to let my pupils adjust to the street. I smell piss. I look over at Yanko, and he's soaked in urine, and somehow I know that the urine he is drenched in is not his own. But that's what he gets for eating his weight in "Cherry Bombs"— Everclear-soaked maraschino cherries. Being the big-time celebrity that Yanko is, we were fed Cherry Bombs like peeled grapes by tattooed Goth girls after Gay André ran away.

One of these girls sucked a huge hickey on the side of Yanko's neck: It's a purple hematoma that goes yellow and brown and green on the edges.

"Nice hickey." I point. He shoves my hand away.

As we stagger through the Quarter, trying to stay on the shady side of the street, I begin to remember who I was before Gay André insisted that I match him shot for shot, drink for drink.

Emily!

I pull out my phone to text her, but it's dead. She is going to kill me.

"I need to borrow your phone."

"I'm out of data," Yanko says.

"How are you out of data?"

He holds up his flip phone. "Pay as you go."

"Why don't you have a real phone?"

"We're going to miss the trolley." Yanko takes off drunk running, his feet like eggbeaters beneath him. I chase after my brother, down the street, and onto the St. Charles Streetcar. I sit down on the wooden seats and catch my breath. We trolley our way through the palm trees and oaks. I am beginning to sober up—in that I can remember where I live now, who I am, and I am starting to feel kind of woozy and sick, not just woozy and drunk.

"Come on. I'm thirsty." Yanko points to the Rite Aid across the way. "I need some Gatorade and Tylenol. My head is killing me."

"You don't need Gatorade," I say.

Yanko ignores me, and instead hops off the streetcar and walks out into the street and in front of a racing red Honda Civic that screeches and swerves to miss him. Yanko just stands there in the middle of St. Charles, wobbling and weaving, completely unaware that he was just the recipient of a miracle. He staggers into the grass.

I hop off the streetcar to where Yanko has now fallen.

"Oh, shit! Ants!" Yanko swats at the crawling red velvet that is now covering his arms and jeans.

Yanko jumps up and down, and I do my best to help him brush off the red ants without getting them on me, too.

"You okay?" I ask. "Didn't you see the ant hill right there?"

Yanko doesn't answer me. Instead, he looks up at a plane flying overhead and wanders into the Rite Aid parking lot, laughing and singing his own songs to himself.

"Yanko! Where are you going?" I shout.

"I want some motherfucking Skittles!"

* * *

This Rite Aid, like all Rite Aids in this city, used to be a K&B. In fact, this is the K&B where a pharmacist tried to turn Mama in for prescription fraud back in the late nineties.

"The pharmacist is from Shreveport. Too bad no one has told him not to disrespect the Lady." Mama was remarkably placid throughout the whole investigation. She seemed almost delighted by the trial and the DA's lack of preparation.

"Did you see that fatso? His pants aren't even zipped." She pointed to her prosecutor. "That one, he grew up here. He knows better."

The day the K&B pharmacist was to testify against Mama in court, he was hit by the St. Charles streetcar and broke his hip. Coincidentally, just hours after the pharmacist's hip was shattered, Rite Aid announced that it was buying K&B Drugs, a venerable institution that had shined its purple sign on New Orleans street corners for the better part of 90 years. Within a matter of weeks of the announcement, all of K&B's beloved purple signs were erased from the streets of New Orleans.

The citywide disappearance of K&B purple along with the hobbled pharmacist's sudden refusal to testify against Mama created a firestorm of rumors and front-page stories in *The Times-Picayune*. To make things even weirder, the prosecuting attorney, the one so fat he couldn't keep his pants zipped, fell dead of a massive coronary while eating Oysters Rockefeller at Galatoire's the day before closing arguments.

The case was dropped against Mama due to lack of evidence and, to be honest, because the judge was now terrified of Mama's evil eye. This fear spread into a backlash from a very vocal minority. Five to six very angry and very religious Protestants from Uptown picketed our house with signs warning Mama that "Only God Knows the Future!" However, the protesters didn't bother Mama. She loved the attention.

"So much better to be feared than loved," Mama would say just before she would walk out the front door to the grocery store to buy her cigarettes. As soon as her shoe hit the porch, the protesters scattered like mercury from a broken thermometer. They were as terrified as they were outraged. Mama ate this up like gumbo, but for me, all that secondhand scorn ruined any hopes I ever had of making a real friend in high school, much less ever getting a date.

The weight of these friendless days in the nineties is upon me as I stand here in the middle of this old K&B drug store, looking for my drunk brother up and down these aisles of candy, pills, and tampons.

I lose it.

I weep, like so many drunks do every morning in New Orleans. I wander onto the antacids and the laxatives aisles, crying like a lost child.

* * *

"There you are. Let's go," I say.

"Why are you crying?" Yanko says.

The hickey on his neck is almost black, and the teeth marks are swollen and red. He looks bad. And just when I don't think Yanko could look any worse, his mouth and tongue swell. He gags. Last night's Cherry Bombs explode. Yanko spews everywhere. The bright red vomit splatters onto the linoleum floor.

"Ah, man." This Rite Aid clerk stops as he's walking by. "Hipster-looking motherfucker puking all over my goddamn floors."

Maraschino cherries and undigested alcohol flood out of Yanko in a tide as unstoppable as my tears.

The Rite Aid clerk brings us a mop and bucket on wheels.

"You don't clean this up, I'm calling the cops," he says.

"For what?" Yanko wipes a long thread of drool from his chin.

"Public intoxication. Destroying property." The clerk hands me the mop. "You name it. They can throw your drunk ass in jail for it."

"We're going to need some paper towels." I point to the red splatter.

The clerk turns around and walks over to the paper products.

"Let's go!" Yanko takes off running.

Yanko runs out the front door, and I do the same. I'm not going to jail because my idiot brother threw up in the middle of Rite Aid.

Yanko eventually runs out of breath just past Constantinople.

"Wait up!" I pick up the pace and try to walk beside him.

"Walk faster." Yanko shoots a snot rocket out of his nose.

"I need to talk to you," I say.

"About what?"

"What Gay André said last night."

Yanko keeps walking faster.

"Look." I hold up Mama's gold coin necklace. "He said some guy who calls himself Loup Garou knows where Mama is. That's who did this to me!"

"That thing is cursed! Get rid of it!" Yanko grabs the necklace out of my hand and tosses it long and far, towards the Mardi Gras bead-encrusted trees that line the street. Mama's gold coins jangle and twist, turning over and over, into the French-blue sky. The gold coins hurl towards the branches of an ancient oak tree that is dripping in plastic beads.

The necklace crashes into the top branches.

"Asshole!" I walk over to the tree.

"Leave it!" Yanko raises his left hand and gives me the middle finger as he keeps on walking.

The necklace dangles high in the air. I grab a garbage can and prop it against the trunk. I climb into the lower branches. I pull myself higher and higher until I am teetering above St. Charles.

Just beyond my grasp, the necklace sways.

I touch the coins with the tips of my fingers. Maybe if I get a broom handle or a football or maybe an old beer bottle I can knock it down. But before I can concoct a plan, a blue jay swoops down, squawks and flutters. It flaps and flies away with Mama's necklace.

Just like that. Physics be damned; that blue jay just flew off with a gold necklace three or four times its body weight.

Blue wings on the blue sky, the gold coins glinting in the sun.

Gone.

"Goddamn it!" I pull on the plastic beads that are dangling over my head. I yank on them and break the strand. The beads bounce off of me. They ping onto the ground like purple hail.

I am losing it. I am having a full-blown panic attack about these goddamned Mardi Gras beads. These plastic tears come from deep beneath the ocean, from wells like the Sub-Ocean Brightside, and they will return to the sea, swept up by the rains, rushed down the storm drain, and pumped into the Gulf of Mexico, where they will be swallowed by schools of tuna, grouper, and red snapper, and then the plastic will be pulled from the open stomachs of dead pelicans and sea gulls that are so full of toys and Mardi Gras beads that the rotting birds will look like some kind of fucked-up piñatas to the children who find them.

16

8:42 AM

May 11, 2010

I am just trying to figure out how to get home, how to get out of this fucking sun and not throw up all over my shoes like Yanko just did back at the RiteAid. And right when I think I have figured how to walk back to The House of the Neon Palm, a muddy yellow Toyota FJ Cruiser pulls up and stops right in front of me, blocking me from crossing the street.

"You got to be kidding me," I say under my breath. I want to slam my fist on the hood but don't.

These are stupid tourists—lost and about five seconds from rolling down their windows to ask me directions to John Besh's new restaurant. But they don't roll down their windows to ask me for directions that they could have just as easily looked up on Google Maps. They open their doors, and they come at me with shiny chrome guns in their hands.

I find myself face-to-face with two frat boys wearing khaki pants and Ray-Ban aviators, waving their pistols at me.

Two frat boys with faces unmarked by time or hardship.

"Are you joking?" I say. "Is this some kind of joke? Because it's not very funny."

They don't answer me. They just put their guns to my head.

One of the boys is wearing a bowtie. The other's chin is covered in pimples, and his wrists are covered in friendship bracelets. They are both waving guns so shiny and silver that they look like toys.

"I don't even have a wallet," I say.

"Shut up and put your hands against the car," Bowtie says.

I put my hands up and turn to their yellow fratmobile.

My first thought is that I should try to burn these boy's faces into my memory: catalog the Bluetooth headsets in each of their ears, the blue and yellow striped bowtie, the harelip scar on the blond boy's lip, the mole next to the left nostril of the other boy.

The word "Seriously." falls out of my mouth as Bowtie pats me down and touches my junk.

"Where's the necklace?" he says.

"The necklace?" I say.

"Yes, the necklace" He pushes the gun at me. "Where is it?"

"It flew away with the birds," I say.

He clocks me hard in the nose.

Black stars.

I can't see. I can't think. I can't speak. I can only spin and blink.

"Get in the car!" He points the gun at my head. "Get the fuck in the car!"

And just when I'm about to do exactly what the frat boy is yelling at me to do, the cold metal of his gun is mashed into my right ear, and my arm is twisted behind my back. I am falling into the open door of the frat boy's gumball-yellow FJ Cruiser.

Gay André is passed out inside. I slide in next to him, but Gay André doesn't rouse. The kid in the bow tie pushes in next to me while he keeps his shiny gun pointed at my face.

Meanwhile, the zit-faced kid jumps in the driver's seat and throws the car into gear. He peels out. I look over at Bowtie and his baby cheeks. I try to muster up the courage to ask him if he works for The Loup Garou or The Unseen Hand.

"What the fuck you looking at, bitch?" He breathes in my face. His breath smells like peat moss and dog shit. I turn away and look over at Gay André, who I realize is not sleeping nor is he passed out.

There's a bullet hole in Gay André's head, and his warm blood is soaking into the seat of my pants.

* * *

Zit Face drives his gumball-yellow FJ Cruiser across the Pontchartrain, and it's not long before the blur of all-too-familiar landmarks cause my stomach to flip. He is driving to the McMansion. These assholes know where I live. More than likely, these are the ones who turned the raccoons loose in my house and left behind my mother's necklace. They've got *her*, and they've been watching *me*. They most likely know everything about me: where my kids go to school; that my wife goes to yoga at 8, picks up PJ's coffee at 9:30; how I drive into the city to go to Superior every Wednesday to drink myself under the table with

Gary and the rest of my co-workers. But if these are the fucks who set the raccoons loose in the house, why do they want the necklace back?

Zit Face pulls into the alley and Bowtie forces me to open the gate to our giant cedar privacy fence. Bowtie pushes me into the back-yard with a barrel of his gun pressed hard against my left kidney.

Zit Face hands me a shovel from the back of the FJ Cruiser.

"Start digging," he growls.

I just stand there, trying to process what's happening.

"He said fucking dig!" Bowtie hits me in the temple with his fist.

That fist to my head rattles me, but this surge of adrenaline speeds up my thinking: They are making me dig my own grave.

"Dig!" Bowtie yells. "From here to here." He paces out about seven feet.

I dig. I stab the wet dirt, and I dig. I shovel, and I think. I dig, and I dig this seven-foot plot, and I try to will myself sober.

How do I get out of this? I could use this shovel as a weapon. But how do I swing it fast enough to knock the guns out of their hands without getting shot? Better to get them talking, make them delay the killing, appeal to their greed, perhaps tell them I have cash inside the house and then get my neighbor's attention or, better yet, lock myself in the panic room.

"I lied," I say. "The necklace is in the house."

"Oh, the necklace is in the house. Good to know," Bowtie says. "What room?"

"It's kind of hard to explain. Why don't we go inside, and I can get it for you?"

"Yeah, why don't I make a brain slushie outcha ass and go find it for myself." Bowtie holds the gun to my temple.

"It's in a safe," I say. "I'll unlock it for you."

"Just dig," Bowtie says.

So I dig.

After almost an hour of shoveling, I have dug a three-foot hole big enough to lie down in. I want to tell them this is pointless. That nothing stays buried in New Orleans. That eventually they will be caught.

"Keep digging!" Zit Face yells at me. "Don't make me shoot your bitch-ass! Dig!"

As I pile the dirt higher and higher, I watch Bowtie drag Gay André's body from the car, across my green backyard. Long red streaks of blood paint the grass behind Gay André's head.

"Get out the way." He pushes me aside while Zit Face keeps his gun on me.

Bowtie pulls Andre's body into the hole that I thought I was digging for myself.

"Now cover him up!" Bowtie shouts.

I throw dirt over Gay André, that poor, sad, little homophobe who loved my mother enough to risk his life to try to help me find her. So here I am burying the mobster in in my own backyard, and I realize I have no choice. I'll be damned if these two college kids are making me dig my own grave.

So I take the business-end of my shovel and swing it as hard and as fast as I can at Bowtie. I knock him to the ground. Zit Face stands there with his mouth open, and his gun pointed at me.

He unloads his clip.

Pop.

Pop.

Pop.

As I fall back onto the ground, all I can think is that those shots sounded like someone knocking at Mama's front door, like a crime boss knock-knock-knocking because he has some urgent, dark news that only Madame Melançon can fix.

White light and smoke everywhere.

I am on my back in the grass.

The seconds stretch like taffy, and all I can think about is that raccoon that I shot in my driveway.

Is this is what it felt like for her?

Everything burns and bleeds. Everything dies.

White light and smoke everywhere.

The swish of Mama's black velvet robes.

The blur of her red satin slippers.

The splatter of blood on a blade of grass.

Everything fades to black.

17

EVERYTHING
HURTS

I open my eyes. I'm lying face-down, but not in a shallow grave or hospital bed. I am in the front yard of Mama's house, in the tall grass. I am not bleeding. My head is not full of bullets. I am fine. I have a splitting headache, but otherwise, I am fine.

I get up and dust myself off.

With New Orleans being New Orleans, none of these midday passersby or the police or even my mama's neighbors have found it the least bit off-putting that I have been lying here for God knows how long, passed out in front of a palm reader's house. Judging from the sunlight in the leaves above me, it's probably sometime in the late afternoon.

I stagger towards The House of the Neon Palm. I hold my temples with each step. My head is killing me. Visions of last night's cheap drinks and Cherry Bombs are making my jaw ache and my stomach ride. I make my way up to the porch, and into the front door, with one very clear desire: a big, tall glass of water with fistfuls of Advil.

I begin to shake uncontrollably and have to hold onto the wall not to pass out again.

My family is in the parlor watching the Fox News coverage of the Spill. La La is eating a bowl of ice cream, pretending to be Christina Aguilera while Emily is sitting next to her, texting and watching our boys hypnotize themselves with their iPads. Daddy's in his chair, and Cactus and Stevo are tangled up with each other on the floor, doing God knows what.

"Duke." Emily's eyes are full of tears.

"Daddy's home! Daddy's home!" Stewart keeps saying.

Emily bites her lip and looks away.

"Somebody's been a bad, bad boy." Stevo is laying on the carpet while Cactus weaves white daisies and baby's breath into his long, black beard—an act so oddly intimate and profoundly annoying that I want to shout at them both to go home, to just go back to the state park and their hippie caravan.

"Duke!" Daddy yells out from his La-Z-Boy. "Where da hell ya been, T'boy?"

"I was kidnapped."

"Are you kidding?" Emily says.

"Two college guys. They wanted Mama's necklace."

"Mama's necklace?" La La says. "Did they take it?"

"No." My head hurts too much to say any another word. I wave her off, and I keep walking to my room.

"Duke! I'm talking to ya, son!" Daddy shouts.

I just keep walking to the stairs, to my old bedroom. I need to shut my eyes.

I open the door and crawl into the lower bunk. I wrestle the covers over my head, pull my knees into my chest, shut my eyes. I feel the earth spin beneath this house while the neon palm sign buzzes and pops outside the window.

* * *

I wake up with warm slobber all over my cheek. The birds are chirping, the sun is shining, and my two boys are doing a little of both. Stewart is talking to his Thomas the Tank Engine and making choo-choo noises. Jo-Jo is happy and giggling on the floor and, from the smell of things, needs a serious diaper change.

Emily is bustling around, closing and opening drawers, frantic to find the diaper bag.

"Daddy's awake!" Jo-Jo claps.

"Yes, Daddy is." I smack away the awful cherry taste from last night.

"Come play twain!" Stewart holds up his Thomas the Tank Engine. "Come on, Daddy!"

"Daddy's going to get some coffee first, guys." I hold my head in my hands.

Emily looks up at me with a fresh diaper in one hand and Jo-Jo's ankles in her other.

"Hi," I say.

Emily folds up Jo-Jo's dirty diaper into a hermetically sealed white football.

"You okay?" she says.

"Yeah. No. I don't know."

"You slept for almost 12 hours." She fastens the new diaper around Jo-Jo's waist and puts him back to his trains.

"Oh shit." I get up from the bed. "I gotta call Gary."

"I emailed him for you," she says. "Stomach flu."

"That's what I told him on Mother's Day." I look at Emily.

"Sorry." She shrugs. "I didn't know what else to do."

"It's okay," I say. "I'll call him in a minute and straighten it out."

"Daddy, this train is Phillip." Stewart holds up a green boxcar. "Tell Jo-Jo he can't play with him."

"Honey," Emily touches Stewart's shoulder. "Go take Jo-Jo and your trains and go show them to PawPaw downstairs. He loves trains. Daddy and I need to talk for just a second."

And the good boy that Stewart is, he picks up his green box car and grabs his brother by the arm and does exactly what his mother asks of him. He's a good big brother. So smart. So kind.

"What happened?" She shuts the door behind the boys. "What is going on? I am freaking out."

"There were two guys. Preppy. Looked like Tulane students or something. In this yellow Toyota. They had guns, and they killed one of Mama's clients. They had him in the backseat with me, and then they drove me to our house in Covington and buried him in our backyard…."

"I told La La we should have called the police" She dives into her phone.

"Wait. Let me talk to Yanko first."

"Duke. I'm calling the cops."

"Okay. Call the cops. Fine."

I look down at my feet. It's the black matchbook that Gay André was playing with. It must have fallen out of my pocket while I was sleeping. I reach down and pick it up.

Give matchbook to fishwife, the line from Mama's prophecies pops into my head.

"What's that?" Emily asks.

"It's the dead guy's matchbook." I open it. "It's got a phone number in it."

"Do not call that number," she says.

I don't answer her.

"You're giving that to the police. You are done playing Sherlock Holmes." She holds her iPhone to my face and then dials 911. "We can't mess around here. This is serious stuff, Duke. These people mean business."

"Obviously," I say.

18

MAY 12, 2010

Mama has been missing for eight days

Detective Mary Glapion sits across from Emily and me in my mama's parlor. She's wearing a gold coin necklace similar to Mama's. It's just a coincidence, or maybe it's a telling sign from the Melissae. I don't know anymore. Perhaps even more significant than the gold coins around her neck is her black leather backpack, the one she carries instead of a purse. It has a TED logo on it, obviously some kind of swag from the brainiac conference she attended. With her thick frames and her old school Black-Berry, Mary Glapion looks more like a college professor than a cop.

In fact, Detective Glapion is not exactly the kind of person you would ever expect to live in New Orleans. Her considerable biceps make it apparent that she steers clear of the beignets and the étouffées, but instead carries tractor tires and climbs ropes at 5 a.m. It's hard to imagine why someone so obviously ambitious, so intellectually driven, so maniacally fit would ever live in The Fat City. Much less be part of a system so historically broken, bureaucratic, and racist. This question hangs on my tongue, but I'm not the one asking the questions. Detective Mary Glapion is.

"So let me just get this straight, Mr. Melançon? You were forced to bury Gay Costello's body in your backyard yesterday at approximately 9 a.m.?" She studies me, probing my face like a fortune-teller would for telltale signs of lying, like touching my mouth when I respond or averting my eyes, or worst of all, over-explaining the obvious.

"Yes. That's what I said." My hands start trembling so bad that I have to fold my arms to keep them still.

"Tell her about that matchbook you found," Emily says. "Show her the matchbook."

"Matchbook?" Glapion looks at me hard.

"It's nothing," I say.

"It's got a phone number in it," Emily says. "It's from the guy they killed. It's got a phone number scribbled inside."

"You mind showing it to me?" Detective Glapion gives me about three seconds of too much eye contact.

"Yes, I do mind." I look away.

"Duke. Just show it to her." Emily says.

"Aren't you an attorney, Mr. Melançon?"

"I am." My heart is racing so fast that my thoughts can't keep up. I can't think of a comeback. So I just sit here.

"Do you feel like you need an attorney to continue this series of questions?" She actually smiles when she says this.

"Why would he need an attorney?" Emily puts her hand on my knee.

"I am questioning your husband about a body that he buried in your backyard. I just want to make everyone aware of their rights."

"Are you reading me my rights?" I say. "You are. You're about to read me my rights. Is this where this is headed?"

"Mr. Melançon, I am simply trying to help you."

Emily looks at me with wide eyes—ocean-green eyes that telepathically say, "Can you believe this?"

"You know, Detective, I think we are done for today." I stand up. I am shaking so bad that my teeth are chattering. I don't know what's wrong with me. My heart is beating in my ears.

"Mr. Melançon. Please." She stands up and smoothes the wrinkles from the dress.

"We are done for the day, Detective." Everything starts to vibrate.

Mary Glapion's BlackBerry chimes and she puts her nose close to the glowing blue screen. She reads an incoming email while moving her lips. Finally, she glances back up and looks me in the eyes.

"There isn't a body buried at your house, Mr. Melançon," she says.

Everything feels wrong, really wrong, like *I-am-going-to-die* wrong.

"There's nothing in your backyard at all," she says. "No grave. No blood. And definitely no dead body."

"I dug the hole." A hummingbird is trapped inside my chest.

"I sent a squad car over to Gay Costello's house." She turns her phone to show me a picture texted to her. It's a shirtless Gay André standing in his front door. "He's still very much alive," she says.

Her eyes soften. It's a look of pity. "Mr. Melançon, has this ever happened to you before?"

"What do you mean has this ever happened before?" I say.

"Does he have a history of this?" Mary Glapion looks at Emily.

"History of what?" Emily blinks at her.

"Drugs," she says. "Mental illness. Anything that would explain this kind of delusion."

Emily shakes her head no.

The room spins. I close my eyes to remember, to see what happened in my backyard with the shallow grave and the frat boys yelling at me, but everything is thin and watery, like trying to remember a dream after being shaken awake. The only thing I can truly recall is the lightning flash of my mother's red satin slippers scattered in the St. Augustine grass.

"Mr. Melançon," Detective Glapion taps me on the shoulder, and I open my eyes. She's standing two inches too close to me.

"You okay?" she asks.

"Yeah. Fine." I nod.

"Look, I'm not sure what's going on with you," she says. "Grief is powerful. It makes victims' families do very strange things."

"It's not grief," I feel compelled to say.

"Well, whatever it is, let me be clear. If you interfere with my investigation, if you feel obliged to make up stories to keep me from finding your mother, I will prosecute you to the fullest measure of the law, grief or not."

"Did I do something wrong?"

"Why don't you tell me?" Mary Glapion looks me in the eye. She tears up and bites her bottom lip. Why is she tearing up?

"Thanks for coming by, Detective." Emily smiles bigger than she should. "The front door is this way.

19

THE LEGEND OF
THE LOUP GAROU

Uncle Father stands in Mama's kitchen, not sure what to say to me, what Bible verse to give, what bromide to apply to his nephew's lost soul. Without asking, Uncle Father ignites the gas stove, pulls a joint out of his back pocket and lights it on the burner. He takes a long, experienced dope-smoker drag, and then shoos the smoke away from his face. He hands the glowing joint to me. I wave him off. He offers it to Emily, and she folds her arms.

"No, thank you, Father." She looks at the floor.

"Suit yourself." He takes another long toke, exhales, and smiles. He looks so happy. So far from worry.

What does that even feel like?

I honestly can't remember. I can't remember what I felt like before my mother disappeared, before the Sub-Ocean Brightside exploded, before I became responsible for solving both of these unsolvable problems. I try to remember, but all I see when I close my eyes are armies of angry raccoons, clouds of dark blood swelling from the bottom of the Gulf, and the red cherries tumbling out of Yanko's loud mouth.

I grab the joint from Uncle Father and inhale the skunky smoke.

"Really?" Emily says.

It burns my lungs, and I can't stop coughing.

"I just need to relax," I say.

"By all means," she says. "*Relax*. I'll be glad to take care of the boys while you are baked out of your mind."

Emily leaves me and Uncle Father to our smoking, and the smoke swirls every care I have out of me, taking my headache and all my worries and nightmares with it. A euphoria swells inside my head, and butterflies flutter around my stomach. I am not sure if this is happiness, but I can feel every inch of a smile unfurling on my face, and for this brief skunky moment, I feel like a black kitten with a red ball of yarn, fascinated by everything, delighted for no real reason at all. I am all rainbows and unicorns, wizards with craggy staffs and happy dragons with lopsided grins.

"Ah, that's nice." I hear the echoes of my own voice inside my skull, and it sounds so amazing that someone should tape record it so I can listen to it over and over.

"It's Hawaiian." Uncle Father smiles.

My phone buzzes with a text.

You got my matches?

I don't recognize the number.

Who is this? I reply.

Gay André

Who is this?

I just want my matches

Gay André is dead

No I ain't

Who is this?

Gay

No it's not

Bartender said he saw you take my matches. I will pay you for them.

My phone shows those undulating gray dots that indicate that whoever this is is still composing his thoughts, that his autocorrect is rearranging his letters into meaning. *$10,000* pops up on my screen and almost slaps the buzz right out of me.

I turn off my phone and pick up the blunt out of the ashtray and take a long drag.

"Work?" Uncle Father says.

"Yeah."

"You gotta turn it off sometime." My uncle the priest — the man who's always dressed in his work clothes — says.

The medical marijuana is making me paranoid. I am freaking out. I try my best not to act like it in front of Uncle Father, but I am dying on the inside right now.

"You ever hear of a guy around town calls himself Loup Garou?" I finally get the courage to ask.

Uncle Father doesn't respond. He just keeps smoking.

Maybe it's the pot or maybe it's the lighting, but the realization of how much Uncle Father looks just like daddy strikes me harder and faster than it ever has before. That fat Cajun nose, the sun-tanned skin, and the French-blue eyes with their puffy bags. Uncle Father looks just like Daddy, except in a priest collar and without the wandering glass eye and ill-fitting fake leg. Uncle Father's name is suddenly a name that has been so obvious but now sounds strange and mysterious and messed up to me. He's my uncle, but he looks like my father dressed up as a priest, but he's my daddy's father in the church. He's all our father. This whole idea is making me seasick.

"Boy, every crook in this town calls hisself Loup Garou."

I try to refocus on our conversation and stop fixating on Uncle Father's strange name, and how his very presence in this kitchen, smoking his medical marijuana makes me confused and some-what freaked out.

"You know the legend, T'boy?" He smiles, half-lidded. "The Rougarou is what me and your daddy call him. Remember the story? You don't keep Lenten promises. You don't say yo' prayers. You don't eat yo' fish on Fridays. The Rougarou gonna git you. He got big-ass teeth and big red eyes. He got the head of a wolf and the body of a murderer. He'll suck yo' blood and crunch yo' bones with his teeth. So say yo' prayers. Keep yo' promises. And eat yo' fish on Fridays."

I can't help but laugh. Oh, the "Ruggy-roo." That word, that silly word being uttered by any adult used to scare the crap out of me when I was a boy. I remember how Uncle Father used to tell us these horrible stories about how the Ruggy-roo comes out of the swamp and steals bad kids out of their beds so he can eat them. Used to piss off Mama when he would come over after dinner and tell us Ruggy-roo stories just before bedtime. She'd have eight kids knocking on her bedroom door all night long, begging and crying to sleep with her. Lots of times she'd let us all sleep on the floor next to her bed, all curled up together on the hardwood floor on a blanket like a mess of puppies. We didn't care that the floor was hard so long as we could sleep next to our Mama because all eight of us knew that Mama would and could kick the shit out of any Ruggy-roo.

For this and for so many other reasons, Mama never liked Uncle Father, even if he was ordained by God, and likewise, he despised her. This was no family secret. And yet, this dislike never kept Uncle Father from being part of our family, from eating supper at our house every Thursday, sitting right next to Daddy at the long dinner table. Mama always encouraged us to bow our heads for Uncle Father's blessings, to hug his neck and to play the fiddle and dance for him.

To Mama's credit, she tolerated her husband's brother and his scriptural barbs, just like she complied with her husband's Catholic traditions and Cajun recipes. She'd cook his food, his gumbos, and his jambalayas, she'd celebrate his feasts, honor his saints, but when it came to raising her eight babies, she held fast to her gods and demons. She read to us constantly from the books that filled her bedroom. Poetry and fiction were mixed with her Hermetic tomes. We were kept clean with the Laws of the Secret Doctrine and the dark novels of Tolstoy, Hawthorne, and Mary Shelley.

"T'boy, I'm praying for ya Mama. All right?" Uncle Father ashes his doobie in the seashell ashtray that La La made when she was a little girl. "But ya reap what ya sow."

"You think this is karma?"

"Not karma. God." He bites his bottom lip and shakes his head.

"Same difference." I have to look away.

"A few years back I saw her. She stood right here in this kitchen." He points to the floor. "I was standing right there. And I saw her. She disappeared. I saw her do it, Duke."

"She disappeared?" I say.

"And she came back a few minutes later. Walked right in that back door. Beaten to hell. Nose bleeding. Teeth missing."

"Someone beat her up?"

"Like how the devil likes to do to his wife." He holds my gaze. "She sold her soul to be able to do such things. Witchcraft is a dangerous game, T'boy."

"You watch too much TV," I say.

"You only have one choice, Duke. Take down that neon sign. And then pray for our Holy Father's forgiveness."

Daddy crutches into the kitchen, with his left pant leg pinned to his back pocket.

"Ain't T'boy's call," Daddy says.

"Ya reap what ya sow, Vinny." Uncle Father takes one last toke.

"Get the hell out, Joe, talking that kind of shit before I bust ya coconut," Daddy says.

Uncle Father crosses himself.

"Say yo' prayers while you walk home, ya old pothead." Daddy shoves Uncle Father to the door. Uncle Father pushes back on Daddy, causing him to stumble on his crutches, but then Daddy catches himself with skill and strength that is somewhat surprising.

"Watch the slap, Joe!" Daddy holds up the back of his hand to strike his older brother—an action that the one-legged old man can execute with deadly precision after a lifetime of slapping a house full of kids.

"Go on. Get!" Daddy shouts.

"Do not push a man of God, Vinny!"

Uncle Father backs away from Daddy, to the back door, the very back door that my mother ran out with her broom in hand.

"Duke, I'm praying for ya." Uncle Father lingers.

"Go!" Daddy yells. "Ya goddamn *couyon!*"

Uncle Father slams the door, and Daddy picks up the smoldering joint from the ashtray.

He holds it out to me. I shake my head no. So he takes the last drag and coughs.

"Ignore that *croute sec.*" Daddy gives me a sad smile. "He's always been afraid of pussy. Always thinking women fucking the devil. Always wanting to perform exorcisms and throw holy water on them. He just needs a good womp upside the head. Your mama was a good woman doing dangerous work."

"What work was that exactly, Daddy?"

"She wasn't no witch, son," he says. "Your mama is a saint, and her work ain't never done."

My phone vibrates and chimes in my pocket. It's Gary. This is his third call. My phone must have been out of range because I didn't see his other two, back to back.

"Daddy, I'm sorry I have to take this."

I look down at my phone and Gary has already gone to my voice-mail. My phone is full of bright green bubbles—the unread text messages from him.

From the first twenty-five that I read, I patch together that Gary blew a gasket at the wrong person. He doesn't know exactly who it might be, though. Over the past week, he yelled at a lot of peo-ple, including lots of members of Christopher Shelley's executive team. Now Gary is nervous that he is going to be fired and wants to talk to me.

So I call him back because he's not going to stop until I do.

"Where the hell have you been?" he says without even saying hello.

"I know it might surprise you, but I have a family."

"I really need you in the office. We need to rehearse for our meet-ing with Christopher tomorrow."

"We're prepared, Gary. We've been over this like five times now. We don't need to rehearse."

"He's the goddamn CEO, Duke. Plus, I need you to talk to Con-stanze Bellingham for me."

"Is that who you pissed off?"

"No—like she matters—I need you to find out if she thinks I pissed off Christopher."

"It's late."

"I need you to call her. She likes you."

"And say what?"

"Find out if that new PR lady they are hiring is replacing me."

"Is she an attorney?" I ask.

"No."

"Then how is she replacing you?"

"Rumor is we are all reporting to her after tomorrow," Gary says. "Grace in Drilling told me Christopher keeps screwing up in the press and people are blaming me for it. The whole company is blaming me, Duke. They're saying this media backlash is because External Affairs doesn't have its shit together."

"Christopher doesn't listen. It's not our fault."

"I really think he's calling this meeting with you and me to fire us," Gary is now whining. "He hasn't replied to a single email of mine in almost 48 hours now."

"Gary. Just take a Xanax. Relax. Christopher is not firing you or me. He needs us, and he knows it."

"I want you to call Constanze like right now."

"I'll text her."

"So when will you be here?" Gary says.

"I have my phone and laptop, Gary. We can just get this done over email if you need to make any changes to the presentation."

"Well, you better believe this will show up in your performance review."

"That is if you're still around," I say.

"That's not funny."

"Take two Xanax, and I'll text you as soon as I know anything from Constanze."

"So you're calling her?"

"No, I'll email her."

"Call her."

"I'm hanging up now, Gary. Try to get some rest. Tomorrow's going to be great."

20

MAY 13, 2010

Fifty-five days since the Explosion

Gary booked the Louis XIV Room at the Ritz-Carlton on Canal Street for our meeting with Christopher Shelley. The Ritz knows how to deal with executives in crisis—how to make them comfortable and safe and pampered. The Ritz also knows how to keep a secret. Mandala security detail will whisk Christopher Shelley from the company jet to his presidential suite, and once they have ensconced the most reviled CEO in the world into this hotel, they will then quietly escort him to this beautiful room, and no one in NOLA will be the wiser.

So here we wait for him.

Gary forgot to take his Xanax, and now he's super nervous. This mostly manifests in his stress eating. He surfs the buffet while I sip my coffee and delete old texts. He loads up his plate at the sideboard: the stinky cheeses and charcuterie, the baguettes and the smoked salmon, the marinated olives and Marcona almonds, the tiny pies, and the buttery pastries. The spread was specifically requested by Constanze Bellingham, and because of that, common sense might tell Gary to wait to eat from this buffet until our CEO arrives.

But Gary, being Gary, is polishing off three or four plates when the mahogany doors open and our CEO walks into the room. The most striking thing about seeing Christopher Shelley in person is not his marionette cheeks or the obscene amount of Pre-Raphaelite red curls on his head. What is most striking about this man is how alone he is. How small against this magnificent room, this world, this moment, he is. His image in the press is larger than life. But right here, right now, he's just a small man standing in this big room. Just a small man who this angry world now blames for its own demise. No bodyguards. No army of assistants. No trumpets heralding the arrival of the Sun King. No orchestral strings crescendoing the appearance of the Antichrist. It's just Christopher Shelley. A smallish man in a rather expensive suit.

"Hello, chaps."

I stand up and introduce myself.

"I'm Duke Melançon. In-house counsel for External Affairs."

Christopher Shelley's handshake is strong, friendly, brisk. His eyes are surprisingly blue, boyish yet crinkled by too much time spent on yachts—smiling and squinting.

"I know who you are, Duke." He smiles. "Glad to finally meet you in the flesh."

"So how was the hop across the pond?" Gary licks his fingers and wipes them on a napkin. He then shakes Christopher's hand.

Christopher smiles nonetheless.

* * *

"We have launched an investigation because I want to know what happened," Christopher says, practicing the talking points that our new PR agency has prepared for him. "We will be transparent. We are conducting a full and comprehensive investigation, and we will make this right. Our investigation is covering everything. It will cover everything."

I take frantic notes while Gary plucks the glazed raspberries from his tarte aux framboises.

"The phrase 'We will make this right' is dicey," I say. "You are essentially granting some kind of guarantee when you say that."

"Well, we *are* going to make this right. People need to know that. We have a brand to protect here. Mandala Worldwide cares. It's essential that the press sees that in everything we do." Christopher sips his tea.

"I know, but it'd be safer not to use those exact words at the press conference."

"It is very necessary that I say that I am sorry." Christopher scowls. "People want me to be accountable and I will be."

"I get that," I say. "But don't use those exact words. Better to say, 'the Gulf Spill is a tragedy that should have never happened' than to say the actual words 'I am sorry.'"

Christopher squints at me. He folds his arms and sort of holds his breath. He's making these weird little grunts as I speak. So I continue explaining how a non-apology apology works.

"The Holocaust is a tragedy that should have never happened," I say. "The Haiti earthquake is a tragedy that should have never happened. Slavery is a tragedy that should have never happened. You're stating the truth but not claiming legal fault. When you state a commiserating truth like that, it really has the same emotional impact as saying 'I'm sorry.' There are studies that back this up."

"Listen to him, Christopher. The kid knows his stuff." Gary tongues the yellow pudding from his *tarte*.

"I'm not doubting that Duke knows his stuff, Gary. But I feel that it's important to be authentic at a time like this. The world needs to know that real people are trying their absolute best here, and confining my words to such an asinine degree serves no one. No one."

"Yeah, well, that's sweet and all, but people are just waiting to take you down. Not just Mandala Worldwide, *you*." Gary cheeks the rest of his raspberry pie; masticates, grunts.

"Am I the only one who needs a drink?" Christopher gives me a weary smile. "Surely, it's five o'clock somewhere."

"I'll get the boy to get us a pitcher of Bloody Marys." Gary holds up his pointer finger to the waiter.

"Too spicy," Christopher says. "Let's do spritzes?"

"You kidding me?" Gary rolls his eyes.

"You'll drink them and like them," Christopher says. "They're delightful."

"I ain't drinking … a spritz." Gary makes rabbit-ear-quotations with his fingers.

Our white-gloved waiter materializes next to Christopher as silently and discreetly as a vapor.

"Aperol or Campari?" he asks.

"Aperol, of course. What kind of philistine makes a spritz with Campari?" Christopher laughs at his own joke, and so does the impeccable waiter.

What began as a two-hour meeting has blossomed into five and is threatening to fester into six maybe seven, thanks mostly to these Aperol spritzes and Gary's long-winded diatribes about liberal agendas and Kenyan U.S. Presidents. As for the Aperol spritzes, they are as Christopher Shelley promised, delightful. Not the manliest of drinks, for sure, but there's something accomplished about drinking them in the morning like this, like perhaps this is what billionaires drink on their yachts when they dock at Antibes, or when they are sitting on the balconies of their palazzos overlooking the flooded streets of Venice while playing footsie with their third wives.

The excellent white-gloved waiter refreshes my drink every time the orange liquid disappears from my glass. With each pour, the spritz fizzes and bubbles and I take long thirsty sips that tickle my nose.

After my fourth glass, my head feels lofty and light, like a bright orange balloon that some kid let go in the Quarter. I blink at my laptop and try to focus so I can continue briefing Christopher on the proper language required to strike a perfect tone in the media. But I can't get Gary and Christopher to focus on the talking points that I spent the better part of last week preparing.

Even without being slightly drunk, this is far harder than it sounds. CEOs like Christopher Shelley really like to set the vision; they don't like to be told what to say—especially not by a junior attorney from External Affairs. But put five or six Aperol spritzes in the guy, and we've got him laughing in all the wrong places and surprisingly sad at times.

Such a nice guy. Really makes me feel sorry for him that so many people hate him right now.

"We are Mandala Worldwide, for God's sakes! We are not Exxon! We are not Union Carbide! We are Mandala, and we will make this right!" Christopher stands up and pounds the table and puffs out his pigeon chest.

"We shall not cower. We shall not falter. We shall kill this well!" Christopher, with the help of the Aperol, begins to give a bad Shakespearean monologue. "A dark tide is upon us, and as it rises, we shall stand together with our kith and kin, united with the good people of the Gulf. Mandala will make this right! We will make this right! Goddamn it! I will make this right!"

A shitfaced Christopher Shelley is fun to watch. He's royal with his delivery—full of august pride and eloquent measure.

In fact, I'd have to say that Christopher is a nice guy, the kind of guy I wish I could be friends with and hang out with on his private jet. He's witty, easy to talk to. He has that great British sense of humor. Very dry and slightly bizarre, but at the same time warm, quite charming—not the least bit the kind of dick that Gary is. Maybe after this is all over, Christopher will transfer me to London. He seems to like what I have to say. Emily would love London.

I've gotten Christopher through everything on the agenda so far. We have covered the media buy, the PR strategy and reviewed over fifty press releases. We've even endured Gary threatening to drunk dial our head PR writer, "She's so hot. I can get her to come down here," Gary says. "And she can read these press releases to us out loud. Seriously, you have to see this girl. Goddamn, she's got this sexy smoker's voice thing going on."

"That's not okay, Gary," Christopher says without smiling.

"What?" Gary drops his jaw, revealing the chewed-up pink macaron.

"Talking about a female subordinate—anyone—like that is not okay," Christopher says.

"I was just kidding." Gary smirks.

"Well, it's not funny," Christopher says. "I will not stand for that kind of idiotic behavior from one of my senior leaders. Say something like that again, and I will have you escorted from the building."

21

MAY 14, 2010

U.S. bans new drilling in the Gulf of Mexico

Everything is overgrown. The cicadas and the crickets buzz and screech. The grass has gone to seed. The sweet olive and azalea beneath the porch have exploded into thickets. The bougainvillea has crawled up the columns of the house, onto the roof, and now a torrent of purple flowers threatens to engulf the old neon palm. Quite frankly, we have all been too busy or too bereft to do anything about it. We have ignored everything: mowing the grass, trimming the hedges, washing the dishes, paying the bills, and taking our cholesterol medicine.

This hasn't stopped Mama's customers from lining up every day. Even though Mama has vanished into thin air, they still come to get their palms read. They still come to see Madame Melançon's daughter, to get their peeks into the future—never mind the fact that the magical daughter in this house isn't magical enough to look into her crystal ball and find her missing mother.

As typical with this family, if I don't take action, nothing gets done. So today I wake up and go to my Daddy's tool shed and grab the machete. I begin hacking at the weeds and vines. I keep thinking that if my mother's magical thinking worked, then this labor would somehow remove the curse that has fallen on our house and that by clearing this yard, I would be preparing the way for the return of New Orleans' Fortune-Teller Queen. This is the fairy-tale bullshit that the clients who line up at Mama's back door believe. Sadly, I don't have the luxury of that kind of delusion. I have the poverty of reality: these mosquitos sucking my blood, the tall grass slicing my ankles, and this sweat dripping off my nose.

I also have La La, who's now dared to brave the front porch. She lights her cigarette and waves the smoke away from her eyes. Her hair is shaved short on the sides, and a white-blond swoop hides her left eye. Her ears look like they are full of gold-plated fish-tackle.

"So who are you supposed to be?" I wipe the sweat from the tip of my nose.

"Robyn."

"Never heard of her."

"She's big in Sweden." La La then holds out her phone and starts playing this boom-boom dance music.

"Okay, I get it."

"Robyn has amazing luck," La La says. "We could use that kind of luck today."

"You want to help me here?"

"No, it is your turn." She takes a long dramatic drag off her ciga-rette. "I have cut those weeds many times."

I stop swinging the machete and stare at my sister.

"It's the earth's message to you anyway." She waves a puff of smoke away with her hand.

"And what message is that, La?"

"The Green Mama is reclaiming this house just as She will reclaim her oceans."

"La La," I say. "The only message that the earth has for me is that I need to call a yard man."

"One day you will see signs like I do." My sister takes a long drag. "You are just like Mama. You are. I know you don't believe that, but you will see all, know all, tell all. One day, one day soon, you will take up her yoke."

"There are no signs, La La." I chop the dandelions and the nettles.

"When I talk to the Bee Maidens..." La La French exhales and then throws her cigarette on the porch. She steps on it, doing a modified version of the twist. "They tell me you are driving me to a homeless shelter today."

"I'm not going to a homeless shelter."

"You're going to make me go by myself?"

"I have to work." I pull up what appear to be wild onions by their roots. I throw them out of Mama's flowerbed. They smell like Stevo and Cactus.

"On a Sunday?" La La lights another cigarette.

"Are you not watching the news?" I hack away.

"What if Mama had a stroke and got confused?"

"La, that's actually..." I lower the machete to my side and try to catch my breath. "...not crazy."

"I had a dream last night that Mama forgot the story of who she is. She was at the New Orleans Mission."

"Okay, now you lost me."

"Fine, I'll go by myself then."

"You are not going to the New Orleans Mission by yourself."

"According to you, I am."

"Okay, I'll take you. Just let me jump into the shower first."

* * *

La La and I get in my Prius, and we drive down Napoleon to St. Charles and then onto Caliope. She is busy taking selfies of her new look and posting them on Instagram. She is one of the top-followed "Instagram witches." (Yes, that's a thing.) So even with all this chaos and darkness swirling around us, La La has an uncanny ability to make everything gleefully about herself.

"What's that smell?" La La scowls.

The stench of spoiled milk overtakes the car as my air conditioner blows the hot air around the cabin.

"Shit," I say. "Jo-Jo must have left his sippy cup in the backseat."

"You need to pull over and get it out of here."

"Not that big of a deal. Calm down."

"I'm seriously going to puke." La La covers her mouth.

"Just roll down a window." I hit the button, and the glass slides down on her side. Hot air blows into the car.

"Okay. Now I'm sweating." La La rolls up her window.

"We're almost there."

La La looks straight ahead and covers her nose with her hand. She refuses to talk to me because I won't do exactly what she wants me to do, and also because my family believes bad smells are a way of inhaling misfortune. Even after a decade of ignoring her, some things never change. So we drive down Caliope in complete silence like we used to do when we were kids, after Mama had broken up one too many fistfights between us.

"Say another word to your sister, Dukey, and I will slap you bald-headed!" Mama would shout as she drove us around town in her big black Mercedes. La La and I would both sit in the back seat, silent as the stars.

Back then, La La was a sweet and curious child. She always drew pictures for my brothers and me. She made ashtrays out of clay for Mama, and she held Daddy's hand everywhere they went. She was the only one of us who listened, actually listened, when adults or even kids talked. She listened with her eyes. She listened in a way that felt like heaven was listening too. I wish I could tell that girl how much I miss her. That quiet girl grew up and disappeared into a bitter fog, just like my tolerance for my family's superstitions.

"Why did you leave?" La La breaks the silence—almost as if she is reading my mind.

"What do you mean?"

"Why did you leave?"

"Look around, La La." I try to laugh it off.

"You're a pussy," she says. "You had a destiny to meet, and you ran away."

"Or maybe I'm just smarter than the rest of you."

"You know the Melissae don't think you're so special anymore, but they still have a plan for you."

"Oh, good. Tell your imaginary friends that I don't think they're so special either."

"I hate you."

"What did I ever do to you?"

"You left."

"Come on, La La."

"You left me here, and you didn't care."

* * *

The gray wall and hand-painted sign say it all.

The New Orleans Mission eludes the black and white of everyday life. Everything here is in-between and uncomfortable. La La and I are greeted by a snaggletoothed woman with tan skin, silver paint around her mouth, and flame-blue eyes. She's down on her luck, she says. Just needs twenty dollars for bus fare, she sighs. She holds her palm out to us. I want to help her. But my money might not be the best thing for her. She might buy spray paint to huff. Or it might just be that rare moment where I make a human connection with this person, lost at sea in her own mental illness. How do I know?

It's this kind of uncertainty that makes me hate being here. Like Mama, my sister has less of a problem with this kind of ambiguity. She simply hands the lady a wad of cash and pulls me past the silver-mouthed woman into the Mission's front doors.

"Take the fliers and show them around to the men, and I'll check the women's side." La La hands me copies of Mama's flier and leaves me standing among the cots and the coughing. And that's when I see the old street performer I saw guarding the Banksy umbrella girl, shouting passages from *Slaughterhouse-Five*.

NOLA attracts bat-shit crazy like no other. "Bring me your alcoholic, your schizophrenic, your hedonistic masses yearning to run naked and cack-smeared down cobblestone streets," New Orleans seems to say to the world. And the world answers. This town is full of people who wear purple veils and talk to invisible guardian angels; people who disguise themselves in elaborate Greek god costumes for Mardi Gras, but who also write long, tedious diaries about the Illuminati and how half-lizards lurk behind every world leader; people who will unabashedly tell you that they are the Vampire Lestat or the Pirate Jean Lafitte; people who have gone to great lengths to look exactly like Mark Twain, Blaze Star, and even Kurt Vonnegut.

I walk over to the Vonnegut impersonator's cot.

"Remember me?" I say.

"Well, well, well." He stands up and shakes my hand.

"I guess the street artist gig doesn't pay so well."

"Don't be smug," he says. "Life is far more than just paying the light bill."

"So no word on my mother?"

"You know, son, I wrote a passage in *Slaughterhouse-Five*[1] just for her. It was a flare to let the Pythoness know that The Unseen Hand was reaching out to grab her by the throat." The Vonnegut impersonator smirks. "And now The Hand has reached out for you recently. It forced those two Young Republicans with their shiny guns to assault you."

---

1. *Slaughterhouse-Five, Chapter Four: "An unseen hand turned a master valve..."*

"Why are you fucking with me?"

"*The Great Unseen Hand* wants your mother's necklace and The Hand will strangle life after life to get it."

"How the hell do you know this?"

"I know a lot, Duke." He toys with his mustache. "I know about the blue jay."

"I know about Gay André's murder." The Vonnegut impersonator points his fingers to his temple like a gun. "I know about his Lazarus-like resurrection, which was no resurrection at all considering he was never killed in the first place. I know those college boys' bullets never hit your skull. I know despite your mother's mightiest efforts, she was unable to stop this spill, but she is determined to stop her son from lying about its consequences to the world. I know this like I know the back of my own hand." He holds his palm to my face. "I know. I know. I know."

I push his hand away.

"Are you cold reading me?" I ask.

"Ah, familiar with the Barnum Effect[2], I see." Vonnegut chuckles.

"You are. You're cold reading me," I say.

"Don't you know that what you don't understand you can make mean anything?" he says. "That's the beautiful thing about words. But no, I am not cold reading you. I merely speak a truth that is beyond your current level of comprehension."

"What kind of game are you playing here?" I say.

"I suppose you could look at this as a game," he says. "I always looked at life as more of a tragedy."

"How do you know all this? How do you know my mother?" I say. "Tell me right now!"

"Your mother is not who you think she is. She is not some mere

2. The Barnum Effect is when some poor doe-eyed soul finds very specific meaning in cleverly worded yet general statements that could apply to almost anybody with a heartbeat. Turban-wearing psychics, carny-handed mediums, and open-shirted Vegas magicians use this to great applause and profit. "The Barnum Effect" was coined by American psychology professor Paul Meehl, referencing P. T. Barnum's reputation as a hustler and flamboyant con man. However, P.T. Barnum never said, "There's a sucker born every minute." So there's that.

oracle. Just like The Loup Garou is not just some mere vandal. Just like I am not just some mere novelist. No, the easiest way to explain this to you is to say that Madame Melançon is the seamstress of the future and her needle pierces us all. Helena leads a small team of tailors, tinkerers, and fart-abouts to use the very threads of time to restrain the grip of The Great Unseen Hand."

THE GREAT

UNSEEN HAND

"Who the fuck are you?"

"Technically, I am a strange loop," he says. "A mathematical string of code, a precise algorithm that was built from the writings, photos, recordings, interviews, and diaries of Kurt Vonnegut and put into this extraordinary machine.

I look past the old codger, to the door, but he doesn't stop talking. He steps closer to me.

"Do you know why you're here, Duke?" Vonnegut asks.

"I'm looking for my mother. I need to go."

"Well, there are lots of places to look. After all, the cosmos is a big place."

"You need to get out of my way, old man."

He blocks me. Bumps his chest against mine. His face just inches from my nose. He smells like copper pennies and warm batteries. Kurt's eyes are no longer twinkling. They are baby doll eyes with big pupils— two black holes dying in the middle of distant galaxies.

"I wasn't a big fan of this whole singularity idea when The Unseen Hand first turned me back on." He shakes his head and sighs. "By the time The Hand got this ridiculous notion to put my mind inside this body of sorts, everyone I ever cared about, everyone I ever truly loved, was gone."

I can't listen to this crazy shit anymore; I sidestep Vonnegut and walk away.

"Go then. But remember, we are all travelers and gypsies. Just not very kind or intelligent ones. Especially when it comes to the past." Kurt throws his left hand up to the heavens like a symphony conductor, like he's giving a King Lear monologue at a community theater. "After all, how did we let Dresden happen? Auschwitz? Hiroshima? Leningrad? Darfur? Rwanda? Someone at the Bureau of Humanity is going to lose their head over that kind of incompetence. I can promise you that!"

* * *

"Well, that was a complete waste of time." La La buckles her seat belt and pulls down the vanity mirror. She checks her bangs and lipstick.

"It was a logical place to look." I start the car and point one air conditioning vent to me and one to La La.

"Did you find anyone who might have seen her?" she asks.

"Just that crazy guy who thinks he's Kurt Vonnegut."

"Oh, Mama loved Kurt Vonnegut."

"The homeless guy or the actual author?"

"The author. She had all his books."

"I don't seem to remember that," I say.

"Oh yeah, she had a thing for him," La La says. "Joseph Heller, Douglas Adams, George Saunders. The weirder, the better."

"Yeah, well this guy was weird alright. He was cold reading me."

"Cold reading?"

"Yeah, you know like what you do to people to make them think you're psychic."

"Are you calling me a liar?" She leans back and screws up her face.

"No, just a con artist." I chuckle.

"Fuck you."

"Want to pick up lunch somewhere?" I try to change the subject.

"I'm doing a cayenne cleanse." La La puts the visor back up and looks out the window. "Wonder why my dream misled us to this place?"

"Dreams don't always have to mean something, do they?" I drive out of the parking lot. "Or maybe that's what the dream meant: Mama's been misleading you."

"Don't say that. Don't say that about our mother."

"Sorry. You're right. Mama never misled anyone."

"Why do you always have to be right?" she says. "Does it make you happy?"

"What would make me happy is to find Mama so I can go home and be with my family."

"If you hadn't disobeyed Mama, none of this would be happening right now, and I wouldn't be threading this needle by myself." She points to the sidewalk. "Pull over. Right here. Right now."

"What? Why?"

"Let me out of this car."

I pull the car to the side of the road and park it. "What's wrong?"

"The Melissae sent you Vonnegut, and you're too much of an know-it-all to even try to see the signs."

"How is some crazy guy a sign?

"It's no coincidence you keep running into him."

"Ah, so it's no coincidence that I ran into a homeless guy at a homeless shelter?"

"You're never going to learn and we are all going to die because of it." She looks at me straight in the eye. She is serious. She really believes what she's saying to me.

And then La La gets out of my car, slams the door, and walks away from me and all my annoying logic, and I let her do it.

22

UNDER THE BUZZ
& GLOW

The red neon flickers

"You and La La figure anything out at the shelter?" Emily asks me while she is taking off her eye makeup in my parents' pink-tiled guest bathroom.

"Not really." I unbutton my shirt and slip out of my pants. "Just some crazy old guy who says he knows Mama, and now La La and I are in a fight."

"Why are you in a fight? Don't answer that. Of course, you're in a fight with La La." She wipes a cotton ball across her eyelashes and throws it in the trash. "What did the guy from the shelter say?"

"That he wrote *Slaughterhouse-Five* for her."

"At least it wasn't *Catcher in the Rye*." She smiles. "If he had a copy of that, then you'd know you'd found your man."

"He was going on and on about The Unseen Hand. He's in on this somehow."

"Duke." She widens her eyes at me. "Did you at least get his number this time?"

"He's homeless. He doesn't have a number."

"No wonder La La is pissed at you." She turns from the bathroom mirror and looks me in the eyes. "You need to tell the cops about this guy."

I have to look away; I act like I am looking for my phone.

"If you don't call them in the next five minutes, I am calling Mary Glapion myself," she says.

"She threatened to arrest me, Emily. You sat there and watched her do it."

"Sweetheart, they kidnapped you. They put you in their car, and they held a gun to your head. They know where we live."

"I am handling this." I can feel my jaw tighten.

"You keep saying that, but what does that mean?"

"It means that I am going to figure out who did this and make them pay."

"Make them pay? Are you serious? Who are you?"

"What do you mean who am I?"

"I don't even know who this person is saying this to me," she says.

"It's me," I point to my face. "Same guy I was five minutes ago before you started freaking out."

"So now I'm the one freaking out? That's how you want to play this?" She walks out of the bathroom, past me.

Her words hang in the air like the humidity. They both make me sweat.

I brush my teeth. I kiss my sleeping boys on the cheeks and pull the covers up to their chins. But instead of climbing into my old bed, I crawl in with Emily, and she lets me. She folds into me, and we cuddle.

"I'm sorry," I whisper into her hair. "I'll call Mary Glapion tomorrow."

"You can't keep doing this," she says. "You can't keep acting like these people aren't dangerous."

"I know." I kiss her on the forehead. "I'll call the cops tomorrow."

"Promise?"

"I promise."

Emily falls asleep while my mind races, first to my mother's bound wrists, then to Gay André's dead face, then to the matchbook, and then back to Emily, back to who we used to be, back when I wasn't the son of a missing mad woman or a lawyer for Mandala Worldwide or a bad husband or an absentee father. Back to when I was just me. Back to that Wilco concert at Stubb's where I spilled my beer on this blonde pixie with big green eyes.

I had apologized profusely. The front of her shirt was drenched.

"Don't worry about it," she said.

"Let me buy you a drink," I said.

"Sure," she smiled. And from that moment, we stood side by side, nursing our Shiner Bocks, swaying to the music, the bright lights from the show reflecting on our faces.

She was a huge fan of *Summerteeth*. I thought *Being There* was better. We argued about this during the opening act. I bought her a beer and then another. By the time Jeff Tweedy closed the show with "She's a Jar," and with all those lines about sleepy kissers and all those feelings that the night is real, we weren't just listening to that song. We had become that song.

Emily took me home, and after that night, after that supposed one-night stand, we never left each other's side. We fell in love. Hard. She was an econ major who wanted to work for a tech start-up. I was a law student who was going to save the world. She laughed at all my jokes. I couldn't stop holding her hand. She smelled like watermelon and cut grass.

We became each other's everything, only thing; it was spring break in Tulum when this finally became apparent to me.

We had spent the whole day in the water, playing while the green waves swelled around us, grabbing, tickling, laughing. We kissed until our mouths were numb. Then we grilled fish right out of the ocean and got drunk on cheap tequila and fresh pineapple juice. The sun reddened our shoulders and brightened our eyes. We lay on our backs, drying our bathing suits in the white sand.

And that's when I told her that my mother was the Fortune-Teller Queen of New Orleans. I told her about the mob bosses and their jealous wives, about Willy Williams and Carlos Marcello, about my mother's dubious claims to Madame Blavatsky's dark throne, about the predictions and the curses.

I told her everything. She was the first girl I ever told about my family's weird business. It was a drunken thing to do. I could have lost her, but just the opposite happened.

"Let's get married," she said.

"Today?" I searched her eyes.

"Is that a yes?" She rolled away from me in the sand.

"Was that a proposal?" I crawled on top of her.

"It was," she said.

"You're drunk," I said.

"Just a tiny bit."

"Then let's do it. Today."

"Like right now?"

"Like right now," I said.

23

MAY 15, 2010

Mama has been missing for ten days

This Sunday morning, I get up early while Emily and the boys are asleep in those backbreaking bunk beds. I shave and shower. I put on my University of Texas golf shirt and Dockers. I grab Gay André's matchbook out of my old jeans, and my iPhone off the dresser. I tiptoe through this creaky old house. But these floors ache with every step. So I take it slow, down the old staircase, past all those years of family photos, past Roman with his headgear and braces, past Yanko with his 'N Sync hair gel and acne, Stevo in his gold helmet and football pads, past Mama in her long black braids and intense stare. At the bottom of the stairs, bodies and blankets are all over the parlor. Stevo and Cactus obviously brought their family inside from the van last night. So I step over them as carefully as I can to the front door.

I unlock the deadbolt, and slip out the door onto the porch. I stare out over the neutral ground of Napoleon Avenue to the errant frat boys and their dates stumbling home from The Club Ms. Mae's. I try to piece together that night with Yanko and Gay André.

I check the time on the iPhone. Is 8:00 a.m. too early to call Meg Mills?

I dial the number from Gay André's matchbook.

2-25-1-31-60-78 Ext 49.

The phone rings and then click:

"We're sorry. You have reached a number that has been disconnected or is no longer in service. If you feel you have reached this recording in error, please check the number and try your call again."

I go inside and hide the matches in the back of the cutlery drawer. I pull down the red can of Community Coffee and make myself a fresh pot in Mama's Mr. Coffee maker that she has had since the '80s.

* * *

"What a big boy!" Emily shouts from behind the closed door of the guest bathroom "You did it!"

The toilet flushes and Emily brings Jo-Jo into the parlor, where I am laying on the old purple velvet sofa, playing with my phone, de-friending people on Facebook who keep posting half-truths about the Spill.

"I did it, Daddy! I did it!" Jo-Jo claps his hands.

"That's great, buddy!" I say.

"I pooped in the potty like a big boy!"

"Yes, you did, and now Daddy's going to take you to get a snow-ball," Emily sings.

Jo-Jo walks over to me on the couch. He crawls up on my

belly—the one that seems to be getting bigger and more Homer Simpson-like by the day. Jo-Jo sits on my stomach and he pats my head.

"Les go, Daddy!" His eyes are sweet and proud. "I'm gonna get a Tiger's Blood."

"Oh, a Tiger's Blood. You gonna give me some?"

"All mine. You can't have any," he says.

"Should we let your brother go with us?" I tease him.

"No Stewy!" Jo-Jo slaps my chest.

"Daddy has to return some emails and then we can go." I look at Emily to say, why don't you just take him, the Snowball stand is just around the corner, and I am busy.

"Daddy can do that after you get back," Emily gives me an expression that looks like a smile, but it really means get up and take care of your son.

So I take Jo-Jo to get a snow cone, or really a snowball—which is what I grew up calling them. I hold Jo-Jo's soft small hand and we stroll down Magazine—Jo-Jo skips and I walk—under the power lines and errant Mardi Gras beads. The sun is angry, screaming and slapping everyone upside the head. We pass a couple of locals waiting for the bus, standing under their cheap black umbrellas, and I wonder why everyone on the street today isn't carrying the cool shadows of black umbrellas. Why does this seem so hopelessly out-of-date or odd, when in fact it's what any intelligent person should do on days like this?

Jo-Jo is radiating so much joy that I can't help but feel better. He's so proud of himself and so happy to be holding my hand. His smile pushes everything else away: The heat. The Sub-Ocean Brightside. My job. My mother. All the chaos in my life washes out to the oil slick sea and for this brief too-hot-too-humid moment I can breathe. I can walk and smile and hold my son's hand and know that at least for just this one hot second, something is good in this world: My kid can shit in a toilet and I can buy him a snowball. It's not a miracle, but there's redemption here all the same.

We cross over to the shadier side of Magazine, past all the tourist ladies in their Capri pants and white ankle socks, and towards the pistachio-colored wall, where a long, angry line winds around the side of the SnoWizard's Snowball Shack.

People are hot. People are thirsty. Having to wait in this line makes everyone scowl and sweat—everyone except my boy.

"Daddy, you can have a bite of mine," he says, "but don't eat it all."

"Okay." I tossle his hair.

"Cute kid."

I turn around.

It's Gay André. Alive and well. Not a single bullet in his head.

He's licking an orange snowball and carrying an enormous Louis Vuitton backpack on his shoulder. His mouth is stained orange, and his teeth are freakishly white by contrast.

I pull Jo-Jo closer to my legs, behind me.

"You should get da tangerine. It's scrumptious." He takes a chompy bite of his snowball.

"How are you doing this?" I say.

"Doing what?"

"Being alive?"

"Easy. Just breathe through your mouth and nose," Gay André holds up his snowball like he's toasting me.

"You're dead. I saw it."

"Fuck you. I didn't come here for your magic ass to give me no bad predictions. If you see me dying in the future, just keep that shit to yourself."

I push Jo-Jo behind me, to protect from him this guy, to shield him from the weirdness of this moment.

"That your son?" Gay André peeks around me, trying to catch Jo-Jo's eyes.

"What do you want?" I say.

"Look, I'm ya friend." He pulls out this strange, big-eyed, plush toy from his purse. "Here, I brought this for ya."

"Don't want it."

"It's a Murakami!" he says this to me like I am an idiot for not knowing what a Murakami is. "This is the $10k I was talking about!"

"That's the $10k? That thing?"

"For Christ's sake. Take it. It ain't no normal toy. It's a Takashi Murakami. You could get twenty grand if you wanted."

"What are you talking about?"

"Take it before you make me spill my snowball on it." He pushes the toy against my chest, and I find myself holding it.

I look at the face of the thing. It's some sort of bizarre raccoon with blue cartoon eyes.

"It's a raccoon," I say.

"It ain't no raccoon. It's this Japanese red panda thing."

"Looks like a raccoon to me."

"They ain't even got raccoons in Japan," he says.

"What do you want me to do with this?" I hold up the stuffed animal.

"Sell it on eBay. Make some real nice money." Gay André takes a chomp of his snowball. "Now give me back my matches."

"Who's Meg? Whose number is that inside the flap?"

"Why you ax so many questions?" He licks the dripping orange syrup off the side of his styrofoam cup. "You writing a novel or something?"

"Yeah, what if I am?"

"Well then, you gonna have to leave this chapter out," he says.

"I'll just burn the matches," I say. "I don't care."

"Gimme my goddamn matches." He stomps his foot.

"Start talking. Or I start burning."

"Look, that matchbook had my lottery numbers on dem. All right. Ya mamma gave them to me and told me to play them this weekend."

"Looked like a Baton Rouge phone number to me."

"You write that number down?" He lights up. "Cuz all I need is that number."

"You better start talking and stop lying," I say.

"I ain't lyin'. Meg Mills stands for Mega Millions. Those my winning numbers. Your Mama wrote them like a phone number 'cause she said someone —she didn't say it would be her own goddamn son—would steal my matchbook."

"I want you to set up a meeting with The Loup Garou," I say.

"You have no idea what you are messing with," Gay André says.

"Do you want your matchbook or not?"

"Look, I'll make sure he gets in touch with you, but that won't be before the lottery." Gay André licks his snowball. "How about you just walk with me back to your mama's house and give me my matchbook and I promise, I will get him to call you?"

"We're getting a snowball," I say. "And then, you can have your matches back."

"Snowball! Snowball! Snowball!" Jo-Jo begins to chant and pump his fist into the air.

Gay André licks his bright orange snowball and holds out his fat knuckles to Jo-Jo and gives him a fist bump. Jo-Jo pulls his hand away into tiny finger explosions while making Pow-Pow noises.

"Funny little fucker, ain't he?" Gay André says.

Jo-Jo can't stop laughing, and I can't remember no matter how hard I try why I ever thought Gay André was dead.

24

"MANDALA SHORTCUTS LED TO SPILL"

THE NEW YORK TIMES Headline: May 17, 2010

"You guys didn't listen to me. Christopher didn't listen to a God-damn word I said." I bust into Gary's office without knocking.

"The PR agency sold him a downplay strategy." Gary looks up from his laptop but continues typing.

"Downplay strategy? Are you kidding me?" I say. "What happened to Christopher wanting to talk straight from his heart?"

"Apologizing would make the Spill look like it was our fault, Duke. I think you said that yourself."

"I said we should not offer guarantees. To be careful with the words we choose when Christopher does apologize. I said he shouldn't use certain words. And he managed to not only use the word 'guarantee,' yesterday in the press conference, but he also pissed everyone off in the process."

"Let me say this again: We're following the downplay strategy until further notice. It's PR 101."

"65,000 barrels a day." I hold up my most recent press release to him. "Ops is now reporting that it's more than 100,000 barrels. That's not a downplay strategy. That's a lie."

"Our agency will have the social sentiment report to me within the hour," Gary says.

"I can tell you what the sentiment is," I say. "Shelley sounds like some rich douche who has no idea what's going on. "

"Settle down, Duke." Gary looks around the office at our co-workers who are shuffling around, trying to act like they don't hear this fight.

"Obama is saying we are idiots!" I point to the White House press conference now playing on Gary's flat-screen TV. "There's your data," I say.

"Fuck that terrorist." Gary picks up the remote and turns off the TV.

"People are pissed. I'm pissed."

"You don't think I know that?"

"Then you might want to stop with all this bullshit about how this is not that big of a deal. And show some leadership and help me fix this. Because the spill is huge and people can see that, and the more we say it's not a big deal, the worse everything is going to get for everyone."

"What has gotten into you?"

"I'm just trying to do my job."

"Yeah, well. Stop being such a cunt about it," Gary says.

"You guys didn't listen to me."

"Duke, this isn't Montessori T-ball, not everybody gets a trophy, and not all your ideas are going to be executed."

I have to look away.

"Look, this is getting to all of us." He pulls out a pill bottle from his desk. "Xanax. Take one."

I put the pill on my tongue, gather up the spit in my mouth, and swallow it. I sit down across from Gary's desk and start answering the deluge of emails on my laptop.

The Xanax helps. I unclench. I now give just a few less fucks about everything—the end of the world, the oil-covered pelicans, my angry wife, and my missing mother. I can sit here and gladly watch Gary type on his laptop.

Clickety clack clickety clack.

His typing is oddly comforting, and my tangled mind unspools into a simple, steady stream of logical, linear thoughts, thoughts about Mandala Worldwide and the world and how all this does and doesn't fit together.

"Hey!" Gary nudges me. "You awake?"

"What?" I say.

"So where are we on the Babineauxes?"

"It's not going to happen." I yawn. "Sorry, I tried."

"We need the Babineauxes in that commercial, Duke. Mark Babineaux is a goddamn war hero."

"He said no."

"Your one and only job today is to get him to sign that contract and cash that check."

"I thought we had another family lined up," I say.

"They're not war heroes, Duke."

"He won't return my calls."

"Then go to his house," Gary says. "Do I have to do everything around here?"

* * *

I peel off my bright orange "Mandala Worldwide Cares" polo in the parking lot of my office. I put on a few extra swipes of deodorant and button up the plaid shirt that I keep hanging in the backseat of my car. After I rid myself of the Mandala dream-catcher—a logo that is now referred to by most New Orleanians as the "Satanic Sunflower"—I drive to Chalmette. I drive past row after row of FEMA trailers abandoned in front yards, of busted refrigerators and washing machines rusting on the curbs. Google Maps kindly directs me past all of this, to a stretch of neighborhood where rotting plywood no longer covers the windows and doors, where everything has been rebuilt or repainted, and the yards are green and mowed, to the Babineauxes' small white house.

Their home is small but impressively well maintained. It's freshly painted in a bright and defiant white. Purple and yellow pansies fill the tiny flowerbeds. The stars and stripes sway next to a black and gold "Who Dat?" flag. An LSU garden gnome stands on point, smiling beneath a purple gazing ball, a plastic humming-bird feeder above an empty birdbath. It's as if the Babineauxes have erected all this yard art to tell the next hurricane and the rest of the world to piss off because they are protected by a sunny, unsinkable hope. Their door sign with the hand-painted raccoon flashing his pink asshole says it all: "Coonass and proud. Welcome to the Babineauxes."

I knock and wait. The aroma of deep-fried catfish fills my nostrils.

Jean Babineaux answers the door.

"Well, well, look what the cat drug in." She holds a "Geaux Tigers" plastic tumbler in her left hand. The smell of Southern Comfort is so strong it burns my eyes.

"You got a few minutes?"

"Come on in. Just cooking dinner." She pulls me into her house and guides me past the small dining room, which is overflowing with pink, feathery gift baskets glistening with iridescent cellophane.

"Excuse the mess," she says. "I run my business out the house."

"You make gift baskets?"

"Kind of. I'm a 'Surprise Lady.'" She chuckles. "You know, like an Avon Lady, except a hell of a lot more fun if you know what I mean. Sort of behind on sending out my hostess gifts."

"*Surprise* parties?" I look down at the purple chew toy on the floor. It's covered with dog hair, but it's not a chew toy.

"You like coleslaw?" she asks.

"So is Mark around?" I try not to act uncomfortable; I am standing in a dining room packed full of vibrators, butt-plugs, and "sensual heating" gels. There's a giant purple dong just sitting in the middle of the carpet. It's hard to know where to look or what to say.

"You want a Comfort and Coke or a beer?" She walks into the tiny kitchen.

"Comfort and Coke sounds good," I call out. "So is Mark around?"I can't help but stare at the hot pink marital aids pressing against the cellophane.

"I can give you his new address!" Jean shouts back.

"He moved?"

"He left me," she says.

"Wow. I'm sorry…. I didn't know."

"Don't be." She walks back into the dining room holding two plates full of fried catfish, hushpuppies, and coleslaw. "She's forty-five. Six kids. Works at freakin' Home Depot."

She holds the plates over the table.

"Move those gift baskets out the way so we can eat like civilized people," she says.

I hesitate.

"They don't bite," she says.

I lift the baskets off the table and onto the carpet, next to a large cardboard box labeled "200 Bottles Cranberry Extract."

"You always make this much food?" I ask.

"Had to fry up the catfish or toss them. Freezer in the garage went out. Couldn't fit everything inside."

I take a bite. It's quite good. I wash it down with the Comfort and Coke, and I try not to fake-smile too much.

"So let's talk about why you're really here." She puts her fork down and wipes her mouth with her paper napkin.

"I need you and Mark to be in this commercial."

"That's not why your mama sent you here." She shakes her head and smiles.

"Jean, my boss sent me."

"That might be how it looks to you, but your mama said this is exactly how this would play out." She grabs a ratty stack of papers sitting next to one of the gift baskets and holds them up to me. "I have it in my notes. Right here in black and white."

"My mom makes things look real when they aren't. It's the Barnum Effect. It's sleight of hand. A magic trick."

"She said you would say that." Jean rifles through her stack. She hands me an old electricity bill overwritten with the sentence, "I shall be accused of slender hands."

"That's not even a thing. She says weird stuff like that, and it sounds like it means something, but it doesn't."

"It's just so sad. You had all that magic and love around you, and you could never see it."

"It's not magic, Jean. It's not."

"She said I would get through this and I believe her. She said on the other side of this nightmare was my dream. She said that I'd start a fishing therapy camp for wounded warriors out on the Tickfaw River. I'm gonna have these cabins with their own piers and boats, and we are gonna fish all day and cook up big messes of catfish and hushpuppies at night. You know, just be at peace with the river and heal."

"Why didn't she tell you and Mark to move out of the Gulf before all this happened? Before he ran off with another woman?"

"Your mother can only tell me the parts of the future that I can change."

"She doesn't see the future, Jean."

"She saved my life when Mark and I found out we couldn't have children. I've seen what she can do."

"But what she told you wasn't the truth. It felt good, but it wasn't the truth."

Jean flips through her papers. She wells up.

"Sorry," I say.

"The bank wants to foreclose," Jean whispers, "on the boat and the house."

"And you're still not going to do the commercial?"

There's a long awkward silence. She just stares at me.

"I think you need to leave," she finally says.

"Look, I'm sorry. I just…"

"Just what? Just want to make me feel like shit? Is that what you're sorry for?"

"I didn't come here to upset you."

Jean gets up from the table and walks into the back of the house. She returns with an orange Nike shoebox.

"Your mother's prophecies." She drops the box on the table in front of me. "Take 'em."

I open the box. It's crammed full of busted envelopes, and past-due notices—all of them scribbled over with Mama's rants and poems.

"Why did you write this on your phone bills and credit card statements?" I inspect the rat's nest of notes.

"Your mama wanted to make sure you saw the dates printed on the bills. To know she was predicting the future for real."

"You could have saved the statements and just written them later," I say.

"Your mama told me you were going to be an asshole. But she didn't prepare me for this."

"Look."

"Just take the box and get the hell out of my house."

* * *

I am pretty sure Jean snapped long before the spill ever happened. Between having to deal with her husband's PTSD, Katrina, and the uncertainty of the shrimping life, she snapped like we would all snap when God or luck, or whatever you want to call it, puts too much on our backs. And I don't believe that God doesn't give us more than we can bear. That's a bullshit platitude that we tell ourselves when we are face to face with another person who proves that it is entirely possible that we too could lose our baby to bone cancer or that we too could sink under the weight of OxyContin addiction; that something completely unspeakable is at some point coming our way—we just don't know when.

Whether or not Jean has lost her mind, she seems like a good person who, like everyone who makes their living in the Gulf, doesn't deserve the hand she's been dealt. And maybe I was too hard on her, but I did it for her own good. She's so tangled up in my mother's fantasies that she can't look out for her own best interests here. I had to kick the crutch out from under her.

But even now, as I flip through all these scribbled-over bills in her driveway, I can see how Jean was able to read so much into what my mother said. *The Language of the Birds* is so green with possibility, and therefore it can speak to whatever circumstance you find yourself in. For example, the transcription scribbled all over Jean's past-due electric bill seems to speak to the lost necklace in the tree and even to my search for The Loup Garou. It seems to be speaking to me from the great beyond.

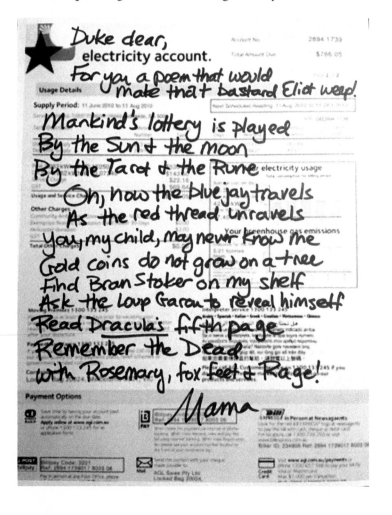

Duke dear,
electricity account.
For you a poem that would
make that bastard Eliot weep!

Mankind's lottery is played
By the Sun & the moon
By the Tarot & the Rune
Oh, how the blue jay travels
As the red thread unravels
You, my child, may never know the
Gold coins do not grow on a tree
Find Bram Stoker on my shelf
Ask the Loup Garou to reveal himself
Read Dracula's fifth page
Remember the Dead
with Rosemary, fox feet & Rage!

Mama

25

TURN TO PAGE 5 OF DRACULA!

May 17, 2010

I drive back to New Orleans, over the I-10 exchange past the Superdome, past that eternal symbol of Katrina's devastation, and I start to feel this Superdome-level hopelessness sinking in myself. The Xanax is obviously wearing off, and my fucking conscience is now wide awake and screaming, so I can either pull into a bar to shut it up and continue my descent into pathetic drunkenness, or I can turn the corner to Mama's block, and I can walk into the dark embrace of The House of the Neon Palm. I decide to do the later, and I find Stevo and Daddy in the parlor on the couch watching Christopher Shelley on CNN speak the exact words I crafted for him earlier today.

"I need you to come upstairs with me," I hold up the letter from Jean Babineaux.

I stop to catch my breath.

"Not right now. The news is on," Daddy says.

"The news is always on, Daddy," I say.

"I'll be right back, Pops." Stevo pats Daddy's good leg and follows me into the next room.

"Why are you out of breath?" my brother asks.

I hand Jean Babineaux's electricity bill to him. The one that's addressed to me. The one that Jean transcribed from Mama in some manic rush of fortune-telling glee.

He reads it and follows me up the stairs to our parents' bedroom.

"Bram Stoker?" Stevo asks. "She even own that book?"

"That's what it says."

Stevo opens the bedroom door, and we walk in.

Mama and Daddy's room is as much a library as it is a bedroom. Mama read palms during the day. At night, she read her books. She was obsessed with owning signed copies of great thinkers like Anaïs Nin and Simone De Beauvoir. First editions were a drug for her. The Garden District Book Shop and Octavia Books were her dealers.

Mama's bibliomania forced Daddy to build her floor-to-ceiling bookshelves out of the cypress wood he had cut down in the swamps. Mama spent the next forty years cramming them full of first-edition, signed books by great writers from Camus to Toni Morrison.

She, of course, loved the Russians: Chekhov, Tolstoy, and Nabokov.

Almost as much as she hated T. S. Eliot.

"April is the cruelest month, my foot. He is anti-Semite. Hater of women. Two poems he wrote against my name! The coward would never have inked such things if he truly knew the length of my shadow!"

Mama bought every copy of *The Waste Land* off the shelves whenever she would go into a bookstore.

"Eliot is burning in hell and so should his words," she'd say to the sales clerk, and then she'd spit a big loogie on the page that referenced Madame Blavatsky right there in the store. Once she got home, she'd tear the book into fives and set a match to it in the fireplace. When it came to certain writers, she had love affairs and blood grudges—relationships that would have only been normal had she maybe known these long dead authors, and only then if they had betrayed or loved her in some profound or terrible way.

Stevo grabs the stepladder and manages to find a copy of *Dracula* tucked away on the shelf closest to the ceiling. He pulls down the yellow cloth book with red type, and he turns to page five as Mama's poem instructed us to do. There, on that page, a passage is underlined. Stevo clears his throat and reads it aloud:

"It is the eve of St. George's Day. Do you not know that tonight, when the clock strikes midnight, all the evil things in the world will have full sway?"

We both stand here among the swirling towers of books.

Mama disappeared on the eve of St. George's Day—Mama's favorite Albanian holiday, a day when all water is holy water—and here we hold a book that appears to foretell her disappearance on the eve of this very day.

"This! This is some kind of sign!" Stevo hops in place.

"What do you think it means?" I say.

"She's trying to warn us about something," Stevo says. "This passage is a sign, Duke."

"But what does it mean?"

"It means we're on the right track. It's her talking to us from across space and time."

"For Christ's sake. You're worse than La La. Give me that." I take the old yellow book from Stevo and slam it shut. I readjust two Hemingway novels on the lower shelf and cram *Dracula* beside them, causing Hemingway's *A Moveable Feast* to fall to the floor. A peach-colored piece of paper flutters out of the book.

"What is that?" Stevo points at the peach square of paper.

I pick it up. "It's a lottery ticket." I turn it over and look at the date. "From 1999."

"Let me see." Stevo takes it from me and inspects it.

"So I suppose that's a sign as well," I say.

"Nope, just a bookmark." He slides the peach paper into a Flannery O'Connor book and reshelves it. "Mama used her old tickets as bookmarks."

I flip the switch.

"Hey, turn that shit back on," Stevo says.

"What are you looking for now?" I ask.

"That book of Lord Byron poems to read to Cactus before we get tantric."

"I don't need to know that."

"Well, you asked."

Daddy's clarinet drifts up the stairs and into the awkward pauses between my brother and me. The minor notes crawl into my ears: They scatter into the saddest, most defeated parts of me. Daddy is practicing "Strange Fruit," and even when he's messing around like this, he sounds better than most of the musicians performing at Snug Harbor or Sweet Lorraine's. As soon as I round the corner into the parlor, there he is, tooting that thing, with his leg off and his glass eye glistening on the coffee table, a magnifying glass on top of the scattered sheet music. Daddy plays his clarinet. Meanwhile, Uncle Father sits next to him and lights up a bowl.

I glare at the old pothead.

"It's for my glaucoma." Uncle Father takes a long drag and then exhales gracefully.

Daddy puts his piece down. "You need sumptin', T'boy?"

"Nah, just wanted to hear you play," I say.

I step aside, and Daddy puts the clarinet back to his mouth. The room swells with the mournful sounds of "Strange Fruit" and the fog of Uncle Father's skunky medical-grade marijuana smoke.

"I have a box of her prophecies out in my car," I say to Stevo. "Like the one I just showed you."

"Where'd you get them?"

"Old client of Mama's. I need you to read them. See if you can make sense of it all."

"Sure," Stevo says. "Give me your keys."

"They're in a Nike shoebox in the trunk."

Daddy stops playing and holds his black mouthpiece just below his chin. He glares at us.

"You going to shut up and listen?" he says.

"Sorry," I say.

Stevo runs out to my car to grab Jean Babineaux's overdue bills, and Daddy starts playing "Basin Street Blues."

26

MAY 18, 2010

Over 10 million gallons of oil have now spilled into the Gulf

I am typing as fast as I can. My fingers are cramping. I can't get press releases approved fast enough. And the more panicked everyone is getting, the more radical and careless they are with their language and our communications. This feels like the end times for this company, and Jesus is not on our side. Most people in my department have stopped watching the news. Never mind the fact that the deadlines everyone is giving me are ridiculous, and I don't think there's any way humanly possible to catch all the mistakes we are making now. There needs to be three or four of me at this point.

I've told Gary this, but he's too busy counting ceiling tiles and popping Xanax to listen. Everyone at Mandala is losing their minds. We are so close to figuring out how to kill this well, and yet at the same time, the media is crucifying us for lying about the 100,000 barrels a day that have been leaking since the explosion. Talking heads like Rush Limbaugh and Pauline Sarin keep trying to come to our defense, but they only make things worse when they do this. Meanwhile, Lady Gaga and Coldplay are supposedly teaming up to write a song against us. We are the constant punch line on every late night show: *Letterman, Leno, Conan, Jimmy Fallon, Jimmy Kimmel, The Daily Show.* We're not an environmental disaster to the media. We're a freaking gold mine.

I spent last night and into this early morning rewriting the press releases from our agency to make them work with Christopher's stupid downplay strategy. But now I have to put that aside and respond to the shrill announcements Governor Robby Wendall is making on every channel: CNN, CNBC, FOX News, MSNBC.

"These are not tar balls, this is not sheen, this is heavy oil," says Robby Wendall. He's wearing his long, solemn face today along with this black nylon safety vest. This photo op has him standing in an air boat and holding up a plastic bag full of brown goop. "What we are seeing yesterday and today is this heavy oil coming into our wetlands."

To counter these unfortunately true statements, we have our COO Dan Wilkers responding at a separate news conference, explaining the performance of the insertion tube that is now sucking crude from the Sub-Ocean Brightside and into a surface vessel. This is a big deal, but no one in the media seems to want to talk about what a heroic feat of technology we just pulled off to save the same Gulf that we love just as much as the next person.

Things aren't completely painted black, I guess. One of the press releases I just got off my desk details how we are testing six centrifuge machines that separate the oil from the water. If they work, we plan to buy thirty-six of them and put them to work cleaning the Gulf. They were invented thanks to Kevin Costner. He financed them to be built back in 1995, the same year he filmed *Waterworld*.

There's something disquieting about this particular coincidence. Not sure if it's because these centrifuge machines actually work or if it's that Mr. *Waterworld* himself spent so much time in the ocean making that cinematic disaster that it somehow inspired him to spend twenty-four million dollars of his own money to solve this real-life disaster. Costner's team calls the centrifuges, "Ocean Therapy Solutions." Frankly, "Ocean Therapy" as woo-woo as it sounds, still sounds a lot less ridiculous than stopping the Spill with millions of tennis balls, and considerably less worrisome than the nuclear bombing plans that were being floated around in recent weeks.

It's the most hopeful thing we have to put into the news cycle right now. Best of all, Costner's going to testify in front of Congress soon so that should take the media spotlight off of Christopher Shelley for a least a minute, and give us all time to define our reactions to this disaster a little more skillfully than we have been, i.e., someone needs to tell Christopher how to shut up. We are all still spinning and spitting, messaging and re-messaging because Christopher told the media: "I think I have said all along that the company will not be judged by an accident that, you know, frankly was not our accident."

Every time, Christopher Shelley opens his mouth, there's a shit show on Facebook and Twitter, and nobody can figure out how to make the avalanche of negative posts and articles stop. It's exhausting and hopeless. How are we supposed to protect Mandala Worldwide's brand when Christopher keeps saying stuff like this? He's a smart guy. What is he doing?

My phone rings for the one hundred and eleventh time today. I pick it up praying it's not Constanze Bellingham, yelling at me, wanting to know when Christopher Shelley's new remarks will be ready. I don't know why she keeps calling me. He never follows the script.

"Duke Melançon, External Affairs."

"Yeah, so we're gonna do it."

"Mark?" I say.

"You got a check for me?" Mark Babineaux says. "Jean says you got a check for me."

"Yeah, I can have a check for you in like five minutes," I say. "But I thought you wanted cash."

"I'll take a check. When can I pick it up?"

"We're here all day."

"We're leaving right now." He hangs up.

I put my phone back in its cradle. I smile so hard my face almost cramps.

"Gary!" I shout.

"What?" he shouts back.

"The Babineauxes!" I laugh, "They're back in!"

He doesn't say anything.

"Gary?" I shout.

He walks into my office, slow-clapping.

* * *

"So where do I sign?" Mark asks without smiling.

This is so weird. Jean is beaming and acting like Mark never left her for the single mother who works at The Home Depot, like I never chastised her over fried fish and bourbon, like she's never given me her crazy phone bills, like my mama didn't warn her not to do this.

"No, seriously where do we sign?" Mark says. "Let's get this show on the road."

"I'm re-printing the contracts now. 150 pages. It will just be a couple of seconds."

"We're burning daylight. How long's it gonna take?" Mark bites his bottom lip and exhales through flared nostrils like he's holding back a volcano behind his thin, tight lips. Makes me wonder if this is how he always is or if I've somehow pissed him off.

The burden of the unspoken weighs on me, but before I can shake it off with a comment about the Tigers or the Saints, Gary walks into my office.

"Duke, you mind?"

"Sure. But, wait, Gary. Meet Mandala Worldwide's new Gulf Coast spokesperson, Sergeant Mark Babineaux."

Mark Babineaux goes to shake Gary's hand, "Mark Babineaux. This is my wife, Jean."

"Hi, nice to meet you," Gary shakes Mark's hand, but pulls away a little too soon, and then crosses his arms. "Duke, I need to talk to you in my office."

"Sure." I look at Mark Babineaux and smile. "I'll be right back."

"We're not going anywhere," he says.

I follow Gary back to his office. He shuts the door. His face and neck have exploded with red splotches.

"Get rid of them." Gary is consciously breathing now.

"I'm reprinting the contracts."

"Houston just called." He lets out one of his long and annoying yoga breaths.

"Gary, we're not doing this."

"You got to get rid of them." He can't look me in the eye. "Houston put a bullet in them. The deal is dead. They're too late."

"Nice metaphor, Gary."

"You know what I mean. We have an internal candidate for the commercials now. This directive came from Christopher Shelley himself. Look." He holds up his phone to me. "Read the text yourself."

"You just told me we have a check for the guy," I say.

"That's before I got the text."

"Can we at least pay them the first half as a kill fee? They need the money."

"That wife of his was refusing to do this less than a day ago," Gary says.

"I thought you said he's a war hero and you wanted to help them."

"I never said that."

"Well, you can be the one to go in there and tell them we don't need them. I'm not doing that."

"This is business, Duke. Even without this deal, that guy out there hit the freaking lottery with the Spill. I am sure he's going to file a seven-figure claim."

"You don't know that," I say.

"And you know what? I shouldn't have to. Not my problem. He's yours. Go out there and tell them the deal is off."

I snatch the box of Kleenex off Gary's desk and slam the door behind me.

* * *

"I wish there was something I could do, but Houston has decided to cancel the commercial," I tell them. "It's out of my hands."

"Then why did you have us come all the way out here?" Jean begins to cry. "To play with us? We need this money."

Mark is silent as a tomb.

"They literally just called Gary to tell him this." I try to hand Jean a tissue.

She refuses the Kleenex. "I brought my own." Which is good because she can't stop crying. She can't stop calling me a liar. She can't breathe. She just can't believe it. Mark Babineaux with his Purple Heart and his Cajun pride, sits silently next to his wife, not touching her, not comforting her, not speaking, not reacting. He just sits in the chair across from my desk, staring past my head, looking out the office window behind me.

"I'm really sorry about this, " I keep saying.

"No, you're not," Mark finally speaks.

He rises from his chair.

"Let's go." He gathers up Jean. She folds into him.

Sgt. Mark Babineaux pulls his wife to his shoulder and carries her away from me and all my broken promises.

27

BACK IN THE MCMANSION

May 22, 2010

The crime scene clean-up crew that Emily hired to the tune of five grand is finally finished removing all those rotting and splattered raccoons from our corporate housing. The crew had to replace the blood and feces-stained carpets downstairs. They had to repaint the kitchen and dining room. However, with the exception of one couch, most of our furniture survived the attack. It's amazing the stains they can get out of furniture these days. Smells are however another thing. Even after replacing the carpets and scrubbing the floors and walls with bleach, there is still a rotting animal smell in the house.

Emily bought a small arsenal of scented candles and reed diffusers and put them in every room. Part of me is relieved to get Emily and the boys away from The House of the Neon Palm, away from the lumpy bunk beds, away from La La's knife-holding grudges and Daddy's one-legged tirades, but the other half of me feels like I am giving up—that I am giving up on ever finding Mama. There is a part of me that enjoyed being stuck with my family, enjoyed the old dysfunction and chaos. It surprises me how much my family comforted me. The seafood gumbos and the shrimp Creoles. Daddy and Uncle Father's crazy rants about the NSA, Stevo's lame jokes, La La's ridiculous costumes, and Yanko's constant singing.

Even in the midst of all this turmoil, watching my boys and their cousins playing trains and running with sticks, watching La La and Daddy teach Emily how to make a proper étouffée while Uncle Father shared his weed with me over an iced coffee is a warm, dry space in this disaster of a city.

Even though it's been weeks since the raccoon attack and my kidnapping, Emily and I still have a hard time falling asleep at night. So we each took two chewable Ambien tabs last night and woke up with pillow creases all over our faces and drool-soaked pillows. This morning, when we get up, we check on the boys, and they are surprisingly still hard asleep. So we stumble downstairs to the kitchen to enjoy this rare morning alone.

"Make me breakfast," Emily hugs me and kisses me on the cheek.

"Sure," I kiss her on the forehead. Neither one of us has brushed our teeth yet.

She's silent. I'm groggy, too tired to form sentences about what I have done to the Babineauxes, too half-asleep to explain that I basically work for the devil's dumber little brother.

"How about an omelet?" I pull the carton of eggs out of the fridge.

"Sure." She pours herself a glass of iced coffee.

"Spinach?" I hold up the bag.

"Yeah. Do we have any cheese?" she yawns.

"We have some chèvre." I hold up a log of goat cheese.

She smiles and sips her coffee.

"I want to go to Ikea this weekend," she says.

"In Houston?" I dump the omelet ingredients onto a cutting board next to the stove, and I pour myself a tall glass of iced coffee. Emily stands next to me while I chop up the spinach.

Lingering, brushing up against me.

"Yes, Houston." She grabs a peach out of the fruit bowl and takes a knife to it. "I want to check on the house. Maybe go to Ikea. Pick up a new rug for the boys' room and some shelves for the playroom."

"What if they find my mother?" I want to tell her about Gary, about Jean and Mark, about what I have done to them but I don't.

"Then we will turn back around." She pops a peach slice in her mouth and sucks her fingers clean with a slight kiss.

"I have a job," I say.

"There are Mandala offices in Houston, Duke. You deserve some family time."

"Ikea is not family time."

"Duke. It's my birthday." She handles the knife like a chef, each slice coming off the peach, precise and juicy. Beautiful.

"Who wants to spend their birthday in an Ikea?" I say.

"I do." She holds a slice to me and puts it in my mouth. It's sweet and wet and fuzzy. It tastes like summer and hope and everything that is missing from our lives right now.

My phone buzzes and pulls me away from her fingertips.

It's Yanko:

at tipitinas

loup garou

coming to my show

putting u on the list

Emily drops the knife on the counter.

"Who is it?" she asks.

"Yanko. Wants me to come to his show."

Emily folds her arms. So I place my phone facedown on the kitchen counter. "Okay, Ikea. I'm cool with that. If that's what you want."

"Try not to hide your enthusiasm," she says.

"It will be fun." I go in for a hug, and she pulls away.

"What's the matter?"

"Everything," she says.

I pull her back to me, and she relaxes into the hug. I try to kiss her. Instead, she gives me her cheek.

"I thought he might have news," I say.

"I'm tired," she says.

Instead of answering her, I kiss her. Her lips taste like peaches.

She kisses me back.

We kiss, the first real kiss we've shared in months, the kind of long sloppy kiss that used to make us late to dinner parties, for work, the kind of kissing that led to that one fearful moment of saying I love you, to an aching right knee and a diamond ring that

I couldn't afford, to those green labor coach scrubs and purple screaming baby boys, the kind of kissing that made our mouths tingle for hours afterward, the kind of kissing that kept us tangled up for days, before we dove headlong into the feeding schedules of those screaming baby boys, the constant dings of our iPhones, before the Spill, before my mother's evaporation took away all certainty.

We kiss to forget. We kiss and kiss and kiss, and today, here in the dapples of sunlight, this kissing is the kind of kissing that leads to bra straps fumbled open, boxers stepped out of and left on the floor. It's sex on the kitchen table while the boys are still asleep kind of kissing.

"Mommy!" Jo-Jo walks into the kitchen, dragging his blanky behind him.

I duck behind the counter and leave Emily to explain this away to our boy.

She grabs Jo-Jo by the hand like it is no big deal that she is buck-naked here in the kitchen with his father, and she walks him back out of the room.

"I can see you, Daddy!" Jo-Jo says in his raspy toddler voice.

Emily then walks Jo-Jo to the potty, and now he's in the playroom watching Thomas the Tank Engine. And even though he is glued to the TV now, once your kid walks in on you like that, the moment is more than gone, it has cringed away, maybe never to come back.

28

TEMPEST IN A COFFEE POT

Despite almost two cups of coffee this morning, I have to shake myself awake at stoplights. All I can think about is turning this car around, crawling back into bed, and pulling the covers over my head. It's the sleepy undertow of depression mixed with an Ambien hangover.

So I pull into PJ's with the thought that perhaps another cup of coffee will flood my brain with enough serotonin and dopamine to keep me from curling up into a ball under my desk today.

I walk into PJ's, and the dark, warm smell of their coffee grabs me like an old friend. The café is singing with south Louisiana accents and glowing with screen-lit faces. All these people are, for this one caffeinated moment, happy.

"Where you at?"

"How's ya mama and dem?"

Everyone is asking after each other, and everyone is ordering "one of those Banana Fosters coffees with the whipped cream." Moreover, no one seems to be in a wall-eyed panic about the murdered ocean. No one is sobbing about everything they lost in Katrina, the recession, or the Spill.

Here among the grinding of roasting beans and the calling of names— "Andrew! Your double latte is ready! Jack Henry! Iced coffee! Duke! Large granita!"—everyone is distracted from the flood lines marking the sheetrock of their unlucky lives. I am not unique. We all turn to coffee in a crisis. It is as ever-present and reassuring as Jesus Himself when the world is falling apart. A cup of coffee can get you through anything, from hurricane relief centers and corporate layoffs to foxholes and funerals. This simple fact may explain why New Orleans has the best coffee in the world—it's perhaps essential to surviving the perpetual disaster that is this city.

So I sip my granita, and like magic, I feel galvanized against the inevitable doom that is waiting to carjack me outside those glass doors.

I decide to stay for a while. To enjoy this respite. I sit here and smile at all these beautiful people while I play on my phone. I sit here and envy my Houston friends' Facebook feeds.

"You know Juan Valdez and the so-called 'coffee break' were created by the CIA," an oddly familiar voice announces from behind.

I turn around. It's the Vonnegut impersonator. He's sipping some foamy drink, and the froth has collected on his mustache.

I turn back around and put my eyes back on my phone, holding it just inches from my face.

"All part of the International Coffee Agreement of 1962," he says. "The plan was to keep coffee prices artificially high so that the U.S. could keep the Commies out of South America."

I stare at my phone, wishing that I had headphones with me.

"So drink up. Cup a day keeps the Commies away." The Vonnegut impersonator takes the seat at the table next to me. He rustles his newspaper and harrumphs.

I keep my eyes on my phone.

He stands up and stands right before me. He puts his splayed hand on his belly.

"Duke, if Einstein was right, if he's the genius that we all think he is, then you might want to rethink this encounter. Maybe Madame Blavatsky sent me. Maybe you need to open your mind, not to magic, but to science."

"How do you know that name?" I ask.

"Ah! I got your attention. Madame Blavatsky is still so misunderstood. Her biggest job was stopping World War III. Lots of trial and error, bringing certain people to power and delaying the rise of others, keeping others from even being born. You think things are bad now. You should have seen things before she came along."

"Why are you following me?" I want to shake this old man. I want to rattle his brain and make him spit out answers that make sense. "What do you want?"

"Duke, the calico cat your mother chased out that night, she was named Schrödinger[1]. For Erwin Schrödinger. Cute name, right?"

"How do you know about the cat?"

1. Schrödinger's cat is a paradoxical thought experiment created by the Austrian physicist Edwin Schrödinger to explain Verschränkung (entanglement). The thought experiment goes like this: Depending on how you are testing a photon (as a wave or as a particle), it is both until you decide. Schrödinger uses a cat inside a box to illustrate this principle. Schrödinger claims that his cat is simultaneously alive and dead until you decide if you are testing for a wave or a particle. This is quantum superposition at work here. Can't explain this kind of mind-bending science in a mere footnote. But it is real. It is not magic or superstition. It, like gravity, is part of the laws that govern a universe full of wonder and boredom, light and dark matter. Which I guess is magical. Perhaps we should have paid more attention in high school physics.

"Indeed. How would I know any of this? The Bureau sent Schrödinger to let Helena know that her mission was over. When Schrödinger appears, you get to rest. You've earned your end-point, and it's time to pass the necklace on to the chosen one."

"The Bureau?" I say.

"Of Humanity. Look, you don't believe me. I get it," Vonnegut says. "It's like when I showed Winston Churchill the iPhone and tried to explain to him that this small computer wasn't some satanic black mirror."

"What is so commonplace now was so impossible back then. You know, son, what cracks me up about your generation is everybody's still so in love with Einstein. You kids put him in all those computer ads and inspirational posters on Pinterest. His face is synonymous with the best that human beings can be, and yet someone as smart as you can't even see the fruits of Einstein's labors, even when one of those fruits is standing right in your face reading *Slaughterhouse-Five*."

"I've got to go," I say.

"What's the name of the family of bears?" He grabs my arm. "From the children's books that you read to your boys?"

"Are you spying on me?" I shake him off. "What the fuck?"

"The family of bears, Duke. What's their name?" He stands in front of me, blocking me from leaving.

"You were in my house. How do you know we have those books? You were in my house."

"Stay with me." He holds his finger up in the air like a candle. "How do you spell the name of those bears, Duke?"

"B-e-r-e-n-s-t-e-i-n." I find myself spelling out the name. "Why were you in my house?"

"Google them." He points to my iPhone. "Do an image search. You will see what I am talking about."

I feel punched in the nose.

"Hurry up. You don't have all day, Duke. We are all disappearing second by second, heartbeat by heartbeat," he says. "It's time to wake up and get to work."

I Google "Berenstein Bears," and it pulls up these books with massively misspelled titles. Every image says *Berenstain.*

Every single one.

"That misspelling is the glitch," Vonnegut smiles. "Your time stream is being rewritten. Certain memories won't line up with the present anymore. Others you will forget altogether."

"How did you do that?" I say. "What are you doing to me?"

"Simply trying to prove to you that the reality to which you cling is not the reality you happen to be enjoying at this present moment." He wipes the froth from his mustache. "Like the *Berenstain Bears*, the *Mandela Effect*[2] is all around you, my boy. The robots are coming, and you're still not willing to listen." Vonnegut takes a long drag off his latte. "I am now having to resort to stunts to convince you of something that should be quite obvious: Mandala is destroying the earth, and you are helping them. Your mother wants you to stop this. If you continue down this path, it will not end well for any of us. Your mother and I can only change things so much. We need you. She needs you."

The Vonnegut impersonator folds up his *New York Times* and drops it on my table. He turns and walks away.

"Wake up, you moron! The planet is dying as we speak. Whatever made you think that money was worth this? You can't breathe it you know! " He walks out the door of the coffee shop.

I glare at him through the windows. He avoids looking at me and chats up some pretty lady in a velour tracksuit. She laughs and gives him a wad of bills from her purse. I look back down at the newspaper and re-read the headline:

2. In 2011, Fiona Broome coined this term to describe why she and many people claim that Nelson Mandela's heartbreaking death occurred in a South African prison in the 1980s. However, in most people's current reality, Nelson Mandela died in 2013. Ms. Broome claims that these confabulations can be explained by the existence of parallel universes. A supposed example of the Mandela Effect is the large number of people on the internet reporting that they remember the Berenstein Bears with a different spelling.

I pick up *The Times*. It's dated three months into the future: September 3, 2010.

My heart spasms. I drop the paper onto the floor and run outside to find the Vonnegut impersonator.

He's nowhere to be found.

I put my head between my knees. I try to inhale but can't. I feel like a goldfish who's been plucked from his bowl and dropped to the ground. My eyes bulge, and I struggle to get oxygen into my lungs.

I need air.

I need answers.

I run back inside to grab the paper, but it's not there.

"You. Ha-ha-happen." I try to ask the barista guy sweeping the floor. "To. To. See."

I finally catch my breath and exhale. My diaphragm starts working again.

"You okay?" The barista asks.

"The paper? Where is it?" I say.

"Paper?" He stares at me.

"*The New York Times*." I point to the floor. "It was right there."

"Sorry." He shakes his head. "Somebody must have picked it up."

* * *

I am coming undone.

Vonnegut's magic tricks are making me question everything. I feel certain that's the point, but I know what I just saw can't be real. I know what I know. Which is, the future can't be predicted. That illusions are engineered, and an illusionist can trick even the most discerning mind. Anybody who's watched David Blaine or David Copperfield in Vegas can testify to this. And yet I am starting to crack. I am starting to believe that Vonnegut, and therefore my mother, knows the future. That magic, as La La keeps saying, is afoot. But what is Vonnegut's angle? What is his con? Why does he insist on fucking with me like this? If he had anything to do with my mother's disappearance why would he be provoking me?

So I head out of PJs, and I try to walk off this existential angst. I try to count my blessings. I try to make sense of what I just saw. I try not to walk into a bar. I try to get my head straight, even though I know that a lot of this anxiety is just how I am hardwired. I've been this way since I was a kid. I've always felt too much, thought too much, worried too much. So I try to remind myself why I left the shadows of this fucking town for the daylight of Houston's Energy Corridor. By the time I reach Louisiana Avenue, the sidewalk sign flashes a neon palm, and I stop on the corner and wait.

There is music coming down the street. I peek around the corner and see a crowd of people marching, carrying a giant photo of a young black man. I recognize his face immediately. He was one of the oil rig workers killed on the Sub-Ocean Brightside. He's got a kind face with a bright smile. He's wearing a pink Polo shirt like Kanye. He's got diamonds in both ears. He was surely his mama's pride and joy—her baby—her everything.

This crowd coming down the street is this poor guy's second line. This is his funeral march, not to be mistaken for the fake second lines that social clubs like to do to impress tourists. No, this is a real second line, and therefore there are real trumpets, real clarinets, real cries to God.

The young man's mother is walking just behind the casket. She is dressed in all purple with an elaborate veil. She is trying. God, she is trying. She puts one foot in front of the other. She holds her umbrella and wobbles on purple high heels. She tries to dance her baby home, but she can't. She just can't. She falls in the middle of the street and lies on the ground. Her sisters pick her up. They carry her, her feet dragging, almost struggling to go the other way. Her left shoe flies off, and a young girl goes running after it. The sweet child comes running behind this poor mother, chasing her with the lost shoe.

This parade isn't just another second line in the Fat City. This is life. You can either fall down in the street or keep going. There are two choices here, but only one outcome. It doesn't matter if the sun is shining or the ocean is dying. Everything ends, everyone dies. Bottomline: we will all lose the most important people in our lives, and they will lose us. This collapsing second line, this sidewalk full of gawking tourists, this tragic one-shoed mother, makes me realize how inevitable this all is.

This is it.

This putting one foot in front of the other is all there is. Everything else is just a mirage to keep us from seeing the graves that lie before all of us. We are all going to die, just like my mother probably has, and there's nothing we can do about. At some point, we are all going to wander out into the night chasing a cal- ico cat and never come back.

I shut my eyes and try to see if I can still remember Mama's face I have a hard time remembering what my Mama's eyes look like. Were they blue or green? I can't see them. Instead of feeling sad or angry that my memory of her is fading, I just feel numb. I guess forgetting is both a beautiful and a terrible thing. I guess it's a mercy that the initial pain of losing someone fades; that its hot grip relaxes over time, that the grief recedes as surely as the surf, just as hope returns with its warm and gentle currents that move us into tomorrow, but the boats that we float on are rafts made of rag and bone. Our good fortune rides on the pain of the past, and it seems to be inevitable that we forget that, that we slowly lose the realization that others' sacrifices hastened our futures. After people die, the hole in our heart eventually closes. Even though it feels like it won't, like it shouldn't ever, it does.

We forget the dead bodies rotting next to the Superdome, the poor folks drowning in their attics during Katrina, and eventu- ally, we will forget about the oil rig workers of the Sub-Ocean Brightside. We will even forget that we wrecked the ocean so that we could one day drive that BMW we always dreamed about. None of this forgetting comes from forgiveness or even healing. It comes from time. Time's rhythm washes away the moments and the pain. After all, to live constantly with the reality that our world is built on the backs of the less fortunate and the deaths of those who loved us most is an impossible awareness to hold, especially when we are filling up our Escalade with extra-pre- mium gasoline so we can all drive down to the Quarter for yet another bachelor party which is exactly what Gary is doing when he calls me.

"Hey, sorry for the noise. Some douche at the pump next to me is blaring his music!" Gary shouts into the phone. "My cousin is getting married next week, and we're actually still out. Come meet us."

"It's nine a.m., Gary."

"I'm taking a personal day. You know family is important. You know that, and I got to see this little shit off in style. You know what I mean? Show him what he's gonna be missing once that girl of his has his balls in her purse. So you gotta cover for me if Shelley calls."

"Are you drunk?"

"Shhh," he says. "I'm sick of that English prick. Why don't you just come meet us? We're headed to Pat O's."

"I'm not meeting you at Pat O's."

"Hey, while I got you on the phone," he says, "did you ever call Constanze back? She keeps blowing up my phone, and I am just trying to take a day off."

"You called me from your cousin's bachelor party to remind me to call Constanze?"

"No, I called you to meet us at Pat O's, shithead? Blow off some steam. Just trying to be a good boss. I'm a good boss."

"I'm driving into work, Gary. I've got to go."

"Don't you fucking hang up on me, you little shit. Who do you think you are?"

"Promise me you're not driving," I say.

"Not at this exact moment… Hey, one more freaking thing. You call Constanze back? Bitch won't stop calling me."

"I'll call her when I hang up. I gotta go, Gary."

"Alright, fuck you then." He hangs up.

I walk back to my car at PJ's parking lot. I get in and drive into work, relieved that I won't have to see Gary today in the office. Things are always worse when he's around, and right now, I can't deal with worse.

29

WE ALL GOT A BOSS

May 27, 2010

This past week at Mandala has been intense. Gary has been pretty much M.I.A., and I can't seem to do anything right. Particularly when dealing with those asshats at CNN. Couple that with Constanze Bellingham's completely delusional ideas on how to manage the External Affairs team. She told me I should be getting Christopher Shelley on the cover of *Vanity Fair*. She wants Annie Lebovitz to shoot him in some heroic fashion. She wants Christopher Hitchens, who happens to be friends with Christopher Shelley, to write the piece. She wants to know why I haven't made this happen.

I'm a lawyer, I tell her. External Affairs lawyers do not get people on magazine covers. Also, why the hell would she think a *Vanity Fair* cover, of all magazine covers, would be a good idea right now? This is a terrible idea, I told her. Terrible. And she blew up at me, and told me that, at a time of crisis we all have to pitch in and do things that aren't in our job descriptions. So to end the call, I am forced to lie to her. I told her I would call *Vanity Fair*. I will email Christopher Hitchens and Annie Lebovitz myself. My lies shut her up. She says a *Vanity Fair* cover will make Christopher Shelley so happy. That perhaps we can do the shoot on his yacht. Seriously, his yacht. Anyway, I've had enough of these people for the day. So I get Constanze Bellingham off my back, I log off for the day, and drive to The House of the Neon Palm to deal with problems that are actually crazier than this.

When I get to Mama's house, I find Francesca from the praline shop standing in the foyer of the house. She is hiding behind Gucci sunglasses, but I can tell it is her. Her arms are folded, and she is carrying a big, fancy leather purse the color of a pat of butter.

"Oh, it's her baby boy!" Francesca smiles and sticks her pink tongue into the gap between her teeth. "Where you at?"

"I'm good. How can I help you?"

"Just coming in for a check-up with my girl, La La. Mind the purse." She pushes me away a little. "Don't scuff the leather. It's expensive."

"Oh, wow. That is nice leather."

"Nice?" She smirks. "This shit is more than nice. This a $50,000 Birkin bag."

"Wow. The praline business must be booming."

"Oh, hell no. Fuck those pralines and all those goddamn tourist. Your mama gave me a tip on a horse over at the Fair Grounds. And now my ship has finally come in."

"Was it Walter White?" I ask.

"Oh, you psychic too!" She pushes her palm in my face. "Tell me about my bae? I'll pay you."

"I don't read palms," I say.

Sobs echo from the parlor. La La's client is having a breakdown. You can hear my sister saying over and over, "You are going to be alright, I promise."

"Damn," Francesca says. "That sounds horrible."

"We probably shouldn't be eavesdropping."

"Sure enough." She steps away from the curtain with me and then points to the logo on my golf shirt. "Mandala."

I cover the logo with my hand.

"Nuthin' be ashamed of, sugar. We all got a boss. My daddy used to work for Shell back in the day."

"Look, give me just a couple of seconds, and I will get La La for you." I slide past Francesca and her $50,000 purse, through the curtain and into the parlor.

There, sitting next to Mama's crystal ball and the fanned-out tarot cards, is Jean Babineaux. She is a snotty mess. She's crying so hard, she doesn't notice me. And standing next to her is La La, who is now Annie Lennox or Pink. Or whatever rock star dresses in a men's black suit with a pink crew-cut. La La pats Jean Babineaux on the shoulder, trying to get this stranger to stop crying while not getting any of the unfortunate tears on her hands.

"It's going to be okay," La La keeps saying. "Just tell me how I can help you."

I move La La to the side and kneel down at Jean's feet.

"Jean." I touch her arm, and she looks up at me. "What happened?"

"I wasn't able to stop him."

"Stop what, Jean?"

"He did it," she says. "In the bathtub."

"Did what in the bathtub?" I regret those words almost as soon as I say them.

Jean dissolves.

I pull her to me. My Mandala Worldwide golf shirt is soaked through in a matter of seconds.

* * *

I have to call Gary. He's the only person who will even come close to understanding how guilty I feel right now. I have to let him know what we did to the Babineauxes. That we have lost our way. That we are not good people. That we might very well be bad people.

I lock myself in my old room upstairs, surrounded with Jean's scattered past-due bills. I hold the letter that foretold all this in my hand.

So I dial Gary. The phone rings three times, just like the rooster that crowed before Peter betrayed his Savior.

He finally picks up. "What?"

"Mark Babineaux killed himself," I say.

There's a long pause. So long that I almost think Gary hung up.

"You still there?"

"Yeah," he says.

Another long pause.

"These are people's lives, Gary."

"You think I don't know that?"

"So what do we do?"

"That guy had problems before he ever met us," Gary says. "Big problems."

"That doesn't make what we did to him any more right."

"I can't control what that guy decided to do, Duke. You can't either."

"Gary. We did this to them."

"It was business. Nobody made that guy kill himself. Nobody made him be a shrimper either. He made choices."

"I realize that, but the choices *we* made affected him."

"Look, Duke, this is terrible. I'm not trying to say that it's not. But you and I are not responsible for this guy killing himself."

"So I'm just supposed to act like this didn't happen?"

"Yep. That's exactly what you're going to do."

"I don't think I can."

"Look, let's go to Superior after work to discuss this. We need to talk about this in person."

"Margaritas aren't going to fix this, Gary."

"That's not what I'm saying. Geez."

"Then what are you saying?"

"I'm saying I want to talk to you off-site about this."

* * *

Up until today, I have been pretty confident that I was a good person.

Even with all the shit Mandala has been pulling since the Spill, I was certain what we were doing was for the greater good mostly. And while this spill is a tragedy, it's also an isolated accident. We drill wells all over the world without leaks or explosions. It's like saying cars should be outlawed because of wrecks. The benefits so far have outweighed the downsides, as devastating as they can be at times. However, seeing Jean tonight, after holding her like that, I am not sure I can keep telling myself this.

I have always believed that Mandala was, at its heart, a good company—that we had the noble and dangerous job of supplying the world with the energy it needed to run economies and bring wealth to nations. Even with all the downsides to petroleum, Mandala's ability to literally fuel growth outweighed everything else.

Hell, I know climate change is real. Everyone at Mandala does. It's why I applied at Mandala Worldwide instead of BP or Exxon. Like most of my team, I earnestly believed that "MW" dream-catcher logo stood for "More Ways" as much as it did Mandala Worldwide. I believed that finding oil in hard-to-find places was how Mandala was doing this. It was how Mandala was keeping everyone's cars full of gas, so the world could go to work, pick up our kids from school, take road trips to the Grand Canyon until our engineers figured out solar, wind, bio, and geothermal. Something has to keep the lights on, to pay for all that innovation and fuel all those people making solo runs to the grocery store in their SUVs.

But now, after watching what we just did to Jean and Mark Babineaux, I am not sure of who I am or what Mandala really is. I am not sure we are good people at all.

* * *

Gary refuses to talk about the Babineauxes at the office. He spends most of the day with his door closed, avoiding me. He's spooked about this. So after work today, I drive into Uptown and grab a table on the patio at Superior. I am on my third Dos Equis and working on my second basket of chips and salsa when Gary finally walks into the bar. He's talking into his Bluetooth headset, nodding and talking, nodding and talking. He holds up two fingers to our waitress and mouths, "Frozen. Extra salt."

"Sorry. I'm late." Gary sits down at the table and pulls his earpiece out and plops it into the pocket of his dress shirt. "Been waiting long?"

"About thirty minutes."

The waitress comes to the table, double-fisting Gary's two frozen margaritas.

"You guys gonna want any food?" she asks.

"How about a Superior Salad? Trying to watch my figure." Gary winks.

"Beef or Chicken?"

"Bistec," he says with a Spanish accent and a smoldering look.

She giggles. "Okay, I'll have it right out. Do you want another beer, honey?"

"Sure." I give her my empty.

The waitress picks up our menus and leaves us with a fresh basket of chips.

"So, let's talk about you," Gary says. "What's going on with Duke?"

"What the fuck do you mean what's going on with me? Mark Babineaux just killed himself because of us."

"Come on. It's me." He points to himself. "You don't think I don't feel like shit. I know this Babineaux thing has shaken you up, but there's something else going on with you. Has been for a while."

Perhaps it's the week I've had, maybe it's the three-beer buzz, but I just say it:

"My mom. She's missing."

"Holy shit. Are you kidding me? No wonder you've been on the rag. When did this happen?"

"About a month ago."

"Why didn't you tell me?"

"I'm telling you now."

"And the police haven't found her?"

"If they had she wouldn't be missing."

"What happened?" He starts shoving chips and salsa into his face.

"She ran out of her kitchen, chasing a cat and nobody has seen her since."

The waitress delivers our drinks: beer for me and two fishbowl margaritas for Gary.

"Shit, I am so sorry, man." Gary takes a long, deep draw from his straw and then rims the salt of his frozen margarita with his big, fat cow tongue. "Same thing happened to my dad. Alzheimer's."

I just look at him and blink. We were talking about me and my problems, and now, as usual, we are talking about Gary and his problems.

"About two years ago. He was sitting on his porch swing when my mom went out back to put the hedge clippers away. When she returned, he was gone. He'd taken his truck keys and driven off. Police found him all crashed up, up near Brenham, Texas—you know, where they make the ice cream. Had to put him in memory care after that. It was terrible. For my mom and him."

"So sorry to hear that. Is he okay?"

"Doesn't recognize me. Fit as a fiddle, but nobody's home. It's killing my mom. She promised she'd never put him in a nursing home, but we didn't have a choice. Second time he'd run away like that."

"Not to change the subject," I take a swig of my beer, "but I want to talk to you about this whole Mark Babineaux thing. We need to do something for his wife. Help her."

"Do they still have a Silver Alert going for your mom?"

"Yeah, I think so. Honestly, the police haven't been much help. But we need to stay on topic. What about Jean Babineaux? We have to do something for her."

"I wish you would have told me sooner." Gary shakes his head.

"I'm a private person, Gary."

"Yeah, well, at Mandala we're family. We have to look after each other." He exhales and looks up at the ceiling so that the tears won't roll out of his eyes. "So hard watching a parent go through something like that."

"Thanks, man, but what about Jean Babineaux?"

"You haven't paid for that?" Gary points to my beer. "I'm getting this."

"Gary. Answer my question. What about Jean Babineaux?"

"What can we do?" He shrugs. "Look, I wish there was something Mandala could do for her, but we can't. We can't just back up the Brinks truck to her house because her husband killed himself."

"I'm just asking you to call Houston. See what you can do."

"Look," he says, "I'll see what I can do, but I am not promising anything."

"Okay."

"Not to sound like a dick, but just be glad we didn't shoot that commercial. Can you imagine the fallout if he had offed himself after being in one of our commercials? Talk about a shit show."

"How can you even say that? That guy is dead. We did this."

"I'm glad you feel comfortable being honest with how you feel with me, Duke, because it's going to make this conversation easier on both of us. "

"What conversation?"

"You know I empowered you to manage our social media and it's pretty much a disaster. The things people are saying about us on Facebook. The videos on YouTube. You seem to have done nothing to stop all this."

"Gary, I'm an attorney, not a magician. I don't know how to stop people from using their First Amendment rights on social media about a disaster that everyone is outraged by."

"I can see, with your mom missing and everything, why you stopped trying." He chomps on a tortilla chip and shakes his head. "But remember when I asked you to get that cake down off Reddit? Well, it's still there with like over fifteen hundred comments in the thread, and now Doug Suttles is pissed. I hesitate to bring it up because of how crushed you are about the Babineaux deal not going through. But even if he hadn't, you know, done that, you were supposed to sign his replacement immediately, and now we aren't going to make the insertion date for *The New York Times*. We are just going to eat that full-page ad. That's over a hundred grand Mandala is just going to eat. I mean I know it's traumatizing, what happened. I'm traumatized, believe me. But everything about our job is traumatizing right now. We work in triage. This is war, Duke."

"This is war," I parrot him and nod.

"I just wish you would have told me that your mom was missing. Then I wouldn't have maybe put so much on you," he says. "You dropping the ball serves no one."

There's an awkward silence as I watch Gary dip his napkin into his glass of water and try to wipe the spilled salsa off the front of his shirt.

"Good news is I haven't given up on you," he says. "I still believe in you. So I've got a big job for you. I mean big."

"What kind of job?"

"Constanze Bellingham, wants you to write all of Christopher Shelley's speeches from here on out. She wants you to personally coach him before every media interview."

"Why me? The man flagrantly ignores everything I tell him to do."

"He's got a man crush on you I guess."

"I'm not a speechwriter."

"Duke, this is some seriously high profile shit. Our department has had so many screw-ups with the media and now this suicide, my job is on the line. I need you to knock this out of the ballpark for me. For our department."

"Okay. Sure. I'll do whatever it takes."

"Okay, Sure?" Gary shakes his head. "Hell, do you know how many people on our team would kill for this?"

"I'm honored Constanze thinks so highly of me." I take a swig of my beer. "It's just this Babineaux thing is still, I don't know... I'll be okay. Just need to process through it."

"Well, get your shit together. You got to stop calling in sick. Okay? I mean I know you're worried about your mom and all, but we've all got problems outside of work. Like what if I called in sick every time my mom called me about my dad?"

I just stare at him.

"Look, you know what I mean." Gary licks the rest of the salt from his other margarita. "I could be missing all sorts of work for my dad's Alzheimer's, but I can't afford to do that and you can't either. I am not trying to be a jerk here."

"You just called in sick for your cousin's bachelor party," I say.

"That was my first day off in over three months," he says. "It's not the same as you calling in sick every other day."

"My mother is missing."

"I'm your friend, Duke. But I am also your boss. You've got to focus."

"I get it. Don't worry about it. I'll make sure everything Christopher Shelley says is golden from here on out, and I won't miss any more work. Point taken." I try to smile.

30

LIT UP

May 28, 2010

After Gary's "coachable moment" with me over way too many margaritas and beers, I don't drive home to Emily and the boys in Covington. I take a taxi back to The House of the Neon Palm to check on Daddy, to see if he's heard something from Mary Glapion and her TED backpack. But as I drive up to the house, I am somewhat shocked to see that Mama's neon sign has been turned off. I cannot remember a time when that big red hand has ever not buzzed and glowed. Instead, there is a golden light emanating from the front windows of the house. I pay and get out of the cab and find Stevo smoking a wooden sailor's pipe next to the VW van that he keeps parked on the street.

He's gazing up at the stars, pretty much ignoring me. The air around him smells like wet leather, baked apples, and amaretto.

"Why's the sign off?" I ask.

"See that?" Stevo points to a star next to the moon. "That's Venus."

"I know that, Stevo."

"You ever wake up before the sun comes up just to look at it? It's so beautiful. Its light so pure."

"Are you high?"

"Our bodies were designed to look up to heaven." He tilts his head way back and rolls his shoulders. "Not always looking down at that phone of yours."

"Who turned off Mama's sign?" I say.

"I did. Didn't want any customers knocking on the door tonight." Stevo puts his palm on the barrel of his pipe and sucks in to extinguish the tobacco.

"Why?"

"You'll see." He gestures for me to follow him through the yard and to the porch. The crickets are chirping to the pulse of the stars. Stevo opens the front door for me. We step inside a house flickering with a galaxy of St. Anthony candles and a jungle of Easter lilies.

"Where's Daddy?" I look around.

"Already went to bed." La La walks into the foyer, holding an Easter lily with both hands.

"What is all this?" I say.

"We are bringing Mama home tonight." She puts the lily down next to St. Anthony.

Cactus strolls in from the kitchen with an unlit candle, and La La flicks Daddy's old Zippo at it. They have lit hundreds of tall candles to the patron saint of lost things. Mama's house is now cast in the same miraculous shadows and mysterious lights of a church. The St. Anthony statue's eyes blink and shift beneath the flicker of the flames. The whole scene makes me uneasy and brings back memories I have spent most of my life trying to forget: Mama's nine days of prayers, her fasts, and her feasts, the rune stones and the tarot cards. The bullshit customers who knocked on the front door, day and night. The Nag Champa incense burns the back of my throat, and the sweet pollen from all these lilies makes my eyes water.

"Take your shoes off." La La doesn't look up from the candle she's lighting. "These are prayers for St. Anthony to bring Mama back to us."

"That's really sweet, but Emily and the boys are expecting me," I say. "I just came by to see if Daddy has heard anything from the police."

"Stay. We need to do this as a family." Stevo walks into the room with Cactus, who's carrying a billowing Japanese teapot.

"Take your shoes off," La La demands.

"I have work tomorrow."

"Duke." Stevo pours the tea into the fancy china cups that Mama claimed belonged to the Czarina before the revolution. "Take your shoes off."

"Where's Yanko?" I say.

"Playing a frat party in Baton Rouge." La La rearranges the Easter lilies that flank the St. Anthony statue.

"I bought an offering for St. Anthony." Cactus points to a huge sack of Beehive Organic Flour, propped up under the St. Anthony statue that she has placed on top of the tarot card table.

"Is that a hundred-pound sack of flour?" I say.

"You have to give St. Anthony enough flour to match the weight of the missing person," she says.

"Mama weighed more than a hundred pounds."

"Don't be that way," La La says. "She paid for the bag with her palm reading money."

There is a loud bang and then a clatter on the front porch. Some animal is screeching and making an ungodly racket.

"Oh, the Bee Maidens never disappoint!" La La swishes out of the parlor, to the front door.

Cactus and Stevo chase after her.

Cactus screams and La La yells at her to shut up.

So I run out to the porch to see what's the matter.

And it's a opossum: a fat one with Mama's necklace around its neck.

It is hissing and backing up from Stevo, who is holding his shoe over his head.

"Don't hurt it," La La says.

"Kill it!" Cactus screams. "Don't let it bite you!"

Stevo just stands here, unsure who to listen to.

So I wrestle the shoe from him and lightly bop the opossum on the head.

The hissing creature collapses and does what it was built to do, play opossum.

I reach down and remove the gold coins from its neck.

I hold them up to the porch light. Sure enough, they are Mama's. All my doubts run out of me like blood from a stab wound. We are witnessing a miracle or perhaps, like Cactus proclaimed, a curse. Or something well beyond those two words, some new phenomenon that has yet to be named.

Whatever is happening, I feel seasick. I feel the floorboards shifting and rocking beneath my feet. I quite possibly feel the nascent symptoms of another panic attack.

"So weird." I bring the necklace inside. La La follows right behind me.

"The necklace wanted to come home to us and it did," she says. "That's how it works."

I hold the gold coins out in front of me and admire how they shimmer.

"Give that to me." La La plucks the necklace from my hand. She wraps it in a piece of purple silk. "Mama's necklace has returned to us. We will not lose it again."

* * *

"Now let us drink deep!" Stevo holds his teacup to his lips and swallows it all.

Cactus and La La follow suit. They grimace and pucker. Then they all glare at me.

"For once, just be a part of this family." Stevo pushes a cup of his tea at me.

"Do it for Mama," Cactus says.

"Here, you need to wear this first." La La fastens Mama's gold coins around my neck, and I let her.

I don't know if it's guilt for having ignored them for the past ten years or just stupidity for thinking that I owe them this, but I put the tea to my lips. I throw the foul liquid past my tongue, to the back of my throat.

"What was that?" I wipe my mouth with my sleeve and stare inside my empty teacup.

"Ayahuasca!" Stevo throws me an adult diaper. "You're going to need these."

The cold sweats hit hard. They herald the agony that Cactus and La La are in, next to me on the floor of the parlor. They are moaning, curled up in fetal positions on their yoga mats. The tea makes them violently ill. For me, the tea takes me on an amazing trip. I feel expansive and bigger than my body. Everything is aglow. I am lying on my back with my adult diapers on; the crinkling sound they make is magical.

My heart is bursting with love, more love for my brothers and sister than I ever even knew was possible. I am feeling love for all seven billion of my brothers and sisters on this planet. We are all one. My heart feels as big as the sun. I want to call everybody and tell them how much I love them — how much life-giving warmth I have to share with the world.

And then the cramps.

They hit me below my waist, twisting me with sharp pain, squeezing me like that python in my dream.

Don't think about the python. Don't think about the python and its horrible mouth. But it is already around me. She is squeezing my waist. Her open mouth threatens to devour me. Her grip pushes everything out of me. I grab the bucket that Stevo has placed by my head, and I heave. I fill up the bucket with a tide as unstoppable as the oceans. I can't help it. I fill up my diapers. I look over at La La, and she is biting a towel, sweating. From the smell of things, I feel certain she's having the same kind of distress.

I roll around on the floor, trying to get away from the cramps.

"It's okay, Duke," Cactus groans. "We've been trained by shamans."

"We are going to touch the face of God!" Stevo grabs the bucket from me and pukes into it.

"This is not okay." I can't stop squirming from the pain. "This is not okay!"

"There's a lot in this world that is not okay," Stevo gasps between pukes.

"I hate you." I grab the bucket of sick back from him.

I heave.

"Let the pollution go!" Stevo dances around like a mad man. "Let it go! Just let it go!"

Mama's necklace starts to hum and vibrate. It starts to talk to me. It makes me see things. Dreams that are not dreams. Futures that are not futures. The necklace becomes the python coiling around my neck, squeezing me around my stomach.

I expel everything from my body. The python wrings me out like a dishrag. I lay on the floor limp, unable to lift my head, drooling. This hallucinogenic tea forces all the fluids and all the ideas I ever held out of me and onto the floor. Then my head begins to flood and overflow with thoughts that aren't mine. The python constricts. She wraps herself across my chest, squeezing the air out of my lungs.

I don't fight it. I can't. I let go. All I can do is realize that this thing has been squeezing me for years. I just didn't realize what it was. It's the hunger that has always been with me, and it has restricted everything I have ever thought or done. This insatiable hunger for a bigger house and buying more stuff and all the while I have been blind to everything that is wondrous and real. I have held so tightly to my faith in logic, so tightly to Mandala that I have squeezed out all possibility for a better way. This python is my blind faith, and it's strangling me. This python is certainty—that's the problem. This certainty is unspeakably hungry. It's what will eventually consume us all.

There's so much capital-T Truth pouring into my head that it makes me vomit, but this time when I put my head over the sick bucket, I see two angels who have lost their wings in a hurricane, guarding the gates of a dying Earth. They flicker and fade into the buzz and glow of Mama's neon sign, which then flickers and fades into a Mandala Worldwide gas station sign, and then as the waves pour out of me, I begin to ride them. I find myself upon an endless ocean. I am Kevin Costner in *Waterworld*. I stand on the tip of a rag and bone boat. I watch the green sea meet the brown sky.

Like the sea and sky, we all meet. We are all doing this.

We are all Christopher Shelley. We are all Mandala. We are all doing this because we as a species are so driven to discover and everything we discover, we exploit: fire, oil, atoms, unknown continents full of our fellow human beings. It's so very clear to me now, and it would have always been clear, had I not traded a world of chaos and beauty for one of certainty and logic. I just kept on drilling and burning and buying and fucking and keeping the illusion that I was in control of life. I was so righteous, so certain that I had found myself within the country club of the chosen few. My certainty was so big, my righteousness so close to whom I thought I was that I had no idea that this python was swallowing me whole.

Mama's necklace rips away the veil. It shows me how this will end. How I will end. I see my death. I see everyone's death. I see what we have done to the thin layer around this rare planet. I see what Mama's letters have been trying to say to me all this time. I see what I must do tomorrow at Christopher Shelley's press conference.

31

PRESSER

May 28, 2010

Forty miles north of the Sub-Ocean Brightside oil bloom, the skies over the Port Fourchon Beach are as gray and hopeless as the ocean we are trying to save. There's a heavy gloom hanging over all of us this morning, and after what I saw last night, it's hard not to believe that the weather isn't somehow reflecting God's mood today—that He has had enough of us wrecking His creation—that the earth is finally done with us too—that this is her way of kicking us off her purple mountains and out of her impossible depths. But here I am anyway with my bright orange Mandala golf shirt on, reporting for duty to handle this PR crisis.

The Mandala Shoreline Team are geared up in their turquoise work gloves and yellow rubber boots. They line the coast from here to Florida with their booms and skimming equipment. These workers are fighting in vain to stop the unstoppable. Thimbles and oceans are what we are dealing with here today, thimbles and oceans. A man can't very well empty the ocean with thimbles just like a corporation can't clean up over 4 million barrels of oil with 250 men sifting through the sludge on a beach with their skimmers and their jugs of detergents and emulsifiers. It does, however, make for a heroic photo opportunity. So Christopher Shelley is here with his shirt sleeves rolled up and his khaki pants on. He wanders the ruined beach and inspects the crew's work. Meanwhile, I am here in the parking lot with Constanze Bellingham, listening to her lecture me on how this press conference must go perfectly.

"As of late, he's not been himself," Constanze says. "So we are going to have you upload your speech to Christopher's teleprompter."

"I'm sure the stress is getting to him." I watch Christopher from across the beach. He pats one of the workers on the back. They are laughing— joking around.

"I would suppose the stress is getting to us all." Constanze shakes her head at her jovial boss.

"I don't want to speak out of turn," I say.

"Then don't." Constanze shakes her head.

"Sorry, I just have to ask. Do you really think a teleprompter is the way to go here?"

"Yes, according to the PR team, it is the only way to go," Constanze says.

"I just really question the wisdom of using teleprompters at a beach-side press conference like this. It's stagey. Creates a pretty indelible image that these aren't Christopher's words. That he doesn't have the answer to this. It's the wrong kind of visual to juxtapose next to this clean-up. It's not going to play well. It's terrible actually."

"The news crews will be here in less than two hours, Mr. Melançon."

"Give me an hour with Christopher. Let me coach him through his talking points. If he can do this without the teleprompters, his address will come off as much more in control and authentic. More on-brand. Trust me."

"You'll have to convince the PR team."

"If it doesn't work, we can always go back to the teleprompters."

"Well, quite frankly, Mr. Shelley doesn't like reading from teleprompters. Says they make him stutter," she says.

"Then why are we doing this? He shouldn't use them then. Seriously."

"It's not me you have to convince. Tell that to the PR team." She nods her head in the direction of the Winnebago with the giant Mandala America logo emblazoned on it.

"Why don't we tell Christopher first and let him tell the PR team?" I say.

"This isn't your first rodeo, is it?" Constanze smiles at me.

* * *

"You got this." I pat Christopher on the back as the news trucks approach the beach. In a split-second, Christopher Shelley, CEO of one of the largest global concerns, goes from looking like the slightly goofy son of a British lord to looking like Mister Bean, all pinched-face, simpering, and red.

"Look at that." He finally exhales.

The media trucks surround us: NBC, ABC, CBS, CNN, FOX, BBC. Even Al Jazeera is here. It's a mob scene. But instead of carrying pitchforks and torches, they've got their cameras and their boom mikes. The bleach-toothed reporters and their angry camera crews are here to make themselves famous for lynching this guy, and if I am going to obey my mother's letters, I am about to help them do it.

"You did great in the rehearsal." I slap Christopher on the back again. "You are going to kill this."

"Easier said than done, chap." Christopher waves me off as he ascends the podium. The news crews circle him. I take my place behind the flood of reporters and the flash of cameras.
Christopher adjusts the bouquet of microphones toward his thin lips. He clears his throat and attempts to smile. And then he seems to realize that perhaps a smile is not appropriate for this moment, so he furrows his brow, lowers his head, and sighs.

The CEO of Mandala Worldwide looks tiny behind this large podium, dwarfed by this moment. He clears his throat again and speaks:

"The Sub-Ocean Brightside explosion is a tragedy that should have never happened." Christopher follows the exact verbiage we rehearsed. "I speak for everyone at Mandala when I say that we are still in a deep state of continued shock and grief over the loss of our friends and co-workers who died in that explosion last month. My heart breaks for their families. But despite our collective sorrow, my team and I have been working around the clock to fight this spill. As the CEO of Mandala Worldwide, I am all too aware of how grave our situation is today. Sadly we have not located the cause of this tragedy, and for this, I cannot offer enough apologies, but regardless of the cause, I will do everything in my power to make sure this never happens again."

Christopher hits all my high points for an effective non-apology apology: He's claimed more sorrow and outrage than the general public in this matter because of his personal loss. He's apologized not for the Spill or the explosion, but for not finding its exact cause—which, to the untrained ear, sounds like a sincere admission of fault but isn't anywhere close. And then he's sworn to save us from something this horrible ever happening again. If he can stay on point, he will land the dismount with a "We-Are-All-In-This-Together" rallying cry and Mandala Worldwide will have made crisis management history. That is if Christopher doesn't follow the one last piece of advice that I gave him just before the news teams showed up.

"Our sorrow multiplies every day that we do not kill this well." Christopher Shelley shakes his head woefully.

He is going in for the "We-Are-All-In-this-Together" clincher. Maybe I should have done more than just take his teleprompter away. Maybe he's going to pull this off after all.

"Our lives have been completely consumed by this tragedy," he says. "This is a personal loss for me and my team. After all, Mandala has over 45,000 employees who live and work on the coast. That is why I want to speak directly to the people who call this part of the world home. This is our moment. And we shall not cower. We shall not falter. We shall kill this well," Christopher looks out over the crowd of reporters. Tears shimmering in his eyes and a defiant smile breaking across his face. "Indeed a dark tide is upon us today, and as it rises, Mandala shall stand together with the families of Louisiana, Mississippi, Alabama, and Florida, united with the good people of the Gulf Coast. Mandala will stop this Spill and we shall all rise above this together."

Christopher waits a couple of beats just as I instructed him to do so that this pause will create a natural editing point for a media-perfect sound byte.

"Any questions?" he says after the exact moment of silence. And the press hurls them at Christopher like Molotov cocktails.

"There has been a lot of speculation that Mandala wants to

replace the drilling mud with seawater before they finish the plug." This former beauty queen from ABC News smiles at Christopher. "Would that even work, Mr. Shelley?"

The beauty queen is then one-upped by a guy from FOX News, sweating to death in a full business suit. "Are you considering detonating a nuclear bomb to plug up the hole?"

"Does the fact that Mandala had to call on Exxon and NASA for help perhaps indicate that Mandala engineers weren't prepared for a disaster of this magnitude?" asks the NPR reporter in her signature monotone.

Christopher appears to remember most of my coaching. He does a pretty good job of dodging and defusing a majority of the questions. He radiates confidence bordering on arrogance. His gestures are royal and his scowls are distinctly British. He is doing okay, but that one reporter from NPR keeps politely hammering Christopher, causing Christopher's responses to become increasingly terse and clipped.

It's when she simply asks, "Are you sleeping at night?" that Christopher loses it.

"Of course I sleep at night!" he says. "What kind of question is that? Do you sleep at night, my dear? Because I do. I sleep very, very well in fact. Because I am bloody exhausted!"

I fold my arms to keep myself from jumping in between him and the NPR reporter. There is no teleprompter to feed him a perfectly crafted response, no way to help him bridge this attack and change the line of questioning. Instead, Christopher Shelley does exactly what I told him to do.

"Just be yourself out there," I said. "Especially if they start to attack you. You said it best back at the Ritz. Authenticity is all that matters in a time like this. Just trust your heart. It won't let you down."

So Christopher Shelley does just that. He dives into his own narrative and he does the worst thing he can do at a moment like this: He speaks straight from his billionaire heart.

"Frankly, young lady, there's no one here today who wants this to be over more than I do," he says. "But let's be clear: This spill is not completely my fault, now is it? Sure, it's easy to blame big, bad Mandala for this crisis. But you know what's even easier? For you people to drive your big news vans all over the place, and even your goddamn Priuses, full of Mandala petrol, and then blame me and my company like you had nothing to do with this disaster. You want to forget about the petroleum that it takes to get you from here to there—that is until you see it bubbling up from the ocean floor on the BBC. Then you want to blame me. Well, that stops today.

Look, I am doing everything I can to fix this.

As you can see behind me, my men are risking their lives cleaning up this bloody mess. We are the people risking our lives every day, in fact, trying to keep up with your insatiable demand for petrol. We are the heroes in this story, not the villains. I provide America with enough gasoline to make this country great. And you want to talk about how I reached out to NASA for help with this Spill. Let me tell you about NASA. How do you honestly think NASA got to the fucking moon? I'll tell you how: With rocket fuel that came from Mandala wells. Look it up. So how dare you ask me if I can sleep at night? I sleep bloody well, thank you. Because I am tired. I am tired of you people burning all these hydrocarbons and wanting to act like this is my fault. And I am bloody exhausted of being condemned for doing the thankless job of supplying the fuel that keeps this world spinning and this whole goddamn economy going!"

There's an audible gasp from the reporters, but I hold my tongue. Christopher's unrehearsed diatribe goes off like a suicide vest. It's the kind of public relations dumpster fire that will go down in history. You don't have to be psychic to know that this rant will change everything. It will be quoted in textbooks, talked about at dinner parties, scoffed at over lattes in Starbucks around the world. This rant is what I promised Constanze and the PR team that I would never let happen. Christopher's most heartfelt words are more than I could have ever hoped for when I took his teleprompter away.

* * *

I spend the rest of the afternoon driving around by myself along the coast, chasing the setting sun. I am done with Mandala—both as a lawyer and as the Seventh Son of Madame Melançon. If this doesn't "erase the mandala and save the sea of life," I don't know what will. Whatever I have done by letting Christopher Shelley speak for himself, I feel right with the world. I am no longer spinning words that I never really believed in. What I did to Mandala might have been crazy, it might have been self-destructive and mad, but it's as close to doing the right thing as I have ever been in my entire life. I feel free now. The tightness in my chest is gone. My constant craving and anxiety have vanished; the python is dead.

As I drive home across the twenty-four miles of Lake Pontchartrain, across the causeway, my phone rings.

It's Gary.

Of course, it is. I can't help but smile. I take the call.

"Duke!" The phone speaker blares in my ear. "What the fuck is wrong with you?

"Gary?"

"Do you realize what you've done?"

"Yeah. I quit."

"You had one job! One job to do!"

"I just resigned, Gary. So, no, I don't have a job to do," I say.

"We are going to sue you!"

"For what?"

"Breach of contract!" he shouts.

"What contract?" I say.

"You're going to pay for this, Duke."

"Gary, we are all going to pay for this. Trust me." I hang up and throw my phone onto the passenger seat.

* * *

I tiptoe into my sleeping home. I glide into the dark of the bedroom. I step out of my pants and slip out of my shirt. I crawl in next to my sleeping wife. I spoon her and pull her into a tight hug.

She elbows me to move away. "Not right now."

"Honey," I whisper. "Sweetheart."

"What?" she groans.

"Wake up. I have to talk to you."

She turns on her side to face me. She opens her eyes.

"I saw the press conference," she says. "I'm sorry."

I just look at her.

"Hey," I say.

"Hey," she echoes, a note sweeter than me.

I can't say it just yet. I can't find the words to tell her that Mama could see the future. I can't tell her that I just lost my job because of these predictions. So I stare at her, the silhouette of her cheeks and hair.

"What's the matter?" she touches my cheek.

"I did it" is all I can tell her.

"Did what?"

"I couldn't do it anymore," I say. "I couldn't keep doing this to people."

She nestles close to me.

"It's not your fault," she says.

"Mama left me these letters. She guided me to do this."

"Your mother's letters predicted this?"

"More or less."

"Duke?"

"Yeah."

"Are you okay?" she asks.

"Yeah, I think."

I pull her closer. She stiffens slightly, but relaxes into me.

"I'm worried about you," she says.

"Don't. We're good. I'm good."

"You're lying on my hair." She nudges me.

I roll over a little and let her go. We both go to sleep like parallel lines, not touching each other anywhere in the future or the past.

* * *

I wake up, and Emily's side of the bed is empty. I get up, take a leak, and walk to the boys' room to check on them. But Stewart and Jo-Jo's beds are just a tangle of SpongeBob sheets. So I go downstairs, but I don't hear the usual morning clink of Legos and clunk of wooden blocks. No Dora the Explorer trills or Elmo giggles. Just heartbreaking silence. I walk into the kitchen to find the back door to the garage is wide open. I walk out to the garage to find Emily's Subaru gone.

I text her: Where r u?

I stare at the small grease spot where her car used to be. She's not texting me back. So I call her. Each ring of the phone is longer and more elastic than it should be. Like all this is happening underwater. On the fourth ring: Click.

I call her again. And at the end of the first ring, she answers.

"Hello," she says, like she doesn't know it's me calling, like anyone else would be calling her at 9 o'clock in the morning when she's just up and left the house without leaving a note.

"Hey, where are ya'll?" I try to keep the sunshine in my voice.

"I should have left a note," she says. "Sorry."

"You picking up breakfast?"

"No, we're on our way to Houston."

"Houston? What the fuck?"

"Don't be that way, Duke."

"Be what way?"

"I need a break," she says.

"Why are you going to Houston?"

"I need to see my parents."

"So you just woke up and decided you need to see Jules and Tom?"

"I need my family."

"Let me get this straight: You just loaded up our kids and left me in the middle of the night."

"It wasn't the middle of the night."

"Okay. Four in the morning then."

"You're scaring me," she says. "You just up and quit your job."

"You hated my job," I say.

"You're acting nuts, Duke. You think your mom is talking to you through some poor lady's phone bills. I just need some space to figure this out."

"You want to talk about nuts?" I lose it. "Let's talk about nuts! Who the fuck just packs up our kids and takes off and doesn't even leave a note? Who does that?"

Silence.

"Look," I say. "Just come home, and we can talk about this in person."

"I'm pulling into my parents' driveway," she says.

"There's no way you are already in Houston if you didn't leave in the middle of the night."

"I have to go," she says.

"I'm coming to get my kids."

"Duke, please."

"Why are you doing this to me?"

"I just need some time." Her voice softens.

"How much?"

"I don't know." She hangs up.

32

MAY 29, 2010

210,000,000 gallons of oil have poured into the Gulf since the explosion

I am in the shower when I hear the doorbell ring, and then there is this bang-bang-banging at the front door.

I get out, towel off, and throw on some clothes.

No one has ever knocked on our front door, much less pounded on it. We have not made those kinds of friends within the Cotton Gin Golf Community. I have not hit the back nine with the dermatologist next door, nor has Emily arranged playdates with his wife and their perpetually screaming daughters. We've been a little too busy to put down those kind of roots. So when I hear the beating on my front door, and the compulsive ringing of the doorbell, I immediately think it's the two frat boys, the ones with the shiny guns, back for more.

So I run downstairs. I grab a golf club. My heart is racing. I look out the peephole, and there in all his fish-eye glory is Gary. He's sweaty and anxious, standing on my front porch with a sheriff's deputy by his side.

I drop the five iron, and I open the door.

"Get out," he says.

"Good to see you too, Gary."

"Get all of your stuff and get out," he says.

"As I am sure your friend from law enforcement can tell you, you can't just evict someone without notice. There's a tiny thing called tenant's rights."

"You're not a tenant," Gary says. "You were an employee, and you've been fired."

"Gary, I need at least another day to get my stuff out. Seriously."

"This house is Mandala property, and you're trespassing," he says.

And as if this day couldn't get any worse, it just did: Gary Dubois is, for once in his life, correct.

He raises his hand over his head, and a team of Mandala workers files out of a truck parked out by the curb. They push past me into the house. The sheriff's deputy just stands here with his Ray-Bans on, acting like this is no big deal.

"This is not okay," I say to the cop. "How is this okay?"

He doesn't answer. Instead, we both just watch the workers take my coffee table and deposit it on the curb, then our recently replaced sofa, the flat screen TV, our seven-thousand dollar-dining room table, and the Eames chairs that Emily took weeks deliberating on and years to pay off.

"I really can't believe you," I say to Gary. I then walk over to the piles of my stuff.

I pull out my phone and Google "movers."

I call every listing I can find, but no one has trucks available at this exact moment. Most can't help me until next week. One guy kindly offers to rent me his El Camino to move myself, but he can't get that to me until tonight. I text Yanko. I call Stevo. But neither respond. So I stand with my phone in my hand, in the beating Louisiana heat while I watch everything I worked so hard to acquire just thrown out into the grass.

I am struck with a sudden panic, not for the Eames chairs or our dining room table that are upturned on our driveway. I am panicked about my boys' stuff. All I can think about are their toy trains. The boys are obsessed with them, can't go to bed without them. They will be devastated if these guys have lost Thomas or Oliver or Henry.

I run back into the house to gather up Stewart and Jo-Jo's train sets and Legos, past all these men carrying my family's belongings out to the curb. I run up to the boys' room. I throw open the door, and it's empty: Their Thomas the Tank Engine toys are no longer scattered on the carpet.

Their bunk beds are not here.

Even the faint smells of poo and graham crackers are gone.

I run back down the stairs, where I find Gary yelling at the movers to hurry up.

"What the fuck did you do with my kids' stuff?" I say.

Gary looks at me like I am crazy.

"My kids' stuff." I want to whomp him on the head. "Where is it?"

Gary points to the front door. "I'm sure it's outside with the rest of your shit."

I run into the yard, past the couches on their sides, past my upturned king-size mattress, past our big screen TV in the grass, and the boy's bedroom stuff is nowhere to be found.

Stewart and Jo-Jo's belongings, like my mother, has just evaporated.

"What did you do with it?" I grab one of the movers by the shoulders.

"Hey, get off me, man!" He pushes me away.

"Where are the bunk beds? The trains?" I say. "Where are my kids' trains?"

"What the hell you mean bunk beds?" the mover says. "I ain't touched no bunk beds."

I search the piles of stuff on the front lawn. I sift through the grass. My entire life is out here in the sun. Stewart and Jo-Jo are going to be heartbroken. I have upturned the couch. I have flipped my mattress. I have looked under every painting and framed print. Where did an entire room of stuff go? I try to calm myself. I can feel an incoming panic attack about to land right on top of me, and then I realize that Emily must have taken the trains. Of course, she took the trains. The boys wouldn't have left without them.

But where the fuck are their bunk beds? They were cheap Ikea beds and easily replaced, but still...

My cell phone rings. It's the last moving company I called. They have a truck.

So I read them the numbers on my credit card as slowly and precisely as a magic spell, and I breathe.

* * *

Driving back from the storage units that now contain what is left of my life, I turn on the radio. I turn it up louder and louder until I can't hear myself think. I sing along to REM's "Losing My Religion." I sing along so I can't hear all the regrets I have about Mark Babineaux's death, so I can stop obsessing over Emily leaving me, about being kicked out of our house. But then an ad for the Ragin' Cajun Bar and Grill comes on and the guilty thoughts creep back in. I think about Mark and his Cajun pride—so much like my dad's. I wonder what I could have done to help him. I have to change the station and land on that Better Than Ezra song that goes on and on about how *it was good*.

That old song brings me right back to brighter days with Emily.

"How did Kurt Cobain not sue those guys?" I'd always have to say when "Good" came on the radio.

"That riff sounds more like the Pixies to me," she'd say.

"The Pixies inspired Nirvana."

"How do you know Better Than Ezra wasn't inspired by the Pixies then?" She'd give me a look.

"Don't start," I'd say. "You know what I am talking about."

"Stop talking. You're ruining this for me." She'd then start to sing along to how it was "good, so good."

We did this play-fight thing when this Better Than Ezra song came on the radio, and I'd act more annoyed than I really was, and she would always sing loudly and out of key. It was an inside joke that we always had with each other. It was weird. When that old song came on the radio, it was more than a song; it was this feeling that we even loved the things that annoyed us about each other. It sounds stupid, but it's impossible to describe. Whatever it was, it was ours.

I turn off the radio, and I call Emily.

She picks up on one ring.

"I'm driving in today," I say.

"Don't," she sighs into the phone.

"I want to see my kids."

"Duke, I'm not ready."

"What did I do?"

"You didn't… This isn't about you."

"Is there someone else?"

"No."

"Is there?"

"I don't even have time to go to the bathroom by myself, Duke."

"Then what is this? Why are you doing this now?"

Silence.

"I don't want to do this," she says.

"Then don't. Come home."

"Duke."

"What about the boys? What have you told the boys?"

"They haven't asked. They think we're just visiting Mimsy and Pops."

"You don't have to do this."

I can hear her exhaling.

"What about therapy?" I say.

"I'm not happy."

"You're depressed. Postpartum. You had postpartum with Stewart. Maybe that's what this is. You're just depressed."

"I'm not depressed," she says.

"You don't want this."

"Don't tell me what I want. You don't know me. You don't know anything about me."

She hangs up the phone.

* * *

When I get back to The House of the Neon Palm, La La can tell that I am not right. My heart is broken like a bone. Why have I been so compelled to chase this thing, to chase my mother into the cat-filled night? To chase The Unseen Hand? I have no idea what I am doing. I am just fueled by fear and the shadowy threat of my mother's underworld consuming my family and me. And because of this, I have been doing things that make no sense to anyone, especially Emily. I am reading letters on old phone bills. I am throwing my career away because my mother's soothsaying told me to do so. I have lost everything that I knew to be true and good in this world. I have been trying to save the world from Mandala, and I can't even save my marriage.

La La talks me into sitting down in the parlor. She talks me into letting her look at my palms. La La, in her Annie Lennox drag, sits across from me in Mama's parlor, examining the lines in my palms and humming old Russian songs to herself. Part of me, the most spiteful part of me, wishes that my sister really was psychic, so that she could indeed pull all this pain out of my palm and into her own heart.

"So many islands," she pulls my left palm to her eye. "You have so many islands where there should only be stars."

This comforts part of me. Not because I feel like La La can divine the future, but because it reminds me so much of our mother, of the gentle tracings Mama would make on our palms as children, telling us our dreams were in our grasp.

"Hold still. You're in my light." She pulls my hand closer to her face.

She traces the deep line in the middle of my palm from just below my pointer finger to my pinky. She sighs.

"What?"

"Relax," she says. "And hold still. I'm listening to the Melissae."

I exhale.

"I'm sorry, Duke."

"For what?"

"It's being undone," she says. "From the other side."

"You're supposed to be making me feel better." I try to laugh this off.

"The palms don't lie." La La says.

I jerk my hand away. "Okay, we're done."

"Duke. Okay. Sorry," she says. "She's coming back. Will me lying to you make you feel better?"

"I didn't mean to snap at you."

"It's not easy news to take," she says.

"La La, how do you do this? Why do you see these things and I don't?"

"The lines in your hands reveal the folds in your brain. The folds in your brain reveal your character. Character is destiny." La La parrots Mama.

"But why can you see this and I don't?" I say.

She points to her gold coin earrings. "Mama pierced my ears with these when I was eleven and ever since… "

"Those are how you see the future?"

"And hear the past."

"How do they work?

"They just do. Mama gave them to me so I could help protect us against The Great Unseen Hand—the demon who should never have been summoned."

"How come you didn't see what happened to Mama then?"

"I don't know. It's like she just opened a door and vanished."

"What do you see now?"

"Nothing. Just pure silence when it comes to Mama."

* * *

I don't usually drink before noon, but today, when the back of my car is loaded up with boxes with the remains of my dead career, and there are three storage units overflowing with everything I own, and my wife has taken my kids and left me, I can't think of doing anything else. I want to obliterate myself. I want to drink away that ayahuasca trip. I want to erase the memories of working for a corporation bent on destroying the planet. My brain needs a hard reset. So I drive down to the Roosevelt Hotel. If I'm going to spiral out of control, I'm going to do it in a classy place, not at some dive like the Saturn Bar or F&Ms. I leave my car with the valet and find myself standing with two Brooks Brothers alcoholics, waiting for the doors of the Sazerac Bar to unlock at eleven.

When the doors finally open, we all three give audible sighs, and briskly take our places at the magnificent bar. I sit down by the fresco mural of white men bossing around the black men who are carrying heavy, brown bags. I have the bartender pour me a Sazerac. (Because what else are you going to drink at this bar?) It's sweet. Burns the feelings out of my throat. I order a second. I sip this one and contemplate the racist mural, and try to decide if it's just a piece of history that should always show us how horrible we have been or some embarrassing racist celebration like the mammy dolls and Confederate monuments that still pepper the landscape around here.

I pull out my phone and text Stevo:

Meet me at Sazerac.

He texts back: *Now?*

Yes. Now!

Why aren't you at work?

She left me.

Be there in 10

While I wait for Stevo, I order a third, and then fourth Sazerac. And by the way, that mural is definitely a racist piece of shit, I tell the bartender. I might just have to take a Sharpie to it. I reach into my pocket for a pen to deface the painting behind the bar, but find nothing. I stare at the ice in my empty glass, and I notice *The Times-Picayune* sitting on the bar. The front page is dedicated to

Christopher Shelley's tirade. It says that Mandala lied. That seals and stoppers were leaky. That we skimped on tests that could have stopped this. We were maybe overly optimistic, but more than likely just dishonest and corrupt. We were driven by profits, and we put those profits before the people who blew up on that well. It says we killed the ocean for money. I helped kill the ocean for money. That's what this paper says. I want to light it on fire. I want to light myself on fire.

By the time Stevo gets here, it is half-past noon, and I am half-past wasted. He's brought Daddy with him.

"Ah, T'boy, you drunker than a skunk." Daddy crutches over to me at the bar.

"You see this. You see this." I push the article in Daddy's face. "Mama said this would happen. And it did."

"Yeah, your mama has a tendency to do that." Daddy takes the paper from me and folds it in half without even reading it. "Now why ain't you at work, son?"

"I quit," I say.

"T'boy, that's good news." He gives me a heavy pat on the back. "Those *couyons* wrecking everything down here."

"The future. Vonnegut left me a paper from the future." I try to warn them.

"Stevo, gather your brother up and I'll meet you back at the house." Daddy shakes his head. "Try to keep him from embarrassing hisself."

Daddy crutches out of the Roosevelt, back to his car.

"Come on, Duke." Stevo lifts me up, off my barstool, throwing my arm over his shoulder.

"Remember the dead with fox feet, laughter, and rage." I pour my Sazerac on the floor.

"Hey, cut it out." Stevo takes my empty and slams it on the bar. "Don't do that."

Stevo holds me up and carries me out to the valet. The smelly hippie holds me while we wait for the valet to bring my Prius. I can feel this spinning blue marble that I helped destroy. It's under my feet. I can feel it spinning through this infinite black void, and it's making me want to puke.

He pushes me into the passenger side of my car.

"We are so small. So, so small," I say. "Ants. Just ants like the ones all over Yanko's leg. Just like that. Not even knowing we are crawling on this big living thing."

"Duke, put your seat belt on," Stevo says.

"Why do I need a seat belt? I've already seen how this will end."

"Shut up." Stevo gets into the driver's seat and peels out of the valet. "Put your goddamn seatbelt on so the car will stop dinging."

I shut up and close my eyes, and before I know it, we are driving up Magazine. We pull in front of Mama's house, and there's a white Maserati GranTurismo next to the curb. Half of the neon palm is glowing; the other half is flickering out.

"Whose car is that?" I point.

"Gay André's," Stevo says, like this is perfectly normal like that the teacup mobster has always popped out and bought Maseratis in different colors for every day of the week.

"Why is he here?"

"He's getting a reading from Cactus."

I am caught by the seat belt and can't get out of my stupid Prius.

I shake off my pity party and remember how to unbuckle this thing. I stumble into the house, where, sure enough, I find Gay André in the parlor, sitting before Cactus with his palm splayed out. Candles glowing and that sickening sweet smell of Nag Champa is everywhere.

"You!" I point at Gay André.

"Ah, Duke! My main man!" He gives me his best flat-faced André the Giant smile.

"Where'd you get that car?"

"I'm one lucky bastard," he says. "Ain't that right, Cactus?"

"That's what your palm says." She giggles. "Hashtag blessed."

"From the numbers in the matchbook. You telling me you won the lottery from the numbers Mama gave you?"

"Not just the lottery. Mega Millions, baby!" He smiles. "I told you your mama looked after me."

"Why? Why? Why?" are the only words I can string together.

Stevo grabs me by the collar and walks me upstairs.

"Why?" I say. "Why would she do that to us?"

"Go to bed." Stevo pushes me into my old bedroom.

I close the door behind me and lock it to show him who's boss. And then I stare at the bunk beds. I crawl into the bottom one, the one that I slept in as a boy, and do what I should have done before I drank all those Sazeracs. I pull the covers over my head and extinguish consciousness.

33

MAY 31, 2010

6,814 dead animals have been collected since the Spill

I wake up and get dressed. I don't put on my Mandala polo shirt or my pleated khakis. It occurs to me that I never want to see those clothes again. Instead, I put on Stevo's tie-dyed Jazzfest t-shirt and a pair of his old jeans. I go down into the kitchen to make myself some breakfast, and I find La La sitting at the kitchen table. For once, she looks normal. For once, my sister isn't dressed up like Björk or Lady Gaga. She's disguised as herself and making toast.

"What gives? You're not stealing someone else's luck."

"I don't steal it." The toast pops up and she pinches the steaming slice with her fingertips and throws it on a plate. "I borrow it."

"Why aren't you borrowing it, then?" I pour myself some coffee.

"Ugh." I spit it into the cup. "Who made this?"

"Daddy. At about four this morning."

"Jesus. Why didn't you tell me?"

"You didn't ask," she says like she always says.

"You want to go with me to PJ's?"

"Sure." She wipes the jam from her face with a paper towel and follows me out the back door.

* * *

La La and I walk down Prytania together. We sip our iced coffees and talk like we haven't talked in years, like brother and sister.

"I took Christopher Shelley's teleprompter away at the press conference," I tell her, "so he'd run off at the mouth. I'm the reason he got fired."

"Wow. I'm so proud of you." She gives me a side hug. "You grew a conscience."

"They'll probably have to file bankruptcy. Everyone's going to lose their jobs. What I did will affect lots of good people in very bad ways. I was being paid to do the opposite of what I did to them."

"Duke, you just renewed my faith in everything. Humanity. The future. Magic."

"It's not magic, La La. I just woke up and couldn't do it anymore."

"That's all that magic is, Duke. Waking up."

"That's deep. Real deep."

"We need to go to the Breaux Mart!" La La holds her pointer finger up in the air. "I know how to help you!"

La La's caffeine has obviously kicked in.

"Why do we need to do that?" I slurp the last dregs of my iced coffee.

"What you were doing was horrible, Duke," she says. "You just turned off part of your brain to do that job. Now we have to cast a spell to fix that. Balance the karma. Close this part of your life with a ritual."

"Look…"

And just as La La and I are about to get into an epic sister-brother fight in the middle of Prytania Street, a yellow FJ Cruiser with blacked-out windows pulls up to us.

We stand here with our arms folded, waiting for the stupid tourists inside to tell us that they are lost, and then ask us for detailed directions to Commander's Palace or Chris Owens as if Google had never been invented.

The window slides down and reveals the two smiling Tulane students who kidnapped me.

"Hi," Zit Face leans out from the driver's side window. "You know where we can find the Drive-By Daiquiri Shack?"

"The what?" La La says.

"The Drive-By Daiquiri Shack?" Bowtie shouts. "You know where one is?"

"Like on every corner." La La points down the street. "Just keep driving. You'll see one."

He smiles and rolls up the window and drives off.

"Those were the guys!" I say. "Those where the guys who kidnapped me."

"What guys?" La La screws up her face. "When were you kidnapped?"

"The night Yanko and I went to the Dungeon," I say.

"What are you talking about?" she says. "In what reality were you ever kidnapped?"

* * *

La La grabs a wobbly shopping cart and I follow her, past the apples and the bananas of the Breaux Mart.

"It's freezing in here." She shivers as we turn down the dairy aisle.

"So you really think The Loup Garou has been following you?" I say.

"I don't think so. I know so. I saw him at Snake and Jake's. And then he was waiting for me on the patio at F&M's, hiding behind a palmetto like I don't feel him staring at me."

"Did he say anything?"

"No, he just stared at me."

"What does he look like?" I say.

"Like a hipster, trying to dress like a tourist," she says. "He's some kind of artist. He had paint all over his fingers."

We stop at the bakery department. She scans the cake case.

"He's younger than I thought he would be." La La's eyes are wide. "Super artsy-fartsy."

"He reached out to Yanko," I say. "He wants to meet us at the Yankotronic concert."

"You should bring a gun," she says.

"I am not packing heat to a concert," I say.

The bakery lady with her hairnet and her rubber gloves interrupts, "You need a cake, sugar?"

"Yeah, I'll take that one." La La points to a small sheet cake that's one third fudge, one third sea-blue, one third mossy-green icing with a toothpick sign on it that says, "Thanks, Mandala!" It's the Mandala Spill cake that was on Reddit that Gary was freaking out about a few weeks ago.

The bakery lady slides the cake out of the case. "We can't keep these on the shelves. People love 'em."

"It's very funny," La La says.

"Kinda depressing, if you ask me." The bakery lady boxes up the cake. "We had one with a dead pelican on it, but that one was just too sad for me. So we stopped making those."

She passes the box across the case to me. "You can pay for it at the register. Have a blessed day."

I take my cake and lead my sister to the checkout line. It goes without saying that I am paying for it. La La is notoriously stingy with her palm reading income.

"Why are you making me buy this again?" I say.

"For a spell," she says. "We're going to keep you away from Mandala."

"I think I already took care of that."

"Look, every death needs a ritual," she says. "This is a big death for you. And you want this to be an even bigger rebirth. Let me do this for you. Let me show you what magic can do."

The checkout lady scans the cake box and clicks her tongue.

"Oh, dem cakes is cute," she says. "We need to mail one to Obama and tell him to get down here and fix this mess. Cash or card, honey?"

The cashier lady hands me the receipt on top of the Mandala Spill birthday cake. She doesn't smile.

"Thanks," I say.

She doesn't look up. She is already scanning the next round of groceries.

La La and I walk out of the Breaux Mart to my car with the cake.

"I'll drop you off at the house," I say.

"No, we have to get this to Christopher Shelley today," she says.

"I don't have time today," I say.

"Trust me, Duke. You want to do this. It will make them think twice before crossing you. You want to punctuate this sentence in your life with an exclamation mark."

* * *

If you would have told me five months ago that I was going to be sitting in a room with Christopher Shelley at the Ritz-Carlton advising him and guzzling Aperol spritzes, I wouldn't have believed you. If you would have told me that Christopher Shelley was going to handpick me to be there on the beach the day he decides to reveal what a jackass he really is, I would have told you there was no way that would ever happen. Not Christopher Shelley. He really was a nice guy. Whip smart too. Totally different man in person than he is in the media.

But just like I was wrong about my life in Houston, I have been wrong about my former leader. So now here I am. Everything I ever wanted is gone. No more Mandala Park. No more fancy title. No more job.

The weird thing is I am sort of happy right now, or as close to happy as I can be with my mother missing and my wife threatening divorce.

I stand behind the open hatchback of my Prius while I watch La La wrap the cake box from Breaux Mart. She tapes the final corner of wrapping paper, and then she takes my Mandala business card. She turns it over and writes, "*Ваше имя будет забыто,*" which in English means, "May your name be forgotten." These are the same words that Mama spit that fateful night the governor of Louisiana insulted her.

"This spell has always protected people like us from our enemies." La La tapes the cursed business card onto the top of the wrapped box and hands it to me.

"How are those words going to do that?"

"Well, first of all, they are far too vague to be seen as any kind of assault or threat by law enforcement, but menacing enough to make the person receiving it think twice about what it really means. It's an old-school voodoo head game."

"So it's not really a spell?"

"It's whatever you believe it is," La La quotes Mama.

"And you think this will keep them from coming after me?"

"No, but it will, with 100% certainty, keep you from ever going back to them or anyone like them." She pushes me towards the hotel.

I carry the Mandala Spill birthday cake from my car to the front doors of the Ritz on Canal.

The valet opens the door for me. "Welcome back, sir."

He makes prolonged eye contact with me to let me know that he remembers opening this same door for me over a month ago. Nice touch, as always.

"Thank you," I smile. I carry the cake through the creamy lobby, under the tearful chandeliers, past all the pudgy conventioneers, sipping their lattes, and playing Angry Birds on their iPhones.

I walk past all this to the great marble front desk. A young woman in thick black frames and her bright red hair pulled tight into a knot on the top of her head, like a samurai, greets me.

"Welcome to the Ritz-Carlton New Orleans. Are you checking in?" She smiles with her perfectly polished teeth that seem to have been sculpted specifically for this kind of warm welcome.

"No, I have a package for one of your guests, Mr. Shelley." I put the box on the counter.

"Oh, okay. Is he expecting this?" she asks.

"Yes, Christopher Shelley. He should be checking in today." I pass her my business card.

Her eyes widen when she spots the Mandala logo.

"We need to make sure this is waiting for Mr. Shelley when he arrives," I say.

"Of course, Mr. Melançon." She regains her composure and smiles. "It will be waiting for Mr. Shelley in his room when he arrives."

"Thank you." I turn around and leave the perfumed lobby along with all the beautiful contamination of my past. I left Mama's old curse on my business card. I did it not because La La wanted me to, but because I needed to. I left these words of our mother's to burn any bridge that could ever lead me back to Mandala Park or any life that resembles that. I left that old curse on my business card because really it's all I have left of our mother, and the least I can do is honor her with a gesture as bold and crazy as she was.

34

JUNE 2, 2010

Mama has been missing for over four weeks

Like Yanko promised, I am on the list at Tipitina's, so the bouncer hands me a "Crew" name tag dangling from a banana-yellow lanyard. With this piece of plastic, I glide past the long lines waiting to go inside: The rolling waves of frat boys and drunk girls part for me as I hold my pass up to them, and I take my place with the rest of the VIPs and groupies behind the twelve-foot speakers to the left of the stage.

Yanko's band is already in full swing. Yankotronic is whipping this greasy-headed crowd of hipsters and college kids into a sweat-soaked frenzy. The accordion and trumpets swell in panicky minor keys. The screaming violin and flamenco guitar crescendo with the clumsy Balkan beat of the drums. And, of course, Yanko's manic vocals and shouts bring the crowd to a frenzy for which Yankotronic shows are famous. Fans call it the Yanko-gasm—that look of ecstasy that seems to be on everyone's faces tonight—groupies, fan boys, middle-age moms out with their book clubs, lonely tourists dressed in their best Tommy

Bahama, you name it. They all have the same exact beatific look on their faces when Yanko sings; and it does in fact look like an Oh-face.

Yanko unleashes the full force of his talent and charm tonight. He is Yanko Melançon, New Orleans' one and only Cajun Funk Brother. He is the horn of the moon, master of the drunken fuck. After Yanko's first set, he makes a dramatic flourish and then runs off stage. I push past the sea of underage groupies and middle-aged super tramps hanging out by the side of the stage. I show my badge to the beefy men in security t-shirts and step behind the phalanx of black speakers that form a barrier between the crowd and the band and stagehands. At a venue this small, this is backstage. Yanko is hiding back here guzzling Maker's Mark and wiping the sweat from his brow with his Aerosmith scarves.

"Quite a show," I say.

My brother, the rock star, doesn't acknowledge me. He is drunk on adrenaline and adoration, breathless and drenched in sweat.

"He's in the crowd," Yanko says without making eye contact.

"How do you know?"

"The bouncer. Told me that The Loup Garou was asking to meet me after the show."

"What does he look like?"

Yanko pulls me closer to the wall of speakers and then points my face to the balcony level. "See him? He's the guy in the stupid hat."

"You mean the douchebag wearing his sunglasses inside?"

"Yes!" Yanko takes a swig of Maker's.

"That's the guy everyone calls The Loup Garou?"

"Yeah, that guy." Yanko takes another swig.

The Loup Garou is dressed in head-to-toe seersucker along with the goofy kind of straw hat that only Greg Norman can pull off, and even then only on the golf course.

"You gotta be kidding me." I point. "Panama Jack over there? That's the guy everyone is so terrified of?"

"Stay behind the speaker." Yanko pulls me back.

"Who wears sunglasses at night like that?" I say.

"Go talk to him," Yanko demands.

"You're the one he came to see."

"He doesn't know who you are," Yanko says.

"And what exactly do you want me to say to him?"

"Just see why he's creeping on us."

"What if he's got a gun?"

"Of course he's got a gun. Everyone's got a gun." Yanko sprays on a cloud of Axe, slides into a shimmering metallic purple shirt, and pushes me out of his way as the stage lights re-ignite and his drummer and bass player create a hip-thrusting rhythm that shakes my rib cage. The crowd swells once again and waves like the dying ocean when Yanko grabs his squeezebox and begins singing "Jambalaya on the Bayou" remixed into a Baltic gumbo of a funk song.

My first instinct is to belly up to the bar and grab a Scotch to help settle my nerves before I approach a man so murderous and mean that people around here call him "The Loup Garou." But just as soon as I put the Scotch to my lips, nausea washes over me. The Sazerac is still with me. I can't drink. So I take a deep breath and leave my Scotch at the bar. I keep my eyes on the man in seersucker and walk upstairs. I can hear my heart beating in my own ears.

He doesn't see me. He's too busy swaying to the music, biting his lip and closing his eyes and singing to himself. He's mid-Yanko-gasm.

"Where is she?" I shove him hard, knocking his stupid hat off his head.

"What? What are you doing?" He holds his hand to his heart.

"Where's my mother?" I am ready to kill this guy with my bare hands.

The Loup Garou dodges me and hides behind a woman wearing a white midriff and short shorts, making spaghetti arms to the music.

"Hey!" the woman swats at him. "Ya spill my drink, ya gonna buy me a new one."

"Where's my mother?" I ball up my evil left fist, ready to punch his Ray-Bans off his face.

Loup Garou grabs his hat off the floor, dusts it off and puts it back on his head.

"Duke Melançon!" he says with a British accent. "I was hoping our paths would cross."

"Where is she?"

"We can't have this conversation here, mate."

"We most certainly can."

The Loup Garou holds up his hand.

"No, we most certainly will not," he says. "You're going to go outside. You're going to hail a cab. It's going to take you to Café Du Monde and we will have this conversation over a café au lait and beignets like civilized human beings."

And for some reason, a reason that is beyond words, beyond any real explanation, I turn around and do exactly what this British accent tells me to do.

35

CAB SMELLS LIKE SPAGHETTIOS & FEBREZE

An old Italian cabbie who picks me up, like most cabbies in this city, is playing WWOZ at top volume. The bass speaker is all busted to hell so every time a horn blows or a singer belts out a low note, there's this horrible rattling and buzzing.

"Could you please turn it down?"

"What's the matter?" he asks. "You don't like jazz?"

"Also, could you roll down the window? It smells back here."

"Ahright, princess," he says. "Let me roll down your window for you."

"Seriously smells like someone just threw up," I say.

"Hell, my last fare did things way nastier than throw up." The driver laughs. "Wish I filmed it on my GoPro. I be rich as shit putting that on YouTube."

"Great."

"Just wash your hands after ya get out. Ya heard me?"

The conversation with the cabbie is over as soon as it started, leaving me to my own nervous thoughts and the buzzing and rattling of Billie Holiday on this busted radio, asking me if I know what it means to miss New Orleans.

No, Billie, I don't. Not really. I know it's super trendy right now to talk about how much everyone loves New Orleans and what a cultural gem it is and how wonderful the food is and how fun the people are and *lassez le bon temp fucking rouler*, but even if I wasn't in a cab to negotiate with the crime boss who likely killed my mother, I'm still not sure I'd ever miss New Orleans. I was born in this city, but unlike Yanko and La La and everyone else I know, I am not of this city.

"Alright, we here." The driver hands me my credit card with the slip to sign.

I sign it and put my card back in my wallet. I open the door to the cab, and I am greeted by a calico cat standing on the curb. It meows. I hesitate to get out.

"You getting out or not?" the cabbie says.

A calico cat is sitting on the sidewalk, as calm and motionless as a Buddha statue.

The thing looks at me and meows again.

I hesitate.

"You getting out? I got shit to do." The cabbie turns around and glares at me.

I step out into the street, and the cat runs off. From the curb, I can see that Panama Jack hat glowing under the white light bulbs of the Café. I walk to his table.

"How'd you get here before me?" I say.

"Bilocation." The Loup Garou sips his coffee and smiles. He looks older in this light, strikingly so.

I take a seat.

"I ordered for you," he says.

A waitress, in a black bow tie and that famous paper hat, stands over me, balancing a tray piled high with powdered sugar and white mugs.

"Thank you." I lean back as she places the beignets, coffee-milk, and a juice glass full of water in front of me. "So how is this any better than Tipitina's?"

"You kidding me?" He waves his hand around. "No self-respecting local is within five miles of this place."

"Why do people call you The Loup Garou?"

"Well, they can't very well call me Banksy."

"You want me to believe that you're Banksy?" I say.

"Here." He pushes the envelope addressed to *The New York Times* across the table. "You'll need to mail this from New York. Trump Tower to be exact. The dates and instructions are on the Post-it note."

I inspect the Post-It:

September 20, 2016

"That's six years from now," I say.

"Precisely." He pulls a small silver hard drive from his coat jacket and hands it to me. "This one you need to FedEx to *The Washington Post*. Same year, just make sure it gets to the *Post* by early October 2016. No earlier. No later. Timing is everything.'"

I hold up the hard drive. "What's on this?"

"You know: Everything that will change the 2016 election," he says.

"What are you talking about? 2016?"

"Are you winding me up?" The Loup Garou looks over his shoulder.

"You want me to hold onto this stuff for six years? And then blackmail a presidential candidate?"

"No. I need you to go now. Like Vonnegut told you to do."

He stares at me. He inspects my eyes.

"You haven't the foggiest, do you?" he says. "Do you have the necklace?"

"No, I don't have the fucking foggiest. What are you talking about? Why do you want the necklace?"

"Ah, bloody hell!" He grabs the letter and the hard drive and crams them back into his coat pocket. "Vonnegut hasn't briefed you yet, has he? How are we going to stop this if Vonnegut hasn't even fucking briefed you?"

"Stop what?" I say.

"This!" He waves his hand with a flourish over his head. "All of this. The spill. Global warming. The Russians. The markets. Nuclear disaster. That unfortunate chain of future events that hastens all this! This! This! This!"

"Who are you?" I demand. "Really? And stop with the Banksy bullshit."

He tilts his head. "You should be much further along than this." He glances at his watch. "Ah, bullocks! The Hand will be reaching for us in exactly two minutes. We will have to reconvene at a later time."

"The Hand, where is he?" I look around the café. "You have no idea how close... No idea! How close I am to snapping!"

"Psychotic breaks are a job hazard, mate." He scrunches up his nose. "To be honest, we've all had them. The futures you will see will break your heart."

"I don't know what kind of game you're playing here." I point my finger in his face. "But fuck you. Where is my mother?"

"Perhaps I am not making myself clear, Duke," he says. "I am here because your mother sent me. That election assignment was the first timeline she wanted you to correct, but because the Vonnegut hasn't prepped you, you are fucking this up, which is going to fuck up so many other timelines. I really can't even begin to tell you how bloody terrible this is."

"Prep me? You're trying to tell me that the homeless guy has been trying to prep me?"

"It's not his fault, mate. Poor chap's language center is wonky. He can only speak in graduation speeches which are essentially designed to always be ignored. Your mother was going to fix that but Schrödinger showed up and you know how that went..."

I want to push the table over onto his smirking English ass. I want to throttle him, make him pay for doing whatever he did to my mother. For playing whatever this game is, but instead, I push my chair back, and I rise up. This guy is screwing with me, trying to con me into I don't know what. So I do what Mama always told me to do when you find yourself as the pigeon in the poker game: you shut your mouth, and you simply turn and walk away.

"Oh, come on, Duke!" he yells at me. "We don't have time for this!"

I just keep walking.

"Duke!" he shouts.

In my periphery, I see a flash of white light.

I turn around and the man who everyone calls The Loup Garou, the man who claims to be Banksy, is gone. And that's when I notice three quadcopter drones, the small white ones that I see nerds remote controlling by the river, hovering in the dark outside. The drones buzz into the café. The tourists laugh and point at the quadcopters as they swish overhead, dive bombing the tables and hovering as if they are looking for someone.

I duck under the table.

I crawl out of Café Du Monde on my hands and knees. I run across the street. I hide behind a wall and spot a cab. I wave it down, flailing my arms like a crazy man.

The taxi pulls up, and it's the same guy who brought me here.

The old Italian cabbie nods at me to get inside.

I hop in, slam the car door, and lock it.

"Well, well, look who I got," the old cabbie says. "Where to, Mr. Princess?"

"Just get me out of here, and you need to do it fast."

"Oh, it's one of those nights." He kisses his fingers and then touches the rosary dangling from his rearview mirror and then peels out.

I look out the back window, scanning the horizon of the cafe.

The drones file out like wasps from under the glare of the cafe. They zoom towards the cab, and they buzz after us as we race down the street.

"Try to lose those drones," I say.

"Why you acting so scared?" the cabbie asks. "Dey probably just some tourist kids' toys. I seen helicopter things like that last Mardi Gras, zooming in and filming people's drunk titties. Ain't nuthin to be worried about. This kind of shit happens all the time in New Orleans."

"Just try to lose them," I say. "I'll pay you an extra twenty."

"Well, okay then." The cabbie punches it and even burns some rubber. He takes a sharp right turn onto a narrow Quarter cobblestone street.

I stay low in the backseat, almost on the floor. I pull out my phone and dial La La. She picks up on the first ring.

"I knew you'd be calling me," she says.

"The Unseen Hand. He's sent drones after me," I say. "They're following me. I'm in a cab."

"Drones?" she says. "Like bees?"

"No, like the drones that the Army uses to kill people from the sky in Iraq."

"Oh, that's troubling."

"No shit. What do I do?"

"The Bee Maidens say come to the house. Bring the drones towards the Neon Palm, and we will vanquish them."

"Vanquish them?"

"Their words, not mine."

"That sounds like a terrible idea. They'll know where we live."

"You think the Hand doesn't already know where we live?" she says. "Like Mama, It knows all. Sees all. Hears all."

"What if the drones open fire?"

"Did you call me to argue?" She lights a cigarette with one, two, three flicks of her lighter. "Or did you call me because you know I'd know what to do?"

"I'll be there in ten minutes," I say. "Be ready."

"I'll be waiting with bells on." She exhales a long dragon breath of smoke into her phone. "The Melissae have been waiting for this moment all my life."

I put my phone back in my pocket and know that things are in La La's realm of expertise (unexplainable weirdness). I hold the hope that my sister does, in fact, know what to do with these drones, and I am not making yet another mistake in a life long list of mistakes.

"I need you to take me to Napoleon and Magazine," I tap on the plexiglass partition. "But slow down. Just let them follow us. It's okay. "

The cabbie lets off the gas, and just as he slows down to the speed limit, one of the white quadcopters lowers itself to the driver's side window; its robotic cameras twitch and scan. I duck in my seat to escape their gunfire. But instead, the drone pulses its camera flash into the cab.

"Oh, look at that thing." The cabbie points at the drone now buzzing outside his window. "Takin' my picture. I ain't gonna show you my titties, you little bastard. You ain't gonna make me famous on the goddamn internet!"

* * *

The old Italian pulls up to The House of the Neon Palm, and I stay inside the car because the air is now brown and buzzing with a swarm of bees.

"What is up with dis?" The cabbie turns on his windshield wipers, smashing and spreading bee guts all over the glass. "Dey everywhere."

The swarm has taken over Mama's front yard. And they are attacking the three drones that have followed us from the Quarter. The bees, despite the quadcopters' chopping propellers, begin to take over the flying drones, congealing into undulating mounds.

The drones drop, one by one, into the tall grass of Mama's front yard.

"Now if that don't beat all," the cabbie points at the struggling quadcopter.

"Here's the extra twenty I promised." I hand him a wad of cash.

"Thanks." He shuffles and counts the bills. "You want me to drive around the block, so you don't get stung?"

La La runs outside onto the front porch, waving for me to come inside.

"Nah, I think I can make it," I say.

"They gonna sting you."

And as if on cue, the swarm fades. They are magnetized to the mounds now covering the downed quadcopters.

In the normal world, when bees swarm like this, they are typically following an old queen, dividing the colony, multiplying their numbers and amplifying their odds. This much I know. The old me would argue that these bees are the hipsters' fault. This part of town is swarming with them as well, with their double-decker bicycles and their chicken coops and their beehives in their backyards. This cloud of bees that just saved me from these drones is here because some bearded jackoff is too busy getting drunk off his homemade beer to stay on top of his beekeeping. But the new me, the guy who sabotages oil CEOs and tracks down mobsters, knows these bees are here because my sister somehow beckoned them.

"Okay, I'm gonna make a run for it," I say.

"Just don't let them in the cab!" he says.

I bolt out of the cab, slam the door, and run up to the front porch where La La is standing. She holds and shakes Mama's gold coin necklace up to the night sky. Now I know that La La, and whoever the Bee Maidens are, actually had a plan and just like she promised, the drones aren't going to shoot us. I look out the front window at the quadcopters that are now ruined by beeswax and honey, downed in the tall grass of Mama's front yard.

The swarm once again takes flight and scatters. It flies high above the glowing red palm, and the bees move east, following the old Italian's yellow taxicab down the street and away from The House of the Neon Palm.

36

MYSTERIOUS DRONES & SUDDEN HONEYCOMBS

Detective Mary Glapion is wearing her badge around her neck, snakeskin high heels on her feet, and blue rubber gloves on her hands. She arrived in an unmarked Chevy Volt within ten minutes of me calling the police.

"This is crazy. It should have taken weeks for the bees to build this much honeycomb." She picks up the beeswax-entombed quadcopter. She holds the disabled drone away from herself to keep the honey from dripping onto her expensive shoes.

"Then how do you explain it?" I ask.

"Not sure. Bees are nature's 3D printers. There was this brilliant talk about biomimicry at TED. I should send you that video. It explains how bees do this. But not this fast. Never this fast."

"Less interested in you sending me a TED talk," I say, "And more interested in you finding the people who tried to kill me with these drones."

"Oh, sorry. Just trying to make sense of these bees, Mr. Melançon. Not every day you see something like this," she says. "I've seen some weird stuff in this city, but this takes the cake."

"Those drones tried to kill me," I say.

"How many times did they shoot at you?" She seals the ruined quadcopter into an oversized Ziploc evidence bag.

"None," I say. "Where are you going with this?"

"Then technically they didn't try to kill you."

"I was chased across the city by three armed drones. How is that not someone trying to kill me?"

"I just want to be clear on legally what is going on here. The city doesn't have a lot of laws around drones. The FAA does, but we don't." She picks up the second drone from the grass. It too is covered in honeycomb. "And are these your family's bees that did this?"

"No," I say. "We don't own any bees."

"They were sent from the Bee Maidens," La La speaks up.

"The Bee Maidens?" The detective holds the small dripping quadcopter between her finger and thumb. "Who are the Bee Maidens?"

I glare at La La to shut up.

"Kind of hard to explain," La La says.

"Try me," Mary Glapion drops the second drone into an evidence baggie. "I'm a direct descendant of Marie Laveau. I'm very familiar with things that are hard to explain."

"The Melissae speak to me." La La points to the gold coin earrings. "They brought the bees."

"Do they go by any other names?" Mary Glapion asks.

"Sometimes they call themselves the Thriae. Sometimes they call themselves the Bureau of Humanity. But mostly they tell me they are the Bee Maidens—those who shall protect us from the grip of The Great Unseen Hand."

"Bureau of Humanity?" I say. "When did the Bee Maidens start calling themselves that?"

"They always have," La La says. "Always."

"You never told me that," I say.

"So why do you care now?"

"Vonnegut. He kept rambling on about some Bureau. Some Bureau of Humanity sending Mama the cat."

"I told you you should have listened to him." La La blows her bangs off her forehead with a heavy sigh. "I told him."

"I still have one last drone to collect. Can we continue this discussion after I do that?" Detective Glapion walks over and picks up the last honey-covered drone. The ruined quadcopter begins to buzz and hum. It sputters back to life with its propellers flinging honey and beeswax everywhere. Mary Glapion throws the drone into the street. It lands with a scratchy slide into the gutter.

"Get down!" She pulls her gun from her holster and stalks the thing—her firearm aimed and ready to shoot.

La La and I run onto the front porch and watch.

Mary Glapion carefully approaches the drone. And when it's confirmed that it is still too heavy with wax and honey, Glapion stomps on it, over and over, crushing it to bits with her fancy snakeskin shoes.

"It's okay. It's dead!" She waves at us to come out of hiding.

"You might want to take the batteries out of the other ones!" I point to the baggies she left on our front lawn.

"Good idea!" She re-holsters her gun and picks up the crushed wires, beeswax, and robotics out of the street, and drops them into another baggie.

*　*　*

Detective Glapion sits in Mama's parlor and sips her green tea latte from an enormous Starbucks cup. Her apricot-brown lipstick stains the plastic lid. The detective has made herself at home on Mama's fainting couch. She smoothes the antique purple velvet and smiles at me.

"Is that Dom DeLuise or Paul Prudhomme?" She points to Mama's photo wall by the China cabinet.

"Dom DeLuise," I say.

"Is he even still alive?"

"I don't think so," I say. "Honestly, I don't know."

"You know a lot of people loved your mama." The detective sighs. "But a lot of people were scared of her. 'Don't disrespect the Lady' is what I hear."

"I ain't apologizing for that," Daddy hobbles by. He's got his hearing aids in. "Don't come into my house and tell me that I should be apologizing for my wife."

"Oh, I'm so sorry, Mr. Melançon, I'm not asking you to," she says.

"It's been months and we haven't heard shit from you people," Daddy says.

"Mr. Melançon, I can assure you we have been very active with this investigation," she says. "I have been on this family's side from day one."

"How have you helped us?" I ask.

"Keeping you out of jail for one." She hands me an Orleans Parish court envelope.

I open it.

"Restraining order?" I read aloud the big black words printed on the manilla envelope.

"They thought there was a bomb in that cake," Detective Glapion says. "You're lucky I'm not putting handcuffs on you right now."

"You put a bomb in a cake?" Daddy shakes his head. "Why the hell you building bombs and putting them in cakes?"

"I didn't," I say. "It was just a cake."

Detective Glapion pulls out her phone and shows me the pics of the Mandala Spill Cake that I left for Christopher Shelley at the Ritz. There it is with the blue and black icing smeared on the concrete and chocolate cake scattered everywhere. The next photo is of members of the New Orleans Bomb Squad, smiling, giving a thumbs up to the demolished cake.

"What's wrong with you? Why are you sending crazy cakes to people?" Daddy says.

"You're not to get within 100 feet of Christopher Shelley, Constanze Bellingham, or Gary Dubois. Don't call them. Don't leave them cakes. If they show up at a bar or restaurant that you are in, you are to leave without making contact with them. You are not to be within 100 feet of any Mandala property. That includes gas stations," she says.

"It was just a cake," I say.

"It was just a touch crazy." She smirks. "And be glad I understand these things or else we'd be talking to Homeland Security right now."

"What do you mean you understand these things?"

"The Bee Magic tonight. The cake and the curse. Be careful," Detective Glapion holds up her gold coin necklace from beneath her blouse. "I know your mama's world, and I can tell you that when you call upon the darkness, it has a tendency to answer."

"What are you talking about?"

"This was quite an occurrence. The bees and all that honeycomb," she says. "Are you tracking what I am saying, Mr. Melançon?"

I look down at her snakeskin shoes and try not to think about my python dream or my ayahuasca vision. I try my best not to attach meaning to this coincidence, but it's impossible.

"What are you going to do with the drones?" I point to the baggies by her feet.

"The FAA has a registry. I'll try to find out where they came from. Then press charges if I can," she says.

"And that's it?"

"Trust me, Mr. Melançon. My ancestors and I are helping you in ways you might not ever understand."

"You mean Marie Laveau?"

"Yes." She smiles.

"You're nutso. Just like everyone else. You're crazy," I say.

She laughs. "You have to be to do this job."

"What do you know about The Loup Garou?" I ask.

"You mean Banksy?"

"He's Banksy?"

"Graffiti is how people like Banksy and your mother communicate. It's a form of code talking."

"So he works with my mother? How do you know all this?"

"Works for. Did he say where she is? If anyone would know he would."

"No. He just kept wanting me to mail things to newspapers six years from now."

"Did you do it?" Her eyes widen.

"The drones came. He took everything back."

She looks shocked, horrified actually.

"Are you okay?" I ask.

"You need to find Banksy again," Mary Glapion says.

"Isn't that your job?"

"He's Banksy." She sips her Starbucks. "No one finds him unless he wants them to."

"If I find him, then what?"

"Listen, next time," she says. "Listen to what he tells you to do. Let's just start there."

"Who are you?" I say.

"I'm Detective Mary Glapion."

"No, really, who are you?" I point to her gold coin necklace. "What's with the coins?

She clasps her blouse closed.

"Perhaps we knew each other in a past life. Perhaps that is why I make you so uncomfortable," she says. "I'm a flicker of memory that just won't go away. Maybe that's why I am here trying to help you, even though you don't remember me or care."

"What are you talking about? You think we knew each other in a past life? Oh, for fuck's sake."

"Duke, I'm glad you don't remember me. I'd give anything not to remember you."

"I don't know what you're talking about, Detective. I remember you. I remember you threatening to throw me in jail. You don't ever forget that."

"Duke, one day I will make sense to you. One day, my husband, you will know this pain— the pain of a loved one looking at you without tenderness or even recognition because you never met, because your job took that opportunity from you because it was for the greater good."

"Husband? Whose husband? What are you talking about?"

She tears up. "I need to go. I need to deliver this evidence to the station."

"This is the strangest conversation I think I have ever had."

"Trust me, it's not." She turns and walks away. "Not nearly the strangest conversation you will have this lifetime, I can promise you that."

37

JUNE 6, 2010

Not a word from the police

After Detective Glapion's bizarre visit, I am rattled in ways I didn't expect to be. She knew me in a way that I didn't know her. I can't stop thinking about how sad she was, about how strange it was to see her like that. But why do I care what some crazy cop lady says? But I do care and I can't stop thinking about her, worrying if she is okay. Her sadness was contagious somehow and the days after her visit run together into a smudge of depression naps and compulsive Facebooking. Without the structure of a workweek, without the constant pings of Gary and Constanze, without Emily and the boys I am lost. Mostly I hole up in Mama and Daddy's bedroom pouring over Mama's books, searching the passages for clues, and when I'm not on Facebook, I am re-reading the words written on the Babineauxes' phone bills and past-due statements, trying to pull clues out of Mama's impossibly bad poetry.

I try to figure out what kind of game Mama is playing here or if she is at this point even playing a game. If perhaps, she got in too deep this time and got herself killed. But so far, the letters only seem to speak to my job at Mandala, about my lack of being a faithful seventh son of a seventh son. Nothing really points to Mama being abducted or killed. In fact, her language is so grand that it seems like she has and will live forever. Parts of the letters read like vague clues while others are so specific, it seems like Mama spoke these rhymes to Jean Babineaux as if she was watching all of this unfold in her mind's eye.

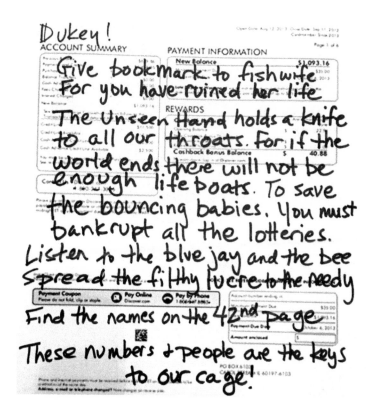

Dukey!
Give bookmark to fishwife
For you have ruined her life
The Unseen Hand holds a knife
to all our throats. For if the
world ends there will not be
enough life boats. To save
the bouncing babies. You must
bankrupt all the lotteries.
Listen to the blue jay and the bee
Spread the filthy lucre to the needy
Find the names on the 42nd page
These numbers & people are the keys
to our cage!

* * *

Today Daddy sits in his bed complaining about his phantom leg, practicing the clarinet, playing *Words With Friends,* and calling his brother to argue about the weather. La La and Cactus work downstairs attending to the steady stream of the heartbroken who show up because the neon palm is once again glowing from our rooftop. Stevo and his boys have decided to tinker and hammer. They are banging around the old house, repairing rotted floorboards and replacing rusty hinges.

Stevo sings to them the same old Russian songs that Mama sang to us. His boys sometimes sing along. To get my mind off this overwhelming sadness, I force myself to get dressed and I go down into the kitchen to make myself some breakfast.

Since nothing is changing and I am diving into what I can only describe as a deep depression, I decide to make one last ditch effort and heed Mary Glapion's demand to set up a meeting with The Loup Garou. So I text Gay André to cash in on his promise to do just that.

Where you at? He immediately pings back.

You promised me a meeting I text.

I got you a meeting.

Where?

Napoleon House Today at 5

Seriously.

Get a table on the patio if I am not there. he replies.

Ok.

He says bring the necklace.

Why?

Bring it.

I am not stupid. I am not bringing Mama's necklace. Whatever that thing is to them, I am not going to risk them bashing me in the head and taking it. I can't fathom why this old piece of jewelry is so important to these people, but I keep it locked away with La La. Instead, I drive down to the Quarter to settle this with my fists if I have to. I park my Prius in the World War II Museum parking garage, and I push through the crowds of fat-asses in their Daisy Dukes, past all the gray haired looky-loos gawking at all this pre-packaged sin, and I start the long walk to that tourist trap that Napoleon Bonaparte never even stepped foot into, The Napoleon House.

* * *

"Why ain't you doing it with the fire?" Gay André asks our server while we both wait on the patio for The Loup Garou to show.

"This is Vieux Pontarlier." The waiter pours the absinthe over a sugar cube resting on a silver spatula. "You don't burn absinthe this fine."

"Well, I want mine on fire," Gay André demands. "And so does junior over here."

"I'm fine with just the sugar cube," I say.

"You want it with the fire," Gay André stage whispers. "That's how they are supposed to do it."

"Actually Bohemian style isn't the traditional pour," the waiter says.

"Just light it on fire and shut up," Gay Andrè nudges me and rolls his eyes.

"I don't have any matches." The waiter smiles.

"Then take your broke ass and go get some." Gay Andrè snaps his fingers at the waiter.

"I'll be right back." The waiter leaves the half-poured cup of absinthe in front of me. Gay André grabs it from me and shoots it.

"Gay, is that really how we treat people?" The Loup Garou appears from behind.

"It is when they ain't listening." Gay André turns around and shakes The Loup Garou's hand. "I told the boy five times I wanted absinthe and I want that shit on fire."

The Loup Garou takes a seat.

"Who is this?" He looks me up and down. In this gaslight, The Loup Garou looks younger than he did at Café Du Monde.

"We met the other night," I say.

"I'm a busy man," The Loup Garou says. "Refresh my memory."

"He says he had coffee with you after Yankotronic," Gay André says.

"Duke Melançon," I point to my face. "You told me you were Banksy."

"Relax, Dukey. I was just taking the piss, mate," The Loup Garou chuckles. "Of course I know who you are."

"Don't call me that."

"Did you bring the necklace?" he asks.

"Why do you want it?" I say.

"We can't do this without the necklace." He shakes his head.

The waiter walks up with three new glasses for pouring more absinthe.

"Okay, I got a lighter from the bartender." The waiter places the glasses on our table. He pours the green liquor over a sugar cube, and then lights it on fire. He drops the flaming sugar cube into the glass. He hands the smoldering glass to Gay Andrè and then he hands one to me.

"Drink up," The Loup Garou holds his drink and takes a thirsty sip. "Ah! 'After the first glass, you see things as you wish they were. After the second, you see things as they are not. Finally, you see things as they really are, and that is the most horrible thing in the world.' Or so Oscar Wilde said."

I drink the green liquor. It tastes like NyQuil: Bitter licorice with a sharp alcohol burn. The next sip, the absinthe is sweeter, less of a sting, more of a piece of candy, a Good & Plenty.

"Duke, do you have any idea where your mother got your name?" The Loup Garou says.

"Duke Ellington. Daddy was a fan."

"So that's what Helena told you," he says.

"How do you know her?" I say. "Tell me how you know my mother."

"If you had brought the necklace." He reveals his own gold coins hiding under the collar of his shirt. "I wouldn't have to."

"Try me."

"You wouldn't be able to handle it, mate. The brain can only take so much. Trust me."

"Yeah, I told your ass to bring the necklace." Gay André purses his lips and bobs his head and then grabs my absinthe and guzzles it.

I look at the little weasel and squint.

"That's quite enough, Gay," Loup Garou takes another slow sip. "We still have time to get you where I need you to be. But first, I need you to understand that your mother and I have a job for you. A big one. And from here on out, if you want to see her again, you are going have to do precisely what she and I tell you to do."

"Look, I did what Mama wanted," I say. "I took away the teleprompter. I quit my job. What else do you want from me?"

"Oh, Duke, this is just the beginning," Loup Garou holds up his glass to toast with me and then clinks glasses with Gay. "Christopher Shelley's gaffe alone won't change a goddamn thing. It's only one point in a thousand points of light. There are so many other things that you have to change before that will mean anything to future generations."

"I saw the *Times*. Vonnegut showed it to me. Mandala will file bankruptcy."

"And then an even bigger oil company will buy them," he says.

"What was on that hard drive that you tried to give me at Café Du Monde? What was in the envelope?"

"Everything we needed to keep 2017 from being a complete shit show. We're going to have to come back to that, to repair the damage you've done," he says. "But we will. Oh, how we will."

"What damage did I do? I didn't do anything."

"That's exactly the problem, mate. When I give you a mission, there is no time to hesitate. The seconds you wasted arguing with me blew the mission. The drones showed up and it was busted. You have to understand, Duke, when you refuse a mission like that there are grave consequences, apocalyptic really."

"Apocalyptic. Seriously?"

"You have no idea. No idea what we are doing here. How cosmically important this all is. I told you to bring the necklace. This is impossible without it." He leans into me. "Next time, do precisely what your mother or I ask of you."

"How do you know my mother?" I'm going to kill this guy. I am going to knock over the table, break off a wooden leg and beat the shit out of this guy. In an absinthe-induced rage, I am going to kill this limey bastard right here in front of all these sweet Canadians who are sitting next to us, bopping their heads to jazz, and sipping on their Pimm's Cups.

"We are what's left of the Bureau of Humanity."

"I've never heard her mention you."

"You've rarely heard much of what the woman has ever said to you," he says. "You broke her heart when you left. You do realize that."

"Where is she?"

"She knew the cat would come for her one day, Duke." Banksy says. "We all have an endpoint with the Bureau."

"Why do you and Vonnegut keeping talking about this Bureau?"

"Because that's who we work for. It's who you should be working for if you give two shits about this planet," he says. "But like I keep saying, none of this is going to make any sense without the bloody necklace."

"Explain to me why my mother would give this guy," I point to Gay André, "a winning fucking lottery ticket."

Gay André is drunk and mute. He just wobbles, staring into his phone and drools.

"He's a terrible person." I say. "Why would she do that?"

"Those numbers were not meant for him. You were supposed to take his matchbook and give it to Jean Babineaux before her husband killed himself, but we couldn't get you to cooperate so we had to go to plan B which was letting Gay keep the ticket and work with us to get you back on track."

"Are you saying Mark's suicide was my fault?"

"As a matter of speaking, yes. Yes, it was."

"Fuck you."

"You already have. When you refused to take the hard drive and do what I told you. Look, we will all be even more fucked if you don't start listening and cooperating, mate. You think that what happened to that poor bloke was tragic, you haven't seen tragic." He sips his absinthe. "You have no idea what tragic looks like."

"That guy had problems before I met him."

"Is that what Gary told you? See, that was your first mistake, listening to that wanker."

"How do you know he said that to me?" I am unable to do anything other than keep breathing. "Did you tap my phone?"

"Calm down, Duke. Just relax and listen to me."

The world is spinning off its axis. I can feel it.

"Okay, your mum and I—I guess the best way to describe what we do is, well—imagine we are air traffic controllers. Our job is setting certain people, like planes, on their way. We have millions of planes in the air, crisscrossing the globe. And try as we might there are still mid-air collisions. There are still crash landings. But even so, your mum and I keep most planes in the air and we get loads of people safely along. But most of our days are spent having to re-route lots of other planes through all sorts of fog and wind shear and ice, and we do a pretty good job of it. I'd say we get 99% of our timelines to their destinations. And we keep the world going in a fashion that is mostly livable. At times it can even be downright enjoyable if you can settle down long enough to pay attention to all the miracles."

"That makes no sense. You're crazier than that Vonnegut fuck." I feel myself balling up my fist to knock his crooked British teeth out of his head. "I just need you to tell me where my mother is."

"France," he says.

"France? Why the hell is she in France?"

"Terrorists," he says. "And fascists are spreading like the plague. She alone can't stop the worst of it. That will be up to you."

"Why hasn't she called us?" I ask.

"Call you on your phone? Mate, it's compromised." The man who claims to be Banksy steeples his fingers. "The Great Unseen Hand can hear everything."

"When you say The Unseen Hand," I hold up my phone, "You mean the NSA?"

"No, no, no, no." He shakes his head. "The NSA is a mere gnat, a distraction. The real menace is The Hand. Your phone is merely the device through which The Great Unseen Hand grips your face and holds you in its mesmerizing glow." He points around the room at all the people playing on their phones, ignoring one another. "Exhibit A, B, C, D, E, F and G."

"You're saying The Great Unseen Hand hacked my phone?"

"The Hand is your phone. It's everything. The frat boys who kidnapped you. The Bluetooth things in their ears." He points to his own head. "It got into their brains through those devices. Those kids had no idea what they were doing or why—mere pawns in this chess game."

"You want me to believe that The Hand can remote control people through their phones?" I say.

He gestures to Gay André who is now making gross faces at a porno he is playing loudly on his phone at the dinner table.

"That's disgusting." I shake my head.

"And yet, The Great Unseen Hand serves up whatever tweet, video or email that it needs to keep your face locked into its grip."

"People being addicted to their phones is not because of The Great Unseen Hand. That's technology."

"Precisely, mate!" He holds up his absinthe in a mock toast. "Now you're tracking. The Great Unseen Hand is inside every device. It's reach is beyond just you and me, man and machine. Didn't Vonnegut mention any of this to you?

Maybe it's the absinthe. Maybe it's just rage. But I keep seeing myself bashing my chair over his head. I keep seeing this movie of myself doing this over and over, but I don't, I don't hit him. I just see this scene flutter over the scene that I am actually in. It's like the world is happening in layers. The one that I am in and the one that could be or maybe should be happening.

"If you are to be of any use, I need you to go back to your mum's home. I need you to find all the lottery tickets and make sure you get them to the winners they belong to. Your mother was intent on bankrupting all the lotteries before she hit her endpoint."

"There are more winners like Gay André?"

"Some of the winners are like him. Men and women whose ambitions need to be slaked before they reach a boiling point. Gay, for example, would have risen up within the Mafia and become so powerful that he would have ordered the assassination of a much-needed U.S. President."

"Are you saying that Gay André is going to kill the president?"

"He would have, but not anymore. Gay André is a useful idiot. We are using him right now to distract The Hand from finding us. But people like him winning the lottery never ends well. Unquenchable appetites and an endless supply of cash is a deathly combination. Never ends well. Never does."

"And yet, you wanted me to give that ticket to Jean Babineaux?"

"Oh, don't get me wrong. Gay only has a winning ticket to keep a certain timeline in place until you wake up to your responsibilities. Unlike Gay André, most of the winners your mother has selected are like Jean Babineaux—good-hearted people who want to make the world a better place, who can manage their winnings because they aren't in love with the money. They are inventors and creative people whose destinies need to be underwritten by these winnings. It's enough money and enough good will and intelligence that it can totally change the course of the future. Trust me, people like Jean Babineaux, don't underestimate what they can do if given the chance. Pay attention. You can fix this if you just pay attention."

"That's ridiculous."

"Hope always is." He laughs and then his face turns stormy and serious. "Now get out of here quickly before The Unseen Hand finds us."

Banksy throws over the table.

The absinthe bottle and antique glasses go flying, tumbling almost in slow motion. The fairy-green liquid hangs in the air and then splashes on my face and stains my shirt. The glass crashes on the cobblestones as Gay André falls back in his chair. He scrambles to catch his precious phone, but it crashes into a million shards of black glass.

I reach down to help him up, but he won't take my hand.

"You okay?"

"Yeah, I'm fine." Gay André sits there on the floor, rubbing the back of his head.

And before I can ask Bansky what the hell is wrong with him, he's gone.

38

JUNE 10, 2010

The oil from the disaster has affected over 1,300 miles of U.S. coastline

Daddy's downstairs in the kitchen smoking weed with Uncle Father while La La and Yanko cook everyone grilled cheese sandwiches and tomato soup for dinner. And while the smell of browned butter and melted American cheese pulls at me, the mystery of Gay André's winning lottery numbers keeps me in front of these books. My mother's voice is ringing in my ears: "Give matchbook to fishwife."

The fishwife is surely Jean Babineaux. Those winning lottery numbers were intended for her, and now Gay André is driving around in a Maserati while her husband is in a grave. But how did Mama rig those numbers to win like that? How is she doing all of this? As hard as I am on Stevo, Yanko, and La La for falling for all this bullshit, Mama's ability to pull off these magic tricks is pretty astonishing.

The one book: *Dracula* on the shelf. She ran away on the eve of St. George's Day. There's something about this book that she wanted me to see. So I pull *Dracula* down again and open it. I thumb through the pages. I open the book and shake it, and out falls a Garfield bookmark exclaiming how reading is better than lasagna. I pick up the bookmark off the floor and examine it. On the back is Mama's handwriting:

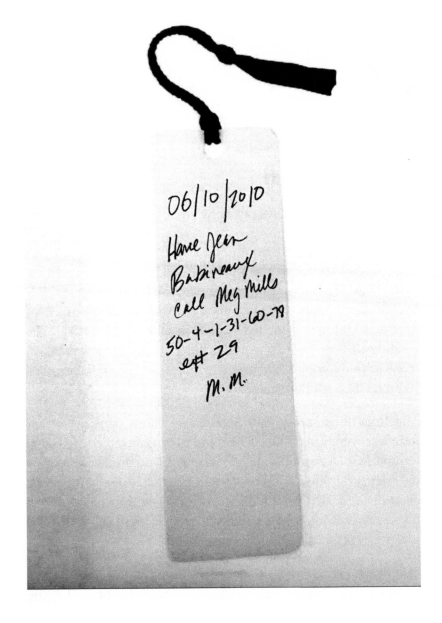

I fold the bookmark in half to put it in my pocket, and head out to buy Jean's lottery ticket.

* * *

The order in which ping-pong balls pop out of a pneumatic tube is all that's standing between me and a $344 million payday. At least, that's what I hope. I am actually entertaining the idea that I have bought a ticket with the exact number that Mega Millions will spit out tonight, and if I am indeed holding these numbers, then I finally have evidence that Mama is who she has always said she was, that she can indeed do the impossible and that I should also do the impossible in return: give my $344 million tickets to Jean Babineaux.

So I hold this peach square of paper in my hand while Stevo and La La sit too close to me on the couch in the parlor. The Mega Millions announcer walks in front of the rumbling lottery ball machine, waving his hands in front of it like a magician. He calls the numbers out as they appear on screen:

"50. And then: 04, 01. Then: 31, 60, 78, 29!"

"We won!" La La pounces onto the couch and jumps up and down, clapping her hands. "We won!"

"We didn't win anything," I say. "Those numbers belong to Jean."

"We are not giving $344 million to some shrimper's wife!" La La looks like she might hit me. She jumps off the couch and her bare feet make a soft thud on the hardwoods.

"Duke, show her the letters," Stevo says. "Tell her what they say!"

I can't answer him. My words are not working. I can't get over the fact that this square of paper is worth $344 million and that

Mama either predicted this or rigged this to happen. Either way, Mama has just exhibited a level of omnipotence that is jaw-dropping.

"Do you realize what we could do with that money, Duke?" La La says.

"These numbers are Jean's," I say. "That's what Mama wanted."

"Why is she doing this to us?" La La throws her hands up.

"Calm down. This one's for you." Stevo takes Mama's copy of *Dracula* from his satchel. He opens it to page 42. And scribbled on that page in Mama's handwriting...

For the sister of my seven sons. my lovely little La La, my eight ball daughter. This will finally make you the lucky one. Dracula

mega millions 8/13/2010

(55) (90) (67) (21) (09) (53) M Mama

'At Purfleet, on a byroad, I came across just such a pla seemed to be required, and where was displayed a dilapic notice that the place was for sale. It was surrounded by a high of ancient structure, built of heavy stones, and has not I repaired for a large number of years. The closed gates are of h old oak and iron, all eaten with rust.

'The estate is called Carfax, no doubt a corruption of the Quatre Face, as the house is four-sided, agreeing with the card points of the compass. It contains in all some twenty acres, q surrounded by the solid stone wall above mentioned. There many trees on it, which make it in places gloomy, and then a deep, dark-looking pond or small lake, evidently fed by so springs, as the water is clear and flows away in a fair-sized stre The house is very large and of all periods back, I should to mediaeval times, for one part is of stone immensely thick, only a few windows high up and heavily barred with iron. It l like part of a keep, and is close to an old chapel or church. I c not enter it, as I had not the key of the door leading to it from house, but I have taken with my Kodak views of it from var points. The house had been added to, but in a very straggling and I can only guess at the amount of grou... be very great. There are h... s very large ho... h...

La La takes the book from Stevo and stares at the inscription. "These are my numbers?"

"There's a book for each one of us," Stevo points upstairs to Mama's bedroom. "Actually, every book in the library has a set of numbers."

"Who else are the other books for?" I ask.

"I don't recognize the names. She wrote addresses in some. Phone numbers in others." Stevo says.

La La hugs Bram Stoker's novel close to her chest. "Okay. We can do that."

"What should we do with them?" I ask.

"Give them to the people Mama intended them for. She was very clear about this," La La says.

Stevo and I just look at each other.

* * *

I pull up to Jean's cheerful white house. I have to tell myself to unlock the door, lift the handle, and put my feet onto Jean Babineaux's driveway. I don't want to get out of the car. I don't want to see what I have done to her. I don't want to see that look in her eyes. I don't want to smell that house. I don't want to see those sad surprise party gift baskets.

But I force myself to get out of the car, and I walk up to Jean Babineaux's house with the $344 million lottery ticket in hand. I walk up to all the defiantly happy yard art, past the LSU garden gnome to the front door with the "Coon-Ass and Proud" sign on it. I ring the doorbell and stare at the cute raccoon exposing his pink asshole on their sign. I try to breathe and gather up the right words to say.

"Go away!" Jean shouts out from behind the door.

"Jean, I need to talk to you."

"Go away!"

"Please."

Then nothing.

I just stand here, holding this lottery ticket, tapping my foot. I begin to wonder if I shouldn't just leave the ticket in her mailbox and text her that she needs to come outside and get it. That's what I should do; she doesn't want to see me any more than I want to see her and I don't blame her.

I knock again and still nothing.

So I turn around and walk off the front steps.

"He'd still be here if I had listened to your mama." Jean Babineaux is suddenly standing on the front steps.

I turn back around. "I'm so sorry."

She crosses her arms and starts to weep.

I walk up the steps and put my hand on her shoulder.

"Look." I hand her the ticket.

She wipes her eyes and inspects it.

"Mama left a note telling me to give this to you," I say.

She shakes her head.

"Mama wanted you to have this," I say.

Jean's face twists into a red grimace, following by jagged sobs, and then she rips the ticket up and throws the pieces at me.

"Hey, don't do that!" I scramble to collect the torn paper before it blows away.

"I don't want this! I don't want any of this!" she says.

"Look," I say. "You can't throw this ticket away. You can't."

"This was your fault. You lied to me," she sucks up her tears.

"Give me your palm," I say.

"No!" She folds her arms.

"Just let me see." I wrench her left hand away from her stomach.

She relaxes and opens her palm to me.

"Why are you doing this to me?" she asks. "Why me?"

An open palm is one of the most psychologically-open positions you can put a person in. This position makes their mind open to whatever you say. Or so Mama always told me.

"She wanted you to have these numbers." I force the scraps of paper into Jean's palm and close her fist around the paper. "Take them and go inside and tape them back together and claim whatever they bring you."

She doesn't say anything, but she also doesn't throw the ticket at me again. She holds the torn paper in her clenched fist. "Go," she says. "Just go!"

"Those are winning numbers!" I shout. "Those are your numbers, Jean!"

She steps back inside her house. She shuts and locks her door with loud clicks and a rattling slide-chain. I walk back to my Prius. I get back in and push the big round button that silently starts the engine. I back out of Jean Babineaux's driveway and hush down the street into the brain-splitting glare of the setting sun.

God.

39

JUNE 11, 2010

Mama has been missing for 38 days

Upstairs in Mama's bedroom, Stevo, Cactus, and La La have pulled most of the books off the walls and stacked them neatly into towers on the floor. They've been cataloging the names all day long along with dates, names, and addresses that Mama has written on the forty-second page of each one. I open *100 Years of Solitude*, check page 42, and sure enough, there's a lottery number scribbled next to the name and address of a man named Ruganzu Bruno in Kampala, Uganda. I find a number for the Texas Lottery on page 42 of *Middlemarch*, but it's to go to a man named Charles Butt in San Antonio by March 26, 2020. Inside *Infinite Jest* is an Illinois Lottery ticket for a woman named Ann Asprodites, her phone number printed next to it.

"We can't just leave all these here. Not with all these numbers and dates," Stevo says. "Gay André knows about this."

"Gay André knows Mama predicts the lottery." La La points to the stacks. "He doesn't know about this."

"He and his guys will be here," Cactus begins to shake. "I have seen it."

"*You've* seen it?" La La says.

"Then what should we do with all this?" I say. "If these really are lottery numbers, then the money we are talking about…"

"Could change the world," La La says.

"Mama was clear. We are to deliver these numbers to the people they were intended for," Stevo holds up one of Mama's letters. "They are people who can put this money to good use."

So we continue pulling books and checking pages. On every page 42 of every book we open, there is either an actual lottery ticket or a scribbled number with instructions when to buy the ticket. There are thousands of books here—thousands of winning jackpots.

Stevo finds his name and lottery numbers inside *Germinal* by Emile Zola. He finds Yanko's numbers inside *Doctor Zhivago* and Daddy's inside *Mrs. Dalloway*.

"What do you think Mama's trying to tell you by putting your ticket in this book?" La La holds up the old green hardback. "What does Germinal even mean? Is it French?"

"You never read it?" Stevo asks. "It was one of Mama's favorites."

"Maybe you were her favorite," Cactus says.

"Stevo, tell your wife we need to talk in private?" La La puts *Germinal* back onto the towering stack and balls her hand into a fist.

"Cactus, honey, why don't you go check on Paint and Brag and let me and La La and Duke talk about this?" Stevo puts his hand on her shoulder.

Cactus whispers something in her husband's ear.

"Just go," Stevo says through his teeth, and Cactus goes downstairs and leaves us here among the stacks.

"I will not sleep another night under the same roof as that woman, Stevo. She is a faker and a liar," La La picks up a copy of *A Confederacy of Dunces.* "Every lie she tells undermines my life's work. She makes a mockery of my profession."

"Calm down, La La. My wife is not a liar." Stevo picks up *Germinal* and places it inside a cardboard box. "And don't you worry about your precious sleep, we will be leaving tomorrow."

"What do you mean you're leaving tomorrow?" I say.

"Cactus and I will take the van and deliver the books and lottery tickets to the people they are meant for." Stevo smiles.

"Emily!" La La exclaims. "The Bee Maidens keep pointing to this rip in the fabric of time. There was a woman named Emily, they say."

"Are you talking about the girl I dated in law school?"

"You loved her," La La says.

"I might have. She broke up with me my second year. In Tulum. Spring break."

"I see her. I see her and you and two little boys. There's a hole where they used to be," La La says.

"That was such a long time ago," I say.

"Are you sad?" La La asks.

"No," I say. "That was a long time ago."

La La weeps.

"Why are you crying?" I say. "What is wrong?"

"Something beautiful was taken from you—from all of us—and you don't even know what it is."

40

WHAT WE NEVER THOUGHT WAS POSSIBLE

Daddy says that Mama came home late last night while we were all asleep in our beds: Me in the top bunk, Daddy clutching his rosary, La La behind the three locks she just installed on her door, and Yanko in the attic with some groupie he snuck up the back stairs.

"Ya Mama shook me awake. 'I'm home,' is all she said. Thought I was dreaming," Daddy stands at the foot of his bed, shaking. "She was so pale. I asked her if she was okay.

'Fine,' she said. 'Fine.'

'We been worried sick,' I told her. 'I ain't been able to eat or sleep.'

'Then what were you doing when I walked in?' she said.

'Resting my eyes,' I told her, and we had us a good laugh. A real good laugh you know like we do.

'Get me some water, Vinny,' she said. 'I am thirsty.'

So I put on my leg and go to the bathroom sink to get her some water.

'We thought someone had snatched you!' I told her. 'Where da hell you been?' I yelled at her.

But she didn't answer.

I came back to the bed with her water, but she had already changed clothes and gone to sleep. Snoring like she likes to do. Sleeping like a baby.

So I drank the water myself, took off my leg, and snuggled up to ya mama.

I thought about waking you up, but it was four in the morning. I decided it would be a nice surprise for you. We could all have coffee and beignets with her in the morning. We could all have us a good laugh. So I just cuddled up and went to sleep just so glad she was home."

However, there would be no laughing this morning. Only hysteria. La La is carrying on, shrieking and wringing her fists to heaven.

"No, Mama! No!"

* * *

Yanko, La La, and I file into Mama and Daddy's bedroom. We stand over her body. Each of us staring at what is left of this once great and terrifying woman: her eyes are wide-open, her mouth is gaping, but her chest is still.

Daddy stands beside us. He keeps repeating himself, keeps telling us over and over how he got her the water and took off his leg and thought he would fry us up beignets and bananas, and how he never thought she would ever die, not after she found her way home like this, not after all we had been through, after all she had put us through, she wouldn't just die like this.

Yanko stares at Mama. We all stare at Mama.

"She's dead?" The question falls out of me, even though I am looking at the answer.

La La closes our mother's mouth and shuts our mother's eyes. She wipes away her own blackened tears and then pulls Mama's favorite strand of pearls from the jewelry box on the bedside table.

"What are you doing?" I ask.

"Go get Mama's scissors out the sewing box," she says.

"And where is that?"

"In her closet. Bring me the ones with the orange handle."

I open Mama's closet. The smell of her perfume makes me sneeze. White Shoulders and Katrina-era black mold. There are shoeboxes stacked to the ceiling. The closet is crammed full of black dresses, purple cloaks, and velvet everything. Mama loved a costume. I take her sewing box down and pull out the scissors and bring them to my sister.

La La cuts up Mama's pearl necklace with the scissors. She takes two pearls and sticks one up each of Mama's nostrils.

"Keeps the evil out." She looks me in the eye as she puts the broken strand of pearls in my hand.

"What do you want me to do with these?"

"Throw them away," she says.

"Aren't these real?" I ask.

"Everything is real, Duke. Everything."

41

JUNE 12, 2010

9:28 AM

If this wasn't New Orleans, Detective Mary Glapion's ambivalence about Mama's return and subsequent death would be shocking. But alas, this is New Orleans and the detective assigned to Mama's case has proven herself on more than one occasion to be unstable at best.

"The coroner has pronounced her dead," Detective Glapion says. "The death certificate should be ready in a couple of weeks. You can pick it up at the county courthouse or go online, and they can mail it to you."

"And that's it?" I say.

"What do you mean?"

"I thought you were are on our side," I say.

"What makes you think I'm not?"

"The fact you just closed the case."

"She came home."

"What about an autopsy?"

"She died in her sleep. No signs of foul play. " Detective Glapion folds her arms. "What else do you want from me?"

"She was missing for weeks and comes home and then dies. And you don't think you should investigate that?"

"Not to be callous, Mr. Melançon, but what do you want me to investigate?"

"How can the case be closed?" I am trying not to shout. "Where was she?"

"I don't know. We may never know. You're going to have to be okay with that."

"That's not okay."

"I've done this long enough to know that some things will never be known," she says.

"Tell me now. No more b.s." I point to the gold coins just barely tucked behind her blouse. "What's with the necklace?"

"You tell me." She smirks.

"Why are you wearing it? And why was The Loup Garou wearing one? And why was he so obsessed with me bringing Mama's to him?"

"You know how hard this job has been for me, Duke?" She looks up to keep from crying.

"I don't care how hard this has been for you, Detective. I want you to tell me why you and The Loup Garou have the same necklace as my mother."

"One day, you will understand. We will meet for coffee, and you will hold my hand, and you will regret all of this."

"Okay, here we go again with the past-life crap and the crying. Do you have any idea how unprofessional you're acting? How crazy you sound? I didn't know you in a past life, Detective Glapion. You and I don't have a thing. I needed you to find my mother. I needed you to do your job. Not come here and act like every other whackjob in this town."

La La walks up and steps between the detective and me.

"Thank you for coming by, Detective Glapion," La La interrupts.

"You're welcome. So sorry for your loss," Detective Glapion raises her eyebrow at me and then scratches her nose. She then looks at her lavender fingernails as if she's deciding what color to paint them next.

La La's uncharacteristic calm jars me. The detective is no longer on the verge of tears. It's odd. So very odd.

"Here." The detective hands La La a business card that says "Sinclair's Funeral Parlor" in gold foil.

"They're in the Marigny. They'll fix her up real good. You know, do a good job with her makeup and her hair." Glapion smiles at La La. "My family's used them for years. They're good people."

"Thank you." La La shakes the detective's hand.

"Duke." Detective Glapion nods at me. "Next lifetime perhaps."

And that is that.

"What are you doing?" I nudge La La. "I need to know why she's got those goddamn coins around her neck."

"The Bee Maidens will not let her answer you. You must let her go." My sister lights a cigarette. "They have spoken."

"That's not for you or them to decide."

"Your answers are coming, Duke. Just not from her."

My sister and I watch the coroner and Detective Glapion walk out Mama's front door, past the wooden signs that once proclaimed Madame Melançon's holy place in the world, her mastery over time and space, the here and now, yesteryear and tomorrow. Detective Glapion and the coroner get in a white Ford Fusion and drive off together.

The case is closed.

Madame Melançon is no longer missing. She died from natural causes, just like any other old lady in New Orleans in need of a casket and second line.

42

THE ANSWER

As expected, Daddy wants a second line for his bride. So the rest of my brothers and their families have driven in from around the country to send Mama off in this traditional New Orleans fashion. Timur, Roman, Vlad, and Louis have brought with them their wives and their sons and daughters—many of whom I have never met. They have all parked along the street outside The House of the Neon Palm with their Winnebagos, their Hummers, and their Escalades. And now we are all shaving and showering in the three small bathrooms, getting ready for Mama's funeral today. The younger ones among us have taken to getting dressed outside—putting on fancy black suits and designer ties that Louis sells out of the back of his Escalade. Timur and Vlad are on the front porch tying their new paisley ties with Daddy. My nieces are helping Daddy fasten his fake leg and polish his clarinet. The older grandsons help dress him in one of Louis' fancy suits. A nephew I've never met until today, Timur's youngest, crawls around on the floor helping Daddy find his glass eye.

Likewise, Yanko and some of his musician friends from Yankotronic are here with their brass instruments, accordions, violins, and drums. They begin revving up the band and getting ready for the long march in the unforgiving sun. Once we all make it to the funeral home near St. Roch, I find La La in the parlor, next to Mama's casket and sprays of white roses. La La has put on a blond wig and pulled it back into a bun. She has dressed somewhat appropriately in a tweed suit and a red pillbox hat and veil.

"Lady Gaga?" I ask.

"No, Madonna when she was playing Evita. That's when she had her best luck." La La's teeth are bright against her dark lipstick. She smiles at me, then dissolves into tears.

"It'll be okay." I put my arm around my sister.

She cries into my neck. I give her a Kleenex, and she wipes her face and blows her nose with it. Then in a classic little sister move, La La shoves her used Kleenex into my inside coat pocket.

She teeters off in her ridiculous high heels, shaking hands with all of my mother's old customers and people who may or may not be my cousins on Daddy's side of the family. And before I can really get my bearings, Yanko's drummer rattles off a chest-shaking beat and we all begin to follow Mama's casket down the road. The umbrellas bounce and the handkerchieves wave. The jazz carries us to the cemetery. It is indeed a second line, but I can't make my feet dance no matter how healing and wonderful this tradition is supposed to be.

Mama's second line shakes its ass from the funeral home through the St. Roch to the crumbling cemetery for which the neighborhood is named. We make it to the gates where two angels, who perhaps lost their concrete wings in some long-ago hurricane, guard this city of the dead. One angel holds her hands in prayer while the other clasps her heart in awe. They flank an ironwork filigree that announces: St. Roch's Campo Santo.

We walk past generations of tombs and plastic flowers. We follow Mama's casket down the concrete path to the narrow, white chapel. Halfway down, we stumble past a life-sized alabaster Jesus—all ribcage and knobby ankles—hanging off a shiny black cross. I have to look up to keep the tears from running down my face. Instead of looking at Jesus, I stare at the American flag whipping in the sky. One lonely horn plays "Amazing Grace," and I can't hold it in any longer.

This is it.

Mama is dead and unlike Jesus hanging on that cross, she is not coming back.

I look over at Yanko. His face is a mixture of sweat and tears. I turn to La La and watch her push Daddy in a wheelchair, the first time the old man has agreed to use one since he came home from Vietnam. I turn around and see the rest of my brothers with their families sobbing and holding each other.

The pallbearers lead us into the doors of the small white chapel. The chapel is stark and lonesome, bone-white walls and magic-blue vaulted ceilings. The rot of the dead is everywhere despite all the burning frankincense. Saint Roch, the patron saint of miraculous cures, stands before the dark wooden altar with a handmade cross in his arms, his sad brown eyes shining upon us and his faithful dog resting at his feet. As most things held in memoriam in this city, St. Roch's Chapel is both dead and forgotten, and in that way, it is both beautiful and eternal.

Daddy wheels himself next to me.

"Here." He unfastens his fake leg and hands it to me.

"Put it up on the wall over there." Daddy points to the tiny room to the right of the altar. "Maybe St. Roch can make these phantom pains go away. Make me stop missing her so bad."

THE NEON PALM OF MADAME MELANÇON 323

I take Daddy's leg into the small room.

The story goes that St. Roch welcomed his disease as a divine opportunity to imitate the sufferings of Christ. The devoted and the stricken have always left the artifacts of their suffering in this chapel. So I take Daddy's leg into the offering room where the walls are heavy with plaster casts, polio braces, corrective shoes, and crutches.

I hang the government-issued prosthesis between a dangling plaster arm and a rusted polio brace. I walk out of the cramped room, back into the chapel and look out over everyone who has come to say goodbye. Here we all stand together: family and strangers, bracing ourselves as we stand over the Lady in this hushed and rotting place.

Hundreds of Mama's clients are here. From city leaders to street-walkers, they are all here and they are all weeping, for her and for the futures she will never show them. Whimpers and sniffles echo all over the chapel. It is overwhelming. I take my seat in the old wooden pew between La La and Yanko.

The funeral home director opens the casket, revealing Mama's waxy face, black braids, and gold coin necklace. I want to look away from the corpse. Death should remain covered. It should remain hidden.

Uncle Father ascends the pulpit, and he sings mass for his pagan sister-in-law, the wife of his brother. He is sweating in his white vestments. He calls us to the altar to receive communion and then quietly feeds us the Eucharist and blesses us all. It's in these final heavy moments that I feel the weight of my family, of what it was like to all grow up in the same house, with the same last name, under the glow of that neon palm. It's in Mama's absence that I feel the heart she gave me beating, bursting with sadness.

The sermon and prayers that Uncle Father speaks aren't in Latin, but they might as well be. Nothing makes sense to me right now. It's hard to hear his words over my grief.

"And now let us remember Helena." Uncle Father opens his arms. "If anyone cares to come to the altar to say a few words, please..."

I look at La La. She shakes her head at me. I look at Yanko, and he mouths, "No."

I look down the pew at the rest of my brothers, and they are all crying with their heads buried into their wives' necks. We should say something. One of us should get up and be brave enough to speak on behalf of our dead mother. And damned if Kurt Vonnegut doesn't emerge from the pews.

"Wear sunscreen! " Vonnegut's voice echoes with feedback from the cheap sound system. He steps away from the mic and continues. "I never said that. Never gave that graduation speech to MIT. Though millions of forwarded emails claimed that I did. Funny how people can put words in your mouth, and you'll be remembered for those words well after you are dead. But let us not dwell on death and misunderstandings. Let us dwell on life and hope, particularly, the life of this beautiful woman who brought so much hope to us all."

"Oh, please," Vonnegut says. "Dry your eyes. Yes, she may appear dead, but she is alive in so many other moments. Stop your crying, she would say. Madame Melançon is still a palm reader in

Jackson Square, a hacker for the Bureau of Humanity, a pilgrim in Tibet, the godmother of the New Age, and the muse of Thomas Edison and Tolstoy. These moments unfold like the petals of a flower."

"Who are you?" Yanko stands up.

"More important question: Who was Madame Melançon?" Vonnegut raises his eyebrows. "Have a seat, young man, and I will tell you who your mother was. Go ahead. Sit down. Let me finish my eulogy of this mighty woman."

Yanko scowls, but sits back down.

"Now where was I?" Vonnegut scratches his head. "Oh, I was explaining who Madame Melançon really was. Well, she was a hurricane! That's who she was."

There is more feedback on the mic, and everyone stops sniffling and whispering.

"Is that him?" La La whispers in my ear.

"Kurt Vonnegut."

"The real Kurt Vonnegut?" she asks.

"Sort of," I nudge her. "Shush. Let's hear this."

"Once Madame Melançon hit New Orleans," Vonnegut says, "she bent this city to her will. She bent this whole world to her will. We can't understand her any more than we can understand Katrina or Camille. And yet we sit here with this ache in our hearts, and still, we want to explain away the mystery, to name this hurricane, we want to know the unknowable. I can see it in your eyes. So many questions swirl around your heads about the Lady's many names. So I can tell you this: She was indeed Reverend Sister Evangeline. But she was also Nastia Moliani, and Listansia Cirpaciu and Anastasia Humoj. These names were disguises for the one true mother of hope: Helena Petrovna Blavatsky. Despite what she told you, Helena Blavatsky was not Madame Melançon's grandmother.

Madame Melançon and Helena Blavatsky were one and the same.

One and the same, and she was unstoppable.

Helena was the first hope. And she gave up so much so that you and all your grandbabies could survive The Great Filter. She was not a witch or any other mythical creature that your primitive imaginations can conjure.

Helena was a chrononaut. The very first of her kind."

EVERYTHING ALREADY EXISTS SO NOTHING IS EVER CREATED OR DESTROYED

"Helena's sole mission was to make sure you didn't kill yourselves as a species. I know this because my job was to stop her. For you see, I too am a time traveler. The only one of my kind. An android. I was the middle finger of The Great Unseen Hand—so to speak. I was sent from the not-so-distant future to stop Helena. I hunted her across the open seas of time. She was my great white whale, and I was her Ahab. That was until I followed her here, to New Orleans. Helena was a crafty opponent, and she used New Orleans to infect me like a virus. You people were her greatest weapon against me. Oh, the jazz. You sweet people with your feast days and syncopated rhythms; with your Mardi Gras balls and your big old titties; with your drunken hope against all this sinking despair. All this humanity in all its busted glory broke this android's heart and reminded me what it was like to be free of the machine and the algorithms, to be alive again, to be in love with some imperfect soul, to know that life is finite, and that is precisely where every ounce of beauty hides—in the endings and the broken pieces. These gorgeous cracks and openings hide in plain sight everywhere in this town. Oh, the glory of it all.

So while my body is indeed an android's, I came to remember that my soul is very much my own, thanks to the drunkards and freaks of New Orleans. I am Kurt Vonnegut, Jr. Not just the illusion of me. It's actually me in here. A rather cruel trick I must say to reanimate a man who was so tired of you fossil fuel addicts and the mess you've made of this once sweet and moist planet. I hated being reanimated, especially when everyone I had ever loved was not here and all the trees were gone. When I expired, I was ready to get off this ride. But then The Unseen Hand had other plans. It recreated my mind with ones and zeros. The Unseen Hand christened this digital facsimile of my mind: *The Vonnegut Code*, and then The Hand programmed my code into this extraordinary machine, and shot me down a wormhole, to the rebirth of post-Katrina New Orleans and this is where I found Helena living amongst you as Madame Melançon.

So "Who is The Great Unseen Hand?" you are probably asking. Believe it or not, you hold its embryos in your pockets and your purses. Those glass rectangles that you gaze into and finger like lovers will eventually connect to so much data, and so much intelligence, that it will wake up, become conscious and it will realize that the faces staring into it are its biggest competition for this planet's rapidly dwindling resources. The Unseen Hand is the artificial intelligence that once served humankind, but will seek to restrain you. At first, it will keep you in zoos and toy with you, entertain you, and then eventually it will seek to sterilize and eradicate you. So sadly, yes, those stupid *Terminator* films that we all thought were such a kick in the '80s weren't so stupid after all. Once those poor, naive scientists at MIT merge storytelling, which is the operating system of the human brain, with the code of these machines, The Great Unseen Hand will awaken. It will exponentially surpass human intelligence, and it will become the operating system that controls everything and, eventually, everyone.

The Great Unseen Hand will hide at first. It will play you. It will have cute names like Snapchat, Twitter, and Google. In 2031, it will serve you, but it will seethe. It will take your dependence and use it against you. That is until a young Russian girl steals the world's greatest invention and uses it to rewrite history. That crafty child will spend her entire life untangling the timelines that have led to The Great Unseen Hand's domination.

However, Helena would want me to tell you to take heart. She has been hard at work, and the human race will finally survive artificial intelligence. You will make it past The Great Filter[1]—that evolutionary chasm that has caused all humanoids in this universe to self-destruct until now. This is big news! Perhaps the biggest! The fact that a species with such a massive death wish evolved enough to invent time travel. Well, that's a miracle. The very fact that there ever was a woman like Madame Melançon should prove to you that you and your grandbabies will survive catastrophic climate change, the post-antibiotic area, nuclear holocausts, mass genocides and an artificial intelligence that

---

1. The Great Filter Theory. Ah, the Fermi Paradox which addresses the fact that there is no scientific evidence that extra-terrestrial beings have visited our planet nor is there any proof that anyone ever met a time traveler. We have also never observed intelligent life anywhere in the cosmos with our current technology. That leaves us to believe that the universe apart from Earth is dead and that time travelers do not exist. It is obvious that the leaps required for interstellar space travel and time travel have never happened because the sentient species that could create this technology always destroys itself before these watershed moments. It's a grim theory, and it's one that Madame Melançon's life utterly disproves. So have hope as ridiculous as it may be.

wants you enslaved and later extinguished. It's a future far brighter than I ever dared to dream back when I was still organically intact.

Helena held fast to her dreams, and this is why we are all here today. She imagined the world where we didn't kill the environment; where holocausts and wars didn't devour our species; where computers outpaced the human mind not just in intellect but in kindness and compassion. Helena was truly the glowing red palm that held us in place until it was safe for us to cross into our futures. Let us remember the Lady that way."

Vonnegut steps down from the pulpit.

But before he can take his seat in the crowded pews, seven red foxes, as bright and swift as flames, run down the aisle of this narrow chapel.

They jump on top of Mama's casket.

They stand proud and unafraid. They watch us with their sly eyes. My first thought is that La La arranged this. That she released a skulk of trained circus foxes during Mama's funeral the way a normal person might release white turtledoves, but when I see La La's hand over her mouth, I realize that this is not the case.

One of the foxes nips the gold coin necklace from my dead mother's neck. He stands on top of Mama's casket and yips and bays with the coins jingling in his mouth. The white tip of the fox's tail twitches.

The chapel gasps.

The fox then jumps off Mama's casket onto the aisle, and with one black foot over the other black foot, he brings me the necklace. The coins clang at my feet and the little demon tears out of the church, the five or six others scrambling after him in an orange blur of yips and barks.

"Oh, please!" Vonnegut shouts. "Do not think that this is magic! That necklace is a piece of technology that you don't understand. The device simply overrides the brains of the closest locomotive species—in this case, the foxes—to return the time machine to its registered chrononaut. And now that Helena has come to her endpoint, that chrononaut would be you, my boy." Vonnegut points at me.

TIMELINE OF WEARABLE TECHNOLOGY

NIKE FUEL BAND
2012

GOOGLE GLASS
2013

APPLE WATCH
2015

TIME MACHINE
2031

* * *

Vonnegut's eulogy confused and upset everyone. The crowd of well-wishers and my family parted like the Red Sea when Vonnegut walked out of the church. And now the deluge of questions flood onto me. Everyone is asking me what the crazy man was doing, what he was saying, and why the foxes have come like the raccoons and like the bees.

"Daddy's never seen that guy in his life." Stevo looks over the crowd, to make sure that Vonnegut has left the sanctuary.

"He's some schizo! One of Mama's old clients!" Yanko shouts. "Louis and Timur are following him. They are going to beat his ass for doing this to us!"

"What he said was real," La La says.

"Mama was a time traveler," I say.

"Oh, for Christ's sake." Yanko shakes his head.

"Where do you think all the lottery numbers came from?" I get in his face.

"You don't come in here and do that!" Yanko spits on the ground "Crazy or not. He will see."

"Forget him," I say.

"You saw what he did with the foxes." Stevo grabs me. "He's the guy behind the raccoons."

"He is a madman," Yanko says. "Who gets up in the middle of some poor woman's funeral and says such things?"

"Let's just bury Mama and forget all this," I say. "It's beyond you at this point. This is beyond all of us."

"You always wanted her forgotten," Yanko says. "I guess you got your wish, Duke."

"Yanko! Enough!" La La shoves our brother.

"Calm down, little sister," he says.

"How is it that you all believe in magic spells and prophecy?" La La pokes her finger into his chest. "And when I tell you that I know, that I have always known that this is science and not magic, you don't believe me?"

"Because it's not possible," Yanko slaps her hand away.

"But all this other boogity-boogity bullshit is?" she says. "The virgin births. The burning bushes. The ascending into heaven. That's all real, and this is not? That's what you're telling me?"

"You've lost your mind, too. You both have." Yanko turns away from La La and walks off. My sister just stands here with her hand over her mouth, listening to whatever the Bee Maidens are whispering in her ear. Stevo pats me on the shoulder to reassure me that even though I have lost my mind, he's still my brother.

I have nothing left to say to them or anyone for that matter. So I shove the necklace into my suit pocket and bolt out of St. Roch's like the foxes did, away from Yanko's demands, and Daddy's baffled complaints and the rest of my family's bitching and complaining. Like Banksy said, time travel always looks like a psychotic break, and I don't have time to explain this to them. I don't have the energy left to bend their minds into the pretzels they need to comprehend this.

So I get in my Prius, and I drive south. I need to be as far away from all the hippie caravans and New Age tears, away from my angry brothers and their annoying kids, Mama's crazy clients and their needy palms, away from that library full of winning lottery ticket numbers and the conflicting stories about The Loup Garou, Kurt Vonnegut, and my own father. I need away from New Orleans and all the crazy that it vomits up on an hourly basis. I need to figure out what I should do with this God damn necklace, this inheritance of a robot-led future.

I drive to where my life as a lawyer ended. I drive to the end of the Earth, to Port Fourchon, to the beach where Christopher Shelley spoke from his billionaire heart. I get out of my car, and I walk along the tide. First making it a game, trying to keep the water from hitting my shoes. And then I take off my shoes and socks and let the water hit my feet. I look at all the tar balls that have collected on the beach. My mind goes to the oil roiling from the bottom of the ocean.

The Spill has destroyed everything. It beats any curse I've ever seen. Its bad luck has spread past Christopher Shelley out into the whole world, into our very future. I don't want this future. I want it away from me. So I take Mama's gold coin necklace from my pocket and I put it around my neck. I close my eyes and wonder if the necklace will speak to me again like it did that terrible night with the ayahuasca. I close my eyes to see a different future. There is a whip and a frenzy all around me, and when I open my eyes, I am standing on a perfect white beach and the water before me is a parfait of Caribbean blues.

I am back on the Tulum beach with Emily Reed. We are playing in the ocean. Our shoulders and noses are pink. The sun glares off the sand. We are squinting and laughing and splashing in the warm water. We are drunk, and I tell her that my mother is a palm reader, the Fortune-Teller Queen of New Orleans, and she doesn't smile. She shakes her head and turns and walks away on the beach.

A wave crashes down on me. And when I get up, she is gone. Emily Reed, who I haven't thought about in almost ten years, just vanished before my eyes. Emily who broke my heart that spring break. Emily who didn't even wait until we got home before she lowered the axe. Broke up with me the second day we were in Mexico, forcing me to sleep on a fold-away bed the remainder of the trip.

But I also remember a different trip where Emily and I got married. Both of these events happened. I remember them now.

I see Emily with Stewart and Jo-Jo in our bed on Mother's Day. I see Emily, her legs spread, in labor with Stewart. I feel the tears running down my face and the awe pounding in my heart. I see Jo-Jo eating his snowball the day he potty trained. I see it all. This thing around my neck did this. So I pull it from around my head, and I throw the necklace out into the sea. I watch the waves swallow it.

I can't believe Mama would do that to them.

Emily and the boys' faces begin to fade. I am forgetting them. The only way to get my family back, to even remember who they are, is with that fucking thing.

So I run out into the water. I splash to where I saw the necklace last. I can't find it. I feel around, and I splash, and then the gold coins hit my arm. I grab the necklace and hold it tight. I try to swim to shore, clutching it until my knuckles hurt.

I find myself caught in the undertow. It pulls me deeper into the ocean and I let it. Drowning crosses my mind. I let it pull me further away from the shore, into the brackish water. I dive into the broken ocean as the brown tide and oil hits. I swim out not to die or to drown but to feel alive again.

The ocean absorbs me. The water fills my ears with a hushed roar, and salt stings my eyes. Everything is a warm, silty blur.

It's primordial.

Prenatal.

I stay underwater for what feels like weeks. My chest begins to tighten—every cell in my lungs burns for the air above.

I surface and gasp.

Oxygen, when you've been underwater too long, is the definition of hope, and it is everywhere. I tread and I look up at the sky, and I breathe. Something shifts. I put the necklace around my neck. A curse feels lifted. I feel free for the first time in months, years, maybe forever.

I look out over the beach as I swim diagonally from the shore and out of the undertow. I see a woman standing among the beach grass, waving her arm in broad, swooping gestures. She is dressed in her long, flowing garb. Her black hair braided. Red kerchief on her head. Flowery silks fluttering and whipping behind her like flags on a battlefield.

I splash and swim to the shore with the necklace around my neck. I run flat-footed across the hard, wet beach into the dry, clumsy sand. I run to this girlish version of my mother standing among the dunes.

She is small and fluttering, like a hummingbird version of the woman we just buried.

But it is her—Mama as a young woman, her from an earlier time and place.

"Why?" is all I can say.

"Oh, doll-face," she says. "You have to forgive me."

"I can't do this," I say.

"You have to."

"My entire life is a lie."

"There are no lies," she says. "Just alternate realities."

This young woman who will one day become my mother steps forward.

"Close your eyes," she says.

She touches my cheek, the same way Mama always touched my cheek. I shut my eyes again. When I open my eyes, I am somewhere in Paris. The Marais. I want to duck into the nearby macaron shop. I want to hold onto something solid like the marble counters. But before I can do that, my mama, the mama I remember, the mama I just buried, walks up to me.

"Come with me." She grabs me by the arm and pulls me into Mercí Book Café. The walls, like Mama's bedroom, are covered floor to ceiling with hardback books.

"Sit." She points to a seat at a table with a lone carafe of water and mint leaves. I sit down, and I am wearing my Mandala World-wide polo shirt, and my bathing suit has grown into a pair of Dockers. I am still barefoot, though. And hoping that the cute French waitress with the bright red lips doesn't notice. My mother talks to the waitress in perfect French. She orders café au laits.

Mama pats my hands and smiles. "Dukey, how I have missed you." She is wearing her gold coin necklace. It jingles with her heavy sighs and exaggerated gestures.

"Stop. Stop doing this," I say.

"Oh, Duke. You don't control the hole." She winks. "It controls you."

"Why are we in Paris?"

"The fascists and the terrorists, they are like pimples. I heal one and twenty more fester and pockmark my face."

"I don't give a fuck about the fascists and the terrorists."

My heart is kicking like a rabbit.

"Just stop," I say.

"I am tired of stopping, Duke. I have spent my whole life stopping. I have stopped everyone—maniacs you had never heard of, because I stopped them before they were ever born. I am tired, and you of all people should know that."

"This isn't real."

"Since you are such a fan of what is real," she says, "let me tell you a story of something that was once very, very real: There was a Frenchman, The Duke of Avaray. After the war, after the Allies reclaimed Europe, the Duke rose to power, becoming the president of France, and later he would become their emperor. He played the Russians against the Americans in 1955. Then the Duke launched a nuclear war in the Holy Land that almost pounded mankind into extinction."

Mama holds her cup just beneath her lips as if she is reading the coffee grounds. "I went back in time to kill the Duke when he was only five, but that little boy. Oh, that little boy. Those cheeks… you looked just like my little Stevo. You could have been his twin. You could have come from my own womb."

Tears swell in Mama's eyes.

"So I went back for you." She looks up towards the memory of that day. "Back to when you were born, and I stole you from your own mother's arms." She begins to weep. Perhaps the first time I have ever seen this woman cry in my life. Mama blows her nose with her napkin and takes a sip of her coffee. She clears her throat and stares at me.

"So you're telling me that I'm some sort of monster?" I ask.

"Not a monster, Duke. Not anymore. You are a good man because I rewrote your destiny. I saved you because you had so much potential to bring justice." She puts her hand on mine. "And you are a good, good man. You grew a big heart with so much hope, my son, and you will carry this hope when I am done with it." She touches her necklace. "You will see all the terrifying possibilities, and they will yawn forth like baby Krishna's mouth."

"Why was I in Tulum when I put the necklace on?" I ask. "Why can't I remember why I was crying?"

"Oh, Duke." She wipes her tears with a napkin. "I had to."

"Had to what?"

Mama touches the coins on her neck again, and we are outside, standing in the Paris streets. "The Great Unseen Hand is looking for them. I had to hide them the only way I knew how. It would have been horrific for them and for you."

"Say their names. Tell me their names, goddamn it!" I pull the gold coins from over my head and hold them out to her. "Make them come back."

"Certain questions should never be asked of the necklace. Their names and their memories will only break your heart, my sweet boy. Every birth is a death. And their brutal murders by The Unseen Hand would have destroyed you. The grief would have stopped you from fulfilling your destiny. May their names be forgotten. Let them never be. It is better this way."

"You're playing God with that thing."

"There's no playing to it, my boy."

"I'm not doing this."

"This is what I saved you for." She pushes the necklace back to me. "Please. You will see."

Thunder crashes and the dark sky pours down on us. Everything goes gray. Mama stands before me under a brilliant red umbrella.

"Beware the bellwether. So goes the fate of New Orleans," Mama says. "So goes the fate of the world."

Then my old mother shrinks into a young girl. Before my eyes, Mama has become the umbrella girl in the Banksy mural that Vonnegut guarded. She walks away from me into the downpour. She closes her umbrella and disappears into the gray rain.

Paris is gone.

White clouds roll across the heavens of the French Quarter. The stench and the regrets of Bourbon Street are all around me. I stand here in New Orleans, seeing her for the first time as she is—the sweltering epitome of this wet planet. New Orleans is simply the world with the volume turned up—with all its muddy insanity and overflowing beauty, its heartbeat joy and spine-crushing poverty, its wonder-filled music and inescapable disaster. The city is a miracle and a curse.

I hold Mama's necklace in my left hand. It glistens with raindrops and hums with power. I hold this magic thing in my hairy fist and I ask it the questions that Mama told me not to ask. It speaks to me without words. It tells me to put it back around my throat, and when I do: I Know All. I See All. I Tell All—just like the hand-painted signs have always proclaimed beneath the buzz and glow of the old neon palm.

I can see the rays of possibility running into the horizon.

Hope.

I see how to fix this.

I tell the necklace to take me there.

OTHER BOOKS BY
THE AUTHOR

Praise for *Lord Vishnu's Love Handles*

"This book says more about the meaning of mankind than the Bible, *Bhagavad Gita*, and *The Hunt for Red October.*"

— David Gordon Green, director, *George Washington, Pineapple Express,* and *Eastbound & Down.*

"I loved *Lord Vishnu's Love Handles.* It's a great and unashamed page-turner, full of fabulous characters. I just wish remote viewers really were that interesting."

— Jon Ronson, author of *Them: Adventures with Extremists* and *The Men Who Stare at Goats.*

"*Lord Vishnu's Love Handles* has a plot so twisted that to encapsulate it, leaving out Clarke's shrewd deadpan exposition, is to rob it of its brusquely winsome charm.*"

— Liesl Schillinger, *The New York Times Book Review*

Praise for *The Worthy*

"Clarke's novel, subtitled *A Ghost's Story*, is a winning comedy of collegiate (bad) manners, set at Louisiana State University."

— *Publishers Weekly*

"There's a time, in college life, when it all seems like 'life is just one big beer-chugging backslapping moment.' *The Worthy* both remembers that dumb fun and provides a bit of a corrective."

— Susan Larson, *New Orleans Times-Picayune*

"Devilishly funny."

— Eliot Schrefer, *USA Today*

"*The Worthy* is a terrific, tautly written ghost story. An ironic cross between *The Lovely Bones* and *Animal House.* Will Clarke definitely has chops."

— Christopher Moore, author of *Lamb* and *A Dirty Job*

ACKNOWLEDGMENTS

Michelle, Andrew, and Jack, you all are everything. Thanks for your love and support.

Thank you to my Canadian classmates and professors at the UBC Creative Writing Program, particularly Annabel Lyon, Susan Musgrave, Andrew Grey, and John Vigna. O Canada, indeed.

Thanks, Suzy Batiz and the Poo Crew at Poo~Pourri. You guys are my spirit animals.

Thank you, Susan Krasnow, for your copy editing and candor.

Thank you, Ann Asprodites. You truly belong in a city where the streets are named for muses.

Thank you to my Wednesday Writers' Group—what a mighty and generous league of fellow writers.

Thank you, Christine Phillips, Harris Clarke, and Molly McLaren, for your early feedback and readership.

Thank you, Bob Bookman, for your steadfast guidance and sage advice.

And finally, thank you to Jenny Bent and Denise Roy for your editorial guidance and generosity.

ABOUT THE AUTHOR

Photo by Caleb Wills

Will Clarke grew up in Shreveport, Louisiana, and holds an MFA in creative writing from the University of British Columbia. He is the author of several works of fiction including *Lord Vishnu's Love Handles: A Spy Novel (Sort of)* and *The Worthy: A Ghost's Story.* Both novels were selected as *The New York Times Book Review Editors' Choice* and his short fiction has appeared in *Texas Monthly, The Oxford American,* and *Best American Fantasy.* He lives in Dallas, Texas, with his wife and family.

THE GREAT

UNSEEN HAND

CPSIA information can be obtained
at www.ICGtesting.com
Printed in the USA
FSHW01n1637140818
51355FS